C000295901

ONLY WHEN IT'S LOVE

HOLDING OUT FOR MR RIGHT

OLIVIA SPRING

HARTLEY PUBLISHING

WANT FREE STUFF?

Join my VIP club and get exclusive content and an
exciting book, all for free!

Find out more at the end of *Only When It's Love*.

Dedicated to my wonderful mum and dad.

CHAPTER ONE

Never again.

Why, why, *why* did I keep on doing this?

I felt great for a few minutes, or if I was lucky, hours, but then, when it was all over, I ended up feeling like shit for days. Sometimes weeks.

I must stop torturing myself.

Repeat after me:

I, Alexandra Adams, will *not* answer Connor Matthew's WhatsApp messages, texts or phone calls for the rest of my life.

I firmly declare that even if Connor says his whole world is falling apart, that he's sorry, he's realised I'm *the one* and he's changed, I will positively, absolutely, unequivocally *not* reply.

Nor will I end up going to his flat because I caved in after he sent me five million messages saying he misses me and inviting me round just 'to talk'.

And I *definitely* do solemnly swear that I will *not* end up on my back with my legs wrapped around his neck within minutes of arriving, because I took one look at his body and couldn't resist.

No.

That's it.

No more.

I will be *strong*. I will be like iron. Titanium. Steel. All three welded into one.

I will block Connor once and for all and I will move on with my life.

Yes!

I exhaled.

Finally I'd found my inner strength.

This was the start of a new life for me. A new beginning. Where I wouldn't get screwed over by yet another fuckboy. Where I wouldn't get ghosted or dumped. Where I took control of my life and stuck my middle finger up at the men who treated me like shit. *Here's to the new me.*

My phone chimed.

It was Connor.

I bolted upright in bed and clicked on his message.

He couldn't stop thinking about me. He wanted to see me again.

Tonight.

To talk. About our future.

Together.

This could be it!

Things *had* felt kind of different last time. Like there was a deeper connection.

Maybe he was right. Maybe he *had* changed…

I excitedly typed out a reply.

My fingers hovered over the blue button, ready to send.

Hello?

What the hell was I doing?

It was like the entire contents of my pep talk two seconds ago had just evaporated from my brain.

Remember *being strong like iron, titanium and steel* and resisting the temptations of Connor?

Shit.

This was going to be much harder than I'd thought.

TWO WEEKS LATER...

CHAPTER TWO

'Morning, Stacey,' I said, entering the kitchen. 'Morning, Alex!' she replied as she poured hot water into her mug. Stacey looked lovely as always, wearing a pair of wide emerald-green trousers and a simple white T-shirt with her blond hair resting on her shoulders. 'Coffee?'

'You read my mind.' I plonked myself down on the silver stool in front of the charcoal breakfast bar, unbuttoned my navy trench coat, then smoothed down my high-waisted grey pencil skirt. I really should've gone straight to my desk first so that my boss Steve could see that I'd arrived on time, but I couldn't function without coffee.

'*Love* your hair!'

'Thanks!' I said, pleased that Stacey had noticed whilst also wincing inside as I remembered how much it had cost to have my long chocolate extensions reapplied at the salon on Saturday.

'So, how was your weekend?'

'Hmmm…' I sighed. 'Could have been better.'

'Oh no!' Stacey pulled a stool closer to me and sat down. 'Why? What happened?'

'Think I've been ghosted again,' I said, rolling my brown eyes.

'Shit, sorry to hear that. I remember that feeling. It's *awful*.'

'Yep. Happens every single time I meet someone. If they're not ghosting me, then they're benching me whilst they continue shopping around on dating apps.'

'I remember that too.'

'You're married now, though, aren't you?'

'Yes!' Stacey grinned wildly. 'To the man of my dreams! We just celebrated our first anniversary!'

Lucky lady, I thought. At this rate, it'd be a miracle for me to celebrate one *month* with a guy, never mind one year. And here was Stacey, all loved up.

'Congratulations! Both on meeting your soul mate and leaving the depressing dating world behind.'

'Thanks! He really is *amazing*. Sorry! I don't mean to sound smug, especially when you're going through such a shitty time. Just because I'm happily married now doesn't mean I don't remember what it's like. I used to have *terrible* luck with men. However rubbish you think you are at dating, I bet that I was ten times worse.'

'Impossible!' I said, slamming my mug down in protest.

'*Believe me…*' Her green eyes widened. 'I have a back catalogue of experiences that will make your hair curl.'

'Oh, I doubt that. I've got enough stories of disappointing dates to fill a hundred encyclopaedias,' I huffed. 'I just don't get it. I meet a guy online, we have a nice date, we're getting on well, we sleep together, the sex is good, it feels like we have chemistry, and then afterwards they either don't call at all, or they come round a few more times and I never hear from them again. *Nothing*. I try calling and texting but zilch. It's like they've disappeared off the face of the earth. Except for the zombies like Connor.'

'So tell me about this Connor. He sounds like an arsehole.'

'He *is*,' I sighed. 'We date, he disappears like a bloody ghost, I spend ages wondering what I did to upset him. A few months later, just at the point where I'm about to get over him, he rises from the dead, messages me as if nothing ever happened, and suggests we "meet up". Each time I swear blind that I won't reply, and to my shame, I do. I always say it's the last time. Then I find myself remembering how great the sex was, and I wind up back in bed with him and back to square one.'

'Nightmare!' said Stacey, topping up my mug as if to console me.

'Tell me about it.' I bowed my head. It was so embarrassing to say it out loud. Especially to someone else. Stacey didn't make me feel judged, though. She was really easy to talk to.

Although she'd only joined my sales team at our trade publishing and exhibitions management company a couple of weeks ago, we'd instantly hit it off. You know when you talk to someone and it's like you've known them for years? That was the feeling I'd had when we were introduced on her first day, and we'd been having our morning catch-ups ever since.

With its bright white walls and matching tiles, the kitchen was a nice space and ideal for chats, but there was only really room to accommodate a few people at a time. Normally if our colleagues saw us nattering away, they'd leave us alone or come in and out quickly, which suited us just fine, especially when we were having conversations like these. Our boss Steve wasn't so accommodating. Whenever he found us in here, he'd always order us back to our desks. *Spoilsport.*

'What I'm interested to know is what changed for you? How did you go from Ms Dating Disaster like me to Mrs Married and all loved up?'

'Do you really want to know?' she said, checking the door to see if anyone was hovering outside.

'Of course I do!' I said, throwing my hands in the air. 'Then again, I suppose you're going to spout a load of clichés and tell me that you were just *lucky* and to *hang on in there* like everyone else does. Or that my soul mate will *knock on my door whenever the time is right* and that *you can't control these things*.'

'No, actually, Alex, I wasn't. What if I told you that I believe that there *is* a way to find your Mr Right and that there *is* a guaranteed, sure-fire way to stop all this agonising, heartbreak, benching, zombieing and everything else?'

'I would tell you, Stacey, that you're the world's biggest liar!' I scoffed. 'That where there are men and where there is dating, agonising, heartbreak, overthinking and feeling like shit automatically follow. And *that's* one hundred percent guaranteed!'

'I thought that might be your response.' She crossed her arms. 'Maybe when you've been ghosted and let down a few more hundred times, you might be ready to listen to my suggestion.'

'What? No! *Tell me!*' I pleaded. 'I want to know *now*!

And there's no way I can bear to be ghosted and let down again. I'm already a mess. If I have to endure much more of this, I'll have a nervous breakdown. Seriously: it's got to that stage. I'm willing to try anything.'

'*Anything?*' She raised her eyebrow.

'Yes! Actually…' I rested my finger on my chin. 'When you say *anything*, what sort of thing are we talking here? I'm not into anything too kinky…'

'Oh no, Alex! No need to worry about that. What I'm suggesting doesn't involve any kinky sex, if that's what you're worried about,' she whispered.

'Phew!' I pretended to wipe imaginary sweat from my forehead. 'Well, then, sign me up!'

'In fact, it doesn't involve any sex *at all*.'

'Oh right, cool! Hold on…' I frowned. 'When you say it doesn't involve *any sex at all*, do you mean it just involves straight vanilla sex?'

'No, no. I mean exactly what I said: if you want a guaranteed way to avoid heartache and all the other stuff that comes with dating, and you *really* want to find your Mr Right, then the answer is simple. Just don't have sex with them.'

My mind raced. She was confusing me.

'You mean not on the first date?' I scratched my head and took another gulp of coffee. Maybe I wasn't fully awake yet.

'Not on the first date, or the second, or the tenth or the twentieth…'

'Sorry, what? Twentieth? Wait a second…' I held my hands out and started counting my fingers. 'Let's say we have two dates a week. That's eight dates a month. Sixteen dates is two months, so twenty dates is two and a half months. Are you crazy? Not sleeping with a guy for two and a half months?'

'Actually, try six…' said Stacey.

'Six? Six what? Six *months*? Not having sex for *six months*? Have you lost your mind! That's *impossible*. That's *stupid*. That's *torture*! I mean, what guy in their right mind will wait *six months* to have sex with me?' I really should have kept my voice down in case someone walked past and overheard our conversation, but I couldn't help myself. 'What am I even saying? What guy would even wait six *weeks*—in fact, six *days*? Especially when it's a miracle if we make it past six hours before hitting the sack.'

'And therein lies the problem.'

'Stacey, I don't know what the men you know are like, but if I ever suggested that to the guys I meet, they would laugh in my face. It's a *crazy* idea! It would never work.'

'Worked for me.'

'What?' My mouth dropped open. 'Are you *honestly* telling me that you didn't sleep with your now husband for *six months*?'

'Yep. That's right.'

'How? Why? *What?* Is he religious? Did you hypnotise him? Do you have a vagina made from solid gold? I don't get it!'

'Nope, he's not religious, and no to everything else you asked.'

'Well, then, none of what you're saying makes any sense, Stacey!'

'I get that too. When I first heard about it, my reaction was exactly the same as yours. I didn't believe it was possible. That a guy would wait that long for me. That I could break the cycle. But then I read the book. And then it all made sense.'

'The book?'

'Yep. The book. It's the holy grail. An awakening. Like a bible for every single woman going through what you are now and what I was going through less than two years ago. I read it after I met another girl who recommended it to me, after a conversation much like the one you and I are having now.'

'So there are other women who have followed this advice too?'

'Yes! Thousands all over the world. It works!' she said, tapping away on her phone. 'There! I've sent you the link. Go online right now and order it. Once you've read it, let me know and I'll help you. This book changed my life, and I want to help you do the same. Try it. You have nothing to lose and everything to gain.'

'Well, I wouldn't quite say that I've got nothing to lose. Six months without any nookie seems like *plenty*. My happiness for a start.'

'And you're happy now, are you? Because I'm pretty sure that two minutes ago, you were telling me that you were feeling miserable after being ghosted for the millionth time.'

'True…but *six months*?'

'Yep. Look, at least read the book. Then you can decide for yourself. See if it's for you. If not, then just go back to your cycle of disappointment…'

'Good evening, ladies,' bellowed Steve. He stood at the door, folding his arms above his round stomach, which looked like it could burst out from under his dreary brown shirt at any second. 'I think you'll find that work started seven minutes ago. It's best if you arrive by eight-fifty a.m. Then you'll be all set up and ready to go by nine. Like I always say, if you're on time, you're already ten minutes late. Which means you're seventeen minutes late. *Ooops!* Actually, make that eighteen minutes and two seconds. Chop-chop! Remember, *the early bird catches the worm.*'

'Coming, Steve!' I said, feigning enthusiasm. 'We're just grabbing a coffee and then we'll be in.'

'Forget coffee! Time to seize the day. At your desks, ladies. Come, come. I'll walk you there,' he said, ushering us out of the door with his hands.

Honestly. You'd think we were schoolchildren rather than adult employees. I picked up my coat and bag, and Stacey followed beside me clutching her mug.

'Don't forget,' she whispered. 'Order the book when you get to your desk.'

'Yeah,' I said, having absolutely no intention of doing so.

I was glad Stacey believed that this book had helped her find her husband, but I certainly wasn't going to bother with it. Especially if it involved no sex for six months.

Nope. *No way.*

Each to their own, but I had better things to spend my money and time on. Hell would freeze over before I agreed to read a single page.

CHAPTER THREE

This was my happy place.

Tucked up under the duvet, in my fluffy pink pyjamas, glass of rosé (preferably White Zinfandel) in hand, about to watch a romcom with Cuddles snuggled up beside me.

Cuddles was my adorable British Shorthair cat. I found her at the rescue centre nearly a year ago and instantly fell in love. As her name suggested, she'd been great at giving me hugs whenever I was lonely or feeling down about life in general, but usually about men, as they caused me the most heartache. Stroking her soft blue-grey fur was instantly calming, and she'd been brilliant at keeping me company in the evenings and making me feel like every-thing would be okay.

After a class at the gym, which I tried to do two or three times a week, typically I'd come home, say a quick hello to Audrey, my seventy-seven-year-old next-door neighbour, to check she was okay, make dinner and then curl up with a good book or a film.

I loved retreating to my bedroom. When I'd finally saved up enough money to buy this place six years ago and started decorating, I'd wanted to give it a nice French country boudoir theme. It had lovely sky-blue walls, a white wooden bedframe complete with a large headboard and matching tables on either side, a baroque-style white mirror, dark wooden flooring, a mini chandelier, and lots of white and blue cushions spread across the white duvet to ensure I was nice and comfy.

When choosing what to read or watch, there were two key conditions: firstly, an element of romance, and secondly, a happy ending. *Always*. Not so much because I was a hopeless romantic. More because I needed to escape.

Every day, I had to spend eight and a half painful hours selling exhibition space at a job I no longer enjoyed, endure a horrible commute on two packed, sweaty, smelly tubes from my house in Tooting, South London, to Holborn in West London, plus drive myself crazy trying to figure out a) why a guy hadn't replied to my messages or, if he had, b) what his message meant.

Romcoms allowed me to forget about reality. For a couple of hours, I wouldn't have to think about my shitty job and disastrous love life and could just be transported to a world where the woman always finds the perfect guy. It was my way of staying positive and trying to convince myself that maybe one day, I might find my soul mate.

Silly, really. I knew happily-ever-afters only existed in the films and weren't something that would ever happen to me. I'd have liked to be positive about it and have more faith, but I had to face facts. I just didn't have a good track record with men.

I'd spent much of my twenties in one disappointing

short relationship after another. I'd hoped it would get better in my thirties and that by then, guys would be more interested in settling down, but now that I was thirty-four, it was no different. All they wanted me for was sex.

Of course, as Stacey had alluded yesterday morning, I knew that sleeping with a guy so soon after meeting him wasn't the best idea, so I couldn't blame them entirely. It's just that if we'd got to the point of having a date and were getting on well, going to bed with them seemed like the next logical step. Like the fourth course on the menu. You know: starters, dinner, dessert, then sex.

It was what I'd always done. What I thought was expected. Maybe it was because of my upbringing and my mum's views on the subject. *Who knows?*

Don't get me wrong, I didn't sleep with them completely out of obligation. I enjoyed it. The flirting and build-up during the date. The first kiss, and the suggestion that they come back to mine for 'coffee'. The excitement and frenzied undressing when they ended up in my bedroom, getting down to business, and of course the climax. And not that I'd given them all satisfaction surveys before they left or anything, but I always seemed to receive positive feedback. They'd compliment me on my kissing skills, say that my blow jobs were 'amazing', and they'd always come with gusto.

Sex was one of the few things I was good at. It was the one thing I could offer that would generally keep a guy coming back at least a couple of times. Well, before they inevitably traded me in for a better model, anyway...

Actually, maybe that was the problem. Did my skills need updating? Perhaps if I learnt some new bedroom techniques, they'd like me more?

Oh God.

See! This was exactly why I needed my evening film fix. Just thinking about relationships, or rather the lack thereof, was soul destroying. It always made me feel so shitty.

Enough feeling sorry for myself. Time to get a dose of happiness.

Just as I was about to scan my Netflix list to select tonight's film, my phone pinged, making Cuddles jump off the bed and head to the living room.

It was a message from Stacey.

Stacey

Check your bag.

Me

My bag?

Stacey

Yes! Check it!

I climbed out of bed, pulled my black leather tote out from behind the door and unzipped it. Everything looked the same as usual. Keys, make-up bag, tissues, hand sanitiser…

Wait. The front pocket looked bigger than usual, and I didn't normally keep anything in there. I popped it open and saw a cardboard Amazon envelope. I took it out, ripped the seal and looked inside.

She didn't!

My phone pinged again.

Stacey

Well? Did you find it?

I quickly typed out a reply.

Me

I cannot believe you bought me that stupid book!

I threw the book onto the bed, climbed back under the warm duvet, then glanced at the screen as Stacey typed out her next message.

Stacey

It's not stupid! I knew you wouldn't bother to read it unless I bought it for you.

She's got that right! But I didn't want to sound ungrateful…

Me

Thank you for being so kind, but I just don't think it's for me.

Stacey

How do you know if you don't try? At least read it first and then decide.

Gosh. She was like a dog with a bone. What Stacey wasn't taking into account was that I knew myself and I knew how guys were towards me. They didn't see me as relationship material or someone they'd like to stick with long-term. It wouldn't work, so why bother?

If a man couldn't even stay with me for a few weeks when I was giving them sex, what hope did I have of getting them to hang around for six months without it? If sex was off the table, why would they wait when they could just log onto Tinder and hook up with someone else in minutes? The whole concept of this book was flawed.

I didn't want to dampen Stacey's enthusiasm and positivity, though. So I typed out a reply, hoping that I could be forgiven for telling a little white lie.

Me

I'll try my best.

Stacey

Great! You won't regret it, Alex. See you tomorrow! x

Me

See you tomorrow. x

I glanced at the bright red cover. *Six Months to Love: Seven Sure-Fire Steps to Finding the One*, by Laurie Love.

Seriously? *Laurie Love*? What a convenient surname for a dating expert. Actually, it sounded like the name of a porn star. *Ha!* And she was practically *guaranteeing* that I could find *the one* in seven steps? One of which I already knew included not having sex for six months, which, for reasons I've just explained, would just not work.

Ridiculous.

I flicked through the pages. There was an introduction, then a chapter for each of the steps, and then—*oh, that is so corny!* A whole section towards the end with glossy photos of impossibly happy-looking couples. Some smug wedding-day snaps, other cheesy shots of them looking all loved up, either gazing into each other's eyes or kissing. I was sure if I looked carefully, there'd be one of two lovers skipping off into the sunset. *Purlease!*

And of course, all of them looked perfect. *As if.* She probably paid models to pose for the book, or bought a bunch of photos from a stock image site. Pff!

Does this woman think we're stupid?

Aha, I thought as I glanced over the text on the inside back page. *So she does seminars, does she? I bet this is part of her scheme targeting vulnerable single women. This Laurie Love woman gets you to read the book, and then, when it doesn't work, she probably recommends that you sign up to attend some weekend-long presentation at a fancy hotel that costs thousands of pounds, where she promises she'll teach you how to find* the one, *except you leave significantly poorer, having learnt sweet FA.*

Well, I'm not falling for it. Stacey was just lucky. Her husband was probably the only guy she met that was prepared to wait, and because she didn't want to stay single, she just gave up and thought *he'll do*. Part of me didn't blame her. I knew better than anyone that finding someone special was hard. But why waste my time with this nonsense? Who was to say there was even someone out there for me? And even if there was, which I doubted, I wasn't going to find him reading this. A bloody book couldn't teach you how to find love.

I tossed it onto my bedside table. Tomorrow, I'd add it to the bottom shelf of my bookcase in the living room, which is where I stored all of my *did not finish/take to the charity shop* items. I had no use for it.

I knew Stacey meant well, but that was enough fruitless distractions for tonight. Time to get back to finding a film.

Right on cue, Cuddles jumped back onto the bed.

'Hello again, sweetheart,' I said, snuggling up to her and grabbing the remote control. 'Now, where were we?'

CHAPTER FOUR

Today was sure to go down as the slowest, most mind-numbingly boring afternoon in history. Well, since yesterday afternoon, anyway.

As part of my role as event sales manager, I'd been trying to sell space for the last few stands at the upcoming Beauty & Wellbeing Show, but no one was biting. 'We just don't have the budget for exhibitions anymore, Alexandra,' they'd say, or 'We've allocated our marketing spend elsewhere this year.'

Because the company I worked for, M&E UK Media Group, produced trade magazines for the health and beauty, property and construction sectors, they relied on those publications to promote their exhibitions. Exhibition space and print advertising were the only options we offered our clients to market their businesses. But as I had tried explaining to Steve a million times, that was no longer enough. Even though the company had been around for over fifty years, in order to stay relevant, they needed to move with the times. Invest in their online presence and give clients the option of digital and social media packages. Did he listen? Of course not. Instead he just rattled off a load of clichés, telling me I needed more 'blue-sky thinking' and should 'think outside the box'.

When I pointed out that expanding their online reach *was* thinking outside of the box, he told me I needed to 'spend more time making phone calls and not excuses'. *Ignorant fool.* Sometimes I wondered if he was forty-five or eighty-five. He hadn't got a clue, and his antiquated views were driving the company into the ground.

On the plus side, he wasn't in this afternoon, so I didn't have him breathing down my neck, and there were now less than twenty-five minutes left until I could officially clock off for the day.

I leant back in my chair and thought of all the things I could do to kill time.

Going to the toilet was out of the question. I'd already done that twenty minutes ago, even though I hadn't needed to, and about half an hour before that. If I went again, then people would *definitely* think I had a problem.

I *could* go and see Shirley in accounts to check if all of my clients had settled their invoices. If I took the stairs, that would take at least ten minutes there and back. Then again, everyone knew nothing got past Shirley. If there was a problem with missed payments, *she'd* be the one to call *us*.

I'd checked Instagram, Facebook and Twitter three times this afternoon too. Karen, my long-lost best friend who'd moved to LA three months ago to pursue her dream of becoming an actress, had posted more photos of palm trees and blue skies, which I'd liked across all platforms and commented on. And there were no new messages on the dating apps, so I was all out of distractions.

Sod it. Looks like I'll need to actually do some work. See if there's anyone on our database that I can add to my call list for tomorrow. Chocolate will make it more bearable. I must have an emergency Snickers bar buried in my drawer somewhere…

Damn. Nothing there. Must have eaten it yesterday to get me through the second most boring afternoon in history.

Just as I gazed upwards, hoping the ceiling would open up and start raining M&Ms or transport me to a job I enjoyed, I spotted a ray of sunshine through the glass office walls.

Well, *hello*.

Who was *that*?

Standing at reception was a very tall, very fit man, dressed in a smart grey suit. His brown hair was neatly slicked back. He looked 'expensive'. You know when a man really takes care of himself? The confident type that get manicures and facials and doesn't give a shit whether their mates give them stick for it? *Very polished.* I had no idea why he was here, but he'd already made my dull afternoon significantly more exciting…

I could see Kandi, our receptionist, blushing and playing with her headset as she spoke to him. Don't blame her. He was a sight to behold.

Holy crap! She'd opened the office door for him, and he was coming this way.

'Stacey!' I said, scrambling around in my drawer for my powder compact. I needed a mirror to check I didn't have anything stuck in my teeth, just in case. 'Stacey!' I repeated, trying to get her attention as she stared intently at her screen. I could tell she was concentrating on something important, but it wasn't often we got hot men dropping into our building, so I was sure, like me, she'd be grateful for the distraction.

'Hmmm?' she said, her eyes still fixated on whatever she was reading.

'Hot guy alert!' I whispered. 'Check out the hottie headed our way!' I shut my compact and shoved it back in the drawer.

As Stacey looked up, her eyes bulged out of her head. Clearly she was just as impressed as I was. But then she jumped out of her chair.

'Whoa! Calm down, love!' I said, shocked that she didn't even try to hide the fact that she was into him. 'I know he's gorgeous, but at least play it a *little* bit cool. You are a married woman, after all!'

Completely ignoring my advice, Stacey pushed her chair out of the way to clear her path, rushed towards him sporting a smile that was bigger than the Joker's in *Batman*, then walked squarely up to Mr Hot Stuff and planted a kiss firmly on his lips.

Huh?

He wrapped his arms around her waist as they kissed for a few seconds, then held hands and approached my desk.

WTF?

'Alex, I'd like you to meet Bobby,' she gushed. 'My *husband.*'

Fuck. That's *her husband?*

I knew this was bad, but I'd always assumed that he would be…well, you know? How could I put this politely?

No oil painting. Stacey was amazing. Smart, funny and beautiful, but it was this whole challenge thing she'd done. I'd just thought she'd settled for someone that had trouble attracting ladies. Surely no good-looking guy, who was likely to have women throwing themselves at him left, right and centre, would wait six months for sex? Then again, I was being shallow and just making assumptions based on his looks. Maybe he had an awful personality.

No, that couldn't be true either, as whenever Stacey spoke about him, he sounded really nice. A gentleman.

Shit. I just realised that my mouth was wide open and I was gawping. It was embarrassing enough that I had just been perving over her husband in front of her, and now I was standing here with my tongue hanging out.

'Nice to meet you, Bobby,' I said, pulling myself together and shaking his hand. 'Sorry, I didn't realise…' I stuttered, wishing the ground would swallow me up. 'Stacey has never shown me any pictures of you.'

'Doesn't surprise me!' he chuckled. 'My darling wife is not one for taking photos on her phone.'

'It's not the same!' said Stacey. 'The quality on my real camera trumps anything I could ever take on my mobile. I have been meaning to print off a wedding photo for my desk, but just haven't got round to it yet. And anyway, I get to see the real thing every day, which is *much* better than a billion photographs,' she gushed again.

'Oh, you sweetheart!' he said as he kissed her on the lips once more and gazed into her eyes like she was the most perfect person that had ever graced the earth.

'Ugh! Get a room!' shouted Garth from the desk behind us. 'You're lucky Steve isn't in today. There's *no way* he'd put up with public displays of porn in the office.'

'Oh, be quiet!' I said, rolling my eyes. 'I'm not sure what porn you watch, Garth, but if all they do is peck on the lips, I'd ask for my money back.'

'Whatever,' he hissed.

'Maybe I should have waited in reception?' said Bobby cautiously. 'It's just that I finished work early, so thought I'd surprise you and take you out for dinner. The receptionist said it would be okay to come to your desk, so…'

'Oh, wow! Dinner!' shrieked Stacey. 'That'll be lovely. Thank you!' This time she kissed him on the cheek, probably worried that Garth would tell Steve. Knowing our idiot boss, he'd try and make kissing her husband in the office grounds for Stacey to fail her probationary period. Arsehole.

'I've booked us a table at the OXO Tower,' said Bobby. 'I know it's one of your favourite places, and the views of the Thames will be beautiful tonight.'

'You're *amazing*, you know that?' replied Stacey, stroking his ridiculously smooth, clean-shaven skin.

'*Ah stop*…you're making me blush,' he said as he now started stroking *her* face. 'Nothing's too much for my honey pie.'

They gazed into each other's eyes again like they'd just been hypnotised. Although part of me wanted to throw up at how cringey it was, another, much larger part of me felt my heart melting.

They looked so happy. *Madly in love.*

They were *so* lucky.

I'd like to be that happy. For someone to look at me the way he looked at her.

I'd like to fall in love and have someone fall in love with me. To adore *me*.

I was happy for them both. Of course I was. But I was also envious. I was only human, after all. Why did I get ghosted and Stacey got a husband who was besotted with her? What was I doing wrong? Why wouldn't a guy love me? Why couldn't I find my Bobby? My very own Mr Right?

'Oooh!' said Stacey, glancing down at her watch as I snapped out of my thoughts. 'It's half past five. Clocking off time!' She skipped over to her desk, shut down her computer, then grabbed her coat and bag. 'See you tomorrow, Alex!'

'It was nice to meet you, Alex.' Bobby smiled warmly at me. 'I've heard so many great things about you. Thanks for helping Stacey settle in so well here. It really means a lot. Enjoy your evening.' He wrapped his arm around her waist and they headed out the door.

Could reading this book really help me find a gorgeous, kind and considerate partner like him?

Really?

I very much doubted it. But maybe, just maybe, I'd have another quick flick through it to see what this Laurie Love had to say for herself. You know, purely for research purposes only. And just to say I tried…

CHAPTER FIVE

M ind blown.

As much as I hated to admit it, this Laurie woman surprisingly seemed to make a lot of sense.

I'd only intended to skim through the book again. You know, glance at the first few pages, so that if Stacey asked me if I'd read it, I could quote a few sound bites to reassure her that she hadn't wasted her money buying the book for me. But a few pages became ten and then twenty and then fifty, and before I knew it, I was on page 125 and as it was only 195 pages, it seemed silly to stop. I was tucked up in bed and it was a Friday night after all, so it wasn't like I had to get up for work in the morning or anything.

Laurie started the book off by giving us an insight into her dating history. I thought *I'd* been dumped a lot, but reading her story made me feel like I wasn't doing as badly as I thought. The guys she slept with didn't even *pretend* not to be arseholes. They were literally out the door the second they chucked the condom into the bin.

The final straw came when she was visiting her grandmother to celebrate her eightieth birthday and received a text from a guy she was convinced was the one after dating him for six weeks (which was one of her longest relationships). He told her that he'd slept with someone else the night she'd gone away, and as this woman was not only a *'freak' in the bedroom*, but also gave *world-class BJs*, he decided that she would be a *better option* for him than Laurie.

Can you believe that?

Anyway, unsurprisingly, Laurie broke down in front of her grandmother, who then encouraged her to explain why she was so upset. Not a woman to take being fobbed off, a generic 'man trouble' response wasn't enough. Grandma wanted *details*. When Laurie reluctantly fessed up, her wise gran told her that the secret to securing a decent man was to follow the mantra: *No Cock Without Commitment.*

After she'd picked her jaw off the floor that her dear grandma had used the c-word, Laurie had listened intently to her wisdom. Most men, she explained, were happy to accept sex if it was offered to them, but if they didn't have to do anything special to get the goodies and you hadn't laid out any relationship expectations *before* you opened your legs, then you shouldn't be surprised when you didn't hear from them again (or they traded you in for woman with a master's in fellatio).

Her grandma reckoned that instead of 'fucking first and asking for commitment later,' Laurie needed to apply the approach she'd used with her late husband. Start by taking time to know each other and establishing his intentions. Once you were sure that he was honourable and had fallen in love with you, then and only then should you consider 'letting his train in your choo-choo.'

Laurie learnt a lot about her grandma that night, and although she was sceptical, she decided to take her advice. It hadn't been easy, and it had taken plenty of willpower and cold showers to get through it, but after lots of failed dates, false starts and disappointments, she'd finally met a man that she loved, who'd fallen in love with her and had been willing to commit and wait for six months. They'd now been happily married for fifteen years. And she had her grandma walk her down the aisle, just two months before she passed away.

It was such an amazing story. At first I thought it was a little bit *too* amazing. Too sweet, too perfect. Well, you couldn't blame me for being cynical. But Stacey was right. This woman did seem legit. As I held the book in one hand, I had my iPad in the other, googling her.

Firstly, I wanted to get to the bottom of this whole surname thing. Laurie openly explained that *Love* was just a nickname her clients had given her, so she'd started using it for work. *Fair enough.*

Next, I'd scrolled through pages upon pages of testimonials on her website and looked at all the photos of the happy couples that had followed her advice, which even included a few celebrities. A pop star who'd waited until marriage to sleep with her basketball-player husband, the supermodel who'd abstained from sleeping with her internet mogul boyfriend until he'd proposed… was it really feasible to have paid all of these people to endorse her? Not likely. She'd need to be a very rich woman.

So I read on. I was intrigued to find out what the steps were, to see if it was as straightforward to follow as she'd made it seem.

Step One was all about acceptance. Understanding why you were embarking on the journey.

If you're tired of being ghosted or benched or zombied or treated like you're not worthy of love, then this book is for you. You have more to offer than what's between your legs. You are worthy. You are lovable. You deserve more. You deserve to be loved.

It was like she had been spying on me and had somehow infiltrated my brain. How did she know that was how I was feeling? That I always felt worthless and like I was never good enough to be loved? Everyone at work thought I was confident, just because I always hit my sales targets. But when it came to men, forget it. I was the poster girl for insecurities. Was it any wonder, when I'd never had a relationship that had lasted more than a few months? How embarrassing was that? As the common denominator was me, it must be because I was so flawed.

I could feel myself welling up. It was always painful to think about this.

Don't cry! I told myself. *Listen to Laurie and repeat: I am worthy. I am lovable. I am worthy. I am lovable. I am worthy. I am lovable…*

I was hoping that if I said it enough out loud, I would start to believe it. If only it was that simple.

Deep breath. *Focus.* Back to the book and the other key points mentioned.

As well as the importance of self-love, which I would definitely need to work on, Laurie also outlined dozens of benefits of waiting. Firstly, it helped you stay sane. She explained that sex literally fucks everything up in a woman's mind. Once we give up the goodies, our bodies release a 'love hormone' called oxytocin, which gets us hooked on the guy and sends us doolally. That's why we start obsessing over them, checking our phones every two seconds to see if they've messaged whilst we blinked and desperately trying to translate their texts and conversations to uncover an often-imaginary deeper meaning.

Whereas if we *don't* have sex, our minds can stay calm. By waiting, we can get to know a guy first to see if our personalities click, and *then* we can see whether they're really interested in us or just what's in our knickers. It weeds out the *fuck you then chuck you* guys, so we can focus on the ones worth giving ourselves to—the ones that like us enough to commit to a long-term relationship.

Step Two talked about 'visualisation and goals.' What did you want to achieve? Love? Marriage? When you visualised your dream man or future husband, what qualities did you see (their physical appearance should be a low priority, so that's a no to Tom Hardy or Idris Elba lookalikes, then…).

This step was also about establishing your deal-breakers. Asking yourself, what were the qualities you couldn't tolerate? I'd have to have a good think about that.

Step Three outlined the groundwork. Laurie said we were the boss of our own love lives and likened the process of finding Mr Right to a CEO looking for a business partner. If you were hiring for the position of boyfriend or future husband, after drawing up a job spec (your goals), you'd put the feelers out to recruitment agencies (dating apps) and headhunters (friends). Then, once you had a list of potential candidates, you'd set up the interviews (dates).

So the groundwork process here was updating your online profile, encouraging people you knew (aka headhunters) to set you up with their single friends and being more open to opportunities in real life. For example, smiling at the guy on the tube, chatting to the friendly man in the supermarket queue…that bit sounded slightly weird, but anyway, the point was to try and set up as many dates with potential 'candidates' as possible.

Step Four was the first interviews. Laurie advised against 'overscreening.' Whilst she didn't condone going out with total nutjobs, she stressed that placing too much of an emphasis on looks and sticking to 'your type' would be buying yourself a 'one-way ticket to Single City' and explained that often, we ended up with someone completely different to who we would have imagined for ourselves.

Again, this was something I would need to work on. I always went for the same men. Tall, dark and handsome. I think it's because it gave me a sense of validation. If a hot guy was attracted to me, then it meant I was good enough. That I must be at least a little bit pretty, otherwise they wouldn't even consider me. But it was a catch-22, because when they chose me, I was elated, but when they left me, I felt shitty. It was like they'd realised I wasn't good enough after all, or found someone prettier than me. I knew I should believe in myself more, but I just didn't know how to. Somehow I had to realise that I couldn't keep repeatedly picking Mr Wrong and expecting a different result. Easier said than done, though…

As finding the right candidate was a numbers game, Laurie reckoned the more dates, the better. Her reasoning was that a CEO looking for a partner wouldn't just give the position to the first stranger that applied. They'd host an extensive round of interviews with multiple candidates.

Dating, she reasoned, was no different. With no nookie involved, we should be free to date as many guys as we could. Seemed logical, I supposed.

Step Five was about the survival of the fittest. Laurie advised continuing to shop around and hosting multiple interviews with multiple candidates to get a shortlist of the top three suitors, then top two, until you found the one who treated you the best and showed that he was ready to commit.

Top three? Talk about wishful thinking. Finding one decent guy would be a major miracle, never mind finding two or three. Hilarious! *Okay, Laurie. Whatever you say, love.*

Laurie said that guys were also likely to be 'attending other interviews' during the early months, but once the final selection had been made and you committed to him, you should expect him to also make you his one and only.

Step Six talked about 'probation and padlocking'. Every job has a probationary period, so whilst you got to know each other, you also needed to continually assess whether the candidate was indeed the one. And a key way to help determine this was to *keep your pussy padlocked for at least six months.*

Well, I've already shared my thoughts on this step. I understood the benefits of holding out, but there was no way I could see a guy waiting half a year to get his leg over with me. Then again, some people swear that aliens and unicorns exist, so if that's possible, then maybe I could find a guy who would wait too? *Nope.* Still not really convinced. I probably had a better chance of coming home to see both a unicorn and a little green man chilling on my sofa sharing a bowl of popcorn and a bottle of beer than this abstinence stuff working. But I'd do my best to go along with Laurie's suggestion...*God help me.*

Finally, Step Seven discussed the appraisal and grand opening. This was where Laurie talked about evaluating your man's performance over the six-month period. If it measured up to your original goals and you felt ready, then and only then should you allow *his key to open your treasure chest* and declare the position of future husband permanently filled.

If this imaginary Mr Right fulfilled my original goals and successfully made it to six months, I wouldn't just let his key open my treasure chest, I'd give him a giant medal and a fancy embossed certificate and commission a solid gold sculpture of his dick to honour his willpower too. But let's not get ahead of ourselves. That actually had to happen first, which was as likely as the unicorn relaxing on my sofa asking me if I wanted to jump on its back and have a ride through the sky to a five-star, all-expenses-paid holiday in Bali. *Dream on.*

Laurie certainly had a way with words. As if to underscore that point, there was also a chapter summarising the key rules, all outlined in her colourful language:

THE RULES
Just say *NO* to:

- **Seeking Out Studs:** Pretty guys may be good to look at, but you're seeking a soul mate, not an ornament for your mantelpiece. Forget choosing style over substance. Hunky hotties have a tendency to break your heart, so unless they have a personality that's as beautiful as their jawline, avoid them like the plague.

- **Rebound Relationships:** Avoid guys who have come out of a relationship of a year or longer less than six months ago. They'll need time to get their shit together, and by waiting, you can be more confident they're not using you to make their ex jealous and won't jump back in the sack with them again.
- **Coming Before Commitment:** No dicks after dinner. Buying you a drink or steak and fries does *not* give him an instant all-access pass inside your knickers. Don't put *out* until he proves he's *in*to you.
- **D.I.Y.:** Take your hands out of your panties and put that vibrator back in its box. Masturbation keeps your desires running high, and we need to keep them low, so no doing you or him.
- **Going Downtown:** The only things that should go in your mouth for the next six months are food, drink and your toothbrush. Strictly no dicks or balls allowed.
- **Tongue:** Ditto. Kissing with tongues is a gateway drug. One minute his tongue is in your mouth, next thing it's licking your nipples and, before you know it, circling your clit. *No cunnilingus until commitment.*
- **Coffee:** No coming upstairs for coffee, tea or anything else on your menu. You're not a sick patient waiting for the doctor to call, so no home visits. Date in public places only.
- **Netflix:** Netflixing and chilling leads to rolling on the sofa and screwing. If you really want to see a film, watch it alone or with your

girlfriends, or go to a busy cinema. And remember, sex in public places is illegal. Ask yourself, are a few minutes of pleasure really worth getting arrested?

Say *Hell Yes* to:

- **Extensive Interviews:** Dating multiple candidates.
- **Public Dating:** Being in public places will help you avoid temptation (and no—slipping off to the bathroom together does *not* count as a public place).
- **Being Treated Like a Lady:** Let a man be a man. Let him take you out, pay for dinner and drinks, open doors for you and pull out your chair.
- **Comfortable Underwear:** Closing your gate to visitors is the perfect excuse to pack away those thongs and embrace wearing your biggest, most comfortable, least attractive panties, which also means no G-string chafing. Happy days!
- **Remaining Upright at All Times Whilst in a Man's Company:** And just in case you were wondering, that doesn't mean getting jiggy against the wall or in the shower…
- **Gym Workouts:** A good session releases the same hormones as sex so will give you the high of an orgasm without the lows of being dumped, ghosted, etc.
- **Saying *no*, *no*, and *no* again and again until**

it's love, engagement, marriage or whatever your goal is.

Fuck. That certainly was an extensive set of rules.

I read over the list again, trying to take it all in.

So, Laurie, let me get this straight: not only are you telling me I'm not allowed to sleep with a guy for six months, but I also can't kiss him properly and he's not even allowed to go down on me?

WTF?

That took me all the way back to my early teenage years of only getting to first base. But I wasn't a teenager; I was a hot-blooded woman with needs!

And then, if that wasn't bad enough, I couldn't even please myself? *Give me a fucking break!* I'd just spent £54.99 of my hard-earned cash on a brand-new waterproof vibrator with five speeds and six vibration patterns, and now I wouldn't be able to make use of it? This woman was a sadist.

And what was with her controversial opinions? Some of Laurie's views were politically incorrect and anti-feminist, and she generalised a lot about both men and women, as if we were all clones rather than individuals with different traits and personalities.

But at the same time, if I forced myself to try and look at it more calmly and with a level head, I *supposed* a lot of it rang true. It was as if she had scanned through my back catalogue of dating disasters, as I was guilty of doing literally every single one of the things on the *Just Say No* list. So if I *did* go through with it, to say this would be a challenge would be putting it mildly.

She'd certainly given me food for thought. Whilst I

had been dead against this whole thing when Stacey had first mentioned it, after meeting her husband and reading the book, I'll admit, I was warming to the idea. Best not to make any rash decisions just yet, though. Particularly when I was tired. I'd mull it over this weekend. As Laurie herself said, *act in haste, repent at leisure*, so just as she advised taking your time before jumping into bed with a guy, I needed to think more about jumping into this challenge. Because the last thing I wanted to do was to make a decision that I would later regret.

CHAPTER SIX

I stretched my arms up to the ceiling. That was a *great* sleep. Perhaps a little *too* good. *Can't believe it's 12.07.* Not surprising, considering I'd been up until silly o'clock reading that book.

Normally on a Saturday, I would have risen by 10 a.m. and tried to get the housework over and done with as quickly as possible. Hoovering (which took much longer now that I had Cuddles as her fur got *everywhere*, bless her), mopping the kitchen and bathroom floors, changing the bed sheets and doing goodness knows what else. I should dust and polish every week too, but I didn't, so I was sure one day I'd be sent to hell for crimes against cleanliness.

After the housework, I'd usually put a pizza in the oven (I never cooked on Saturdays), then collapse on the sofa and watch a film. By 3 p.m. I'd vow to go to the gym, telling myself that it was important to stay in shape, but sometimes it was *so* hard to get motivated enough to drag my behind away from my warm cosy house. Much easier going straight after work. So typically I'd fall asleep for a few hours, wake up, watch another film, read a book or log on to the dating apps and swipe and message until I fell asleep again. Lazy, I know, but wasn't that what weekends were for when you were single and didn't have kids?

Sometimes I'd get woken up with a message from a guy asking if he could come over, and *sometimes* I would agree. Not always. Okay. Maybe eight times out of ten? It depended how I felt. Now that I'd read the book though, I'd *definitely* try and say no to booty calls more often.

Yes, *the book*.

I got out of bed, picked it up, headed to the kitchen, switched on the kettle and sat down at the reclaimed pine table. Like most of the house, in keeping with my favourite colour, the kitchen had a blue theme. Rustic blue kitchen cupboards teamed with ivory walls and floor tiles.

I flicked through the pages of the book again, zooming in on the mantras I'd highlighted and circled with pen whilst I was reading:

You are worthy of love
No cock without commitment

Could it *really* work for me? What Laurie said *did* make sense *in theory*. I just wasn't sure if I could find a guy to love me enough to wait, or if *I* could hold out for that long. In the past year, I'd never gone more than a month or two without sex. If you don't want or need it then fine. But if it's being offered to you on a platter by a hot guy, it's much harder to resist. Being able to just say no seemed a bit unrealistic.

I rested the book back on the table, and just as the kettle boiled, the doorbell rang.

I wasn't expecting any visitors, and I looked *a mess*. I

was in my fluffy pink pyjamas, my hair was tangled, plus I wasn't wearing a scrap of make-up, and I *always* had a full face on. Whether I was going to the office or working out at the gym. I didn't like *anyone* seeing me with my skin exposed. Not even the postman. I was prone to breakouts, and if anyone saw me au naturel, they'd probably run for the hills.

I sprinted to the bathroom, grabbed my foundation, pumped it onto my make-up brush and applied big strokes all over my face. Thank God for my eyelash extensions. No need for mascara. I slicked on some pink lip gloss and quickly smudged on some eyeliner. *Much better*. The doorbell rang again.

I stepped out of my pyjama bottoms, pulled the top over my head and dragged on my push-up bra, a tight white vest and a green Lycra pencil skirt that was hanging on the back of the door.

The bell rang again. Then again. *Gosh. So impatient!*

'I'm coming!' I shouted as I gave the ends of my hair a quick brush, checked myself in the mirror, then raced to the door. I looked through the peephole. *What's my cousin doing here? Did we have plans to meet that I forgot about?*

I opened the door.

'Roxy? Hi?'

'Hey, Alex!' she said, bursting into the narrow hallway and kissing me on both cheeks. 'What you up to? Just finished the housework and watching one of your cheesy films, no doubt?'

Am I really that predictable?

'No, actually…'

'Ah, so you must be about to make lunch *before* you watch a film, then. Well, no need. I've bought us pizza,' she said, tossing her long fiery red hair over her shoulders, waltzing into the kitchen and putting the cardboard box on the table.

'Thanks! I hadn't quite got round to making lunch yet, as I woke up later than usual, so good timing.'

'I was just on my way to Shane's house, for some *afternoon delight*, and as it's only around the corner, I thought I'd stop off here first,' she said, unzipping her knee-high black leather boots, putting them under the table and pulling down her red velvet mini dress. Very glam for a Saturday afternoon, but that was Roxy all over. 'So, how come you were up late, then? Heavy night, was it, Alex? Or did you have a guy stay over and you've just kicked him out?' She winked.

'No! I was just up late…reading,' I said, rinsing off two plates and placing one on the table in front of her.

Just as the words exited my mouth, I saw Roxy glance down at the book.

Oh dear.

If there was anyone I would *not* want to see the book, it was her. Roxy was…how can I describe her? A lady who appreciated the company of men…preferably, without their clothes on.

Roxy and I used to see each other fairly regularly when we were teenagers. For some reason, she thought my mum was cool, perhaps because she was so liberal and not as strict as my aunt.

After uni, Roxy got married pretty quickly and moved out of London, and I hardly saw her. But then two years ago, when she hit forty, she got divorced and completely changed. Turned out, her ex was very controlling and she was never allowed to go out or have friends or any form of fun. Sex with her husband was always on his terms, and she never enjoyed it. So when she became single again, Roxy had been determined to make up for lost time and started partying and dating. *Hard.*

Difficult to imagine it now, but in her early days of newfound freedom, Roxy used to come to *me* to get tips on things like setting up a dating profile as she'd never used apps before. Roxy read a load of sex books and got herself back out there, and boy did she put all the theory she'd learnt into practice.

Unlike me, Roxy wasn't one to get attached. She would happily *date* (translation: *sleep with*) multiple guys at a time (on different days, obviously. Roxy hadn't told me of any orgies or swinging parties she'd been to. Then again, I wouldn't put it past her…).

Roxy would tell them from the start that she was only interested in no-strings fun. 'Don't get attached to me,' she'd warn, 'and definitely don't fall in love with me. You'll only end up getting your heart broken.' Can you imagine?

Most were thrilled to find a woman like her who didn't hassle them for commitment. Whenever she felt the need, Roxy would simply text one of her FWBs (friends with benefits) and ask them to pop round. If one wasn't free, there was always someone else waiting in the wings, only too happy to oblige. They'd come over and do the deed, and then she'd ask them to leave. Roxy didn't do spooning, hugs or emotions. She didn't want to cook them dinner, wash their socks, deal with them leaving the toilet seat up or listen to them snoring or farting in bed.

As far as she was concerned, men were there for pleasure. To fulfil a need. Nothing more, nothing less. Without that, they served no purpose. So you can understand why explaining a book which was based on the premise of a) committing to a guy and b) abstaining for six months to my highly sexed, anti-commitment cousin was going to go down like a lead balloon…

'What's this, then?' she said, picking the book off the table. 'Another one of your soppy girly books? *Six Months to Love: Seven Sure-Fire Steps to Finding the One*, by Laurie Love?'

I thought about snatching it away before she'd had a chance to read any further, but then I figured that would only draw more attention. Maybe she'll just put it back down and say nothing…

'Cup of tea?' I asked, hoping to distract her.

'A G&T would be lovely, thanks, Alex. I'm parched.'

She's starting early. I guessed it was almost 1 p.m. I put the kettle down, opened the blue kitchen cupboard and picked up the bottle of gin from the bottom shelf.

'Oh, you have *got* to be kidding me!' she shrieked.

'Oh dear,' I muttered, searching for the tonic water in the fridge and trying to avoid eye contact.

'Please tell me you are *not* thinking about listening to this nonsense, Alex? *No cock without commitment?*' Roxy said as she furiously flicked through the pages, her eyes drawn to the sections I'd circled. "When you've found the one, you need to keep your pussy padlocked for at least six months. Then and only then should you let his key enter your treasure chest?" WTF! Is this woman telling you that you can't fuck a guy for six months?'

'Would you like ice?' I replied, turning my back to her as I took a glass from the dishwasher and completely ignored her question.

'JFC, Alex! Jesus fucking Christ! Where did you get this ridiculous book from?'

On second thoughts, maybe I'd scrap the tea too. If Roxy was going to grill me like a lamb chop, which I now knew with absolute certainty was *exactly* what was going to happen, I was going to need something stronger. I took a bottle of rosé from the fridge and poured myself a large glass.

'Here you go,' I said, putting her G&T in front of her and opening up the pizza box. 'Ooh, you got extra mushrooms and peppers. My favourite!' I took a large gulp of my wine, hoping for the best.

'Nice try, Alex,' said Roxy, folding her arms. 'But now that I know you're deliberately trying to avoid answering the question, I'm even *more* intrigued to find out why you're reading this horseshit.'

Knowing she wasn't going to take no for an answer, I took a deep breath and explained everything to her. The persistent ghosting, the conversation with Stacey, Stacey buying me the book. Me dismissing it, then seeing Stacey's hot husband and deciding to give it a quick skim for research purposes only—and now, having read it, trying to decide whether or not I should give it a go.

With every sentence I uttered, Roxy rolled her eyes and tutted loudly, which is exactly what I would have predicted. When I'd finished what felt like a business pitch, she folded her arms again.

'So let me get this straight: you're not going to have sex for six months because you want to find a man?'

'Well, I haven't decided whether or not I'm going to do it yet. But, yes, that is one of the key principles of the challenge.'

Her frown deepened. Judging by the way Roxy's face was contorting, you'd think I'd just tried to explain quantum physics backwards in German.

'WTF! Sorry, Alex, but I just don't get it,' she said, tossing the book back onto the table. 'Sex is a basic human need. Why would you want to give that up *voluntarily*? People are crying out for more of it and you're telling me that when you've got hotties throwing themselves at you, you're going to turn them down? YOLO, my love. What if you're dead in five months? You would have spent your last days being frustrated. That's no way to live, my darling cousin.'

She just isn't going to get it. I finished chewing my slice of pizza.

'I know it sounds crazy,' I said, taking another glug of my wine for Dutch courage, 'but like I told you, I've tried every dating app under the sun and been out with dozens of guys, and it always ends the same way. We sleep together and I get dumped. I *need* to do something different to break the cycle.'

'I hear what you're saying, Alex,' she said with her mouth full, 'but you don't need to give it up for six months to find the right guy. In fact, maybe you should *increase* the amount you're having. Be safe, obviously, but date *multiple* guys. That way if one drops off, you're not bothered. On to the next. Just grow a backbone, don't catch feelings, and keep dating and fucking until you find the man you like the most. Simple.'

If only. One session in the sack, and as much as I tried not to, I was already wishing this guy was the one, designing my wedding dress, planning the furniture in our new home and what school our children would be going to. The book said women with more testosterone had less oxytocin so were less likely to get hooked on a guy after sex, so maybe that was why Roxy could stay so detached. That just wasn't me. At least it seemed she agreed with the multiple interviews approach Laurie had suggested.

'Yes,' I said, tearing off another slice of pizza, 'if I did the challenge, I *would* be dating multiple guys. Just not sleeping with them.'

'Bollocks!' She slammed her glass on the table. 'Dating multiple guys without checking under their bonnet is pointless. *Try before you buy.* Isn't that what your mum always taught us? You wouldn't buy a new car without test-driving it first. And you only keep a car for a few years, then trade it in for a new version. If you're planning to tie yourself down—which, having been married, I think is *crazy*, but each to their own—anyway, *if* that whole commitment malarkey *does* appeal to you, then you're talking about screwing the same guy over and over again for half a century. Surely you can see why it's important to know what you're getting and whether he'll float your boat? If you can't understand that, then you're insane!'

'I'm not talking about waiting to get married,' I argued. 'Just holding out, you know, waiting a bit. Until I know they're serious…'

'A *bit*?' she shouted. 'What is wrong with you, woman?' she said, slapping her forehead. 'A few days or a few weeks is *a bit*. But six *months*? That's like punishment. People who commit crimes go to prison for much less. Let's say you *do* hold out. You spend half a year getting to know each other, holding hands and planning your happy ever after and then when *D-Day*, as in *Dick Day*, finally arrives, you put on your saucy underwear, dust off your cobwebs and get ready for action, only to find that this perfect guy's manhood is smaller than your little finger and he can't satisfy you. What then?'

'Well, size doesn't always matter,' I muttered half-heartedly. I felt beads of sweat forming on my forehead as I pictured that awkward scenario with a guy called Norm a few years ago, when he'd dropped his pants to reveal a micropenis. I hadn't wanted him to feel bad as I could already sense that he was self-conscious, so we'd carried on kissing and touching. All the while, I was hoping he was a grower and not a shower, but it took a nosedive when, after putting on the condom (which didn't roll down very far), I suggested that he enter me, only for him to tell me that he was already inside. I couldn't feel a thing. *Oh gosh.* That was so embarrassing. In the end, we'd opted for oral, which was actually amazing on both counts. Giving head was a breeze and his cunnilingus skills were off the chart. Now that I thought about it, whilst we hadn't really engaged in penetrative sex again, the couple of other times we'd met up, he was actually very good with his tongue and hands.

See? It's not all about size. Surely it's much better to have a lovely guy with a small peen than a fuckboy with a big one? Right? Right...?

'We'll love each other and find a way to make it work,' I replied optimistically. 'Do other things.'

'Size *does* matter! What other *things* are you going to find to do for fifty years? And size is only the tip of the iceberg, if you'll pardon the pun. Say he *is* a decent size, but when you do it there's just no connection. He doesn't make the earth move. What then?'

She did have a good point. What *would* I do? Just as I

was scanning my brain for a response, as if by divine intervention, the doorbell rang.

Bloody hell. I don't get any visitors for ages, unless it's a booty call, and then today I have two in the space of an hour.

'Is that the door?' I said, hot-footing into the hallway. I looked into the peephole. It was my next-door neighbour, Audrey, clasping an orange pot.

'Hi, Audrey!' I said, opening the door.

'Good afternoon, Alex. Are you busy? Have you eaten? I've just finished cooking some pumpkin soup and I've made far too much, so thought you might like some to enjoy whilst you're watching one of your romantic films.'

I hadn't realised I was that predictable. Literally everyone this side of London seemed to know my weekend routine.

'That's so kind. Thank you. We've just eaten, but feel free to come in anyway,' I said, opening the door fully.

'Oh, I'm so sorry, Alex. I didn't realise you had company. I don't want to intrude. I won't stay long.'

'No, no!' I said, my voice going up several octaves as I realised the benefits of her timely visit. 'You're *more* than welcome. Come in. *Please!*'

Not only did I enjoy Audrey's company, but with her joining us, there was no way that Roxy would be able to continue our conversation. As well as talking about what was going on in each other's lives, sometimes Audrey and I chatted about how things were *in her day*, and Roxy wouldn't last more than five minutes listening to those stories before making an excuse to leave. Audrey's timing was *perfect*.

'Roxy, this is my neighbour, Audrey. Audrey this is my cousin, Roxy.'

'Pleasure to meet you,' said Roxy politely. Such a contrast to the potty-mouthed comments that had tumbled out of her mouth mere seconds ago.

'Likewise,' said Audrey, shaking her hand. She was dressed in a pretty floral three-quarter length wrap dress and a chunky sea-green necklace, with her striking silver bob skimming her cheekbones. She always looked so elegant.

'Please, have a seat,' I said, pulling out the wooden chair and placing the pot on the stove. 'Audrey popped over with some soup and to have a chat. I *do* love our conversations. Particularly the ones where we talk about how things were in the *good old days*,' I stressed. Audrey's face brightened. 'Sometimes our chats can go on for *hours*. We *really* get into it. So if you need to head off to see your friend Wayne, we'll *totally* understand…'

Don't get me wrong, it was good to see Roxy, but we were never going to agree on the philosophy of the book, so her heading off to have fun with her latest fuckbuddy would be better all round.

'Oh, *really*?' said Roxy, sitting up straighter in her chair. 'Sounds *fascinating*!'

'But, what about Wayne?' I said as my heart sank.

'*Shane* can wait. I want to chat with Audrey. Alex and I were just having a very interesting conversation ourselves, which I'd *love* your input in.' *Oh God. Please tell me she isn't about to ask what I think she is…* 'Alex has been reading a stupid book which tells her that to find her perfect man, she needs to not have sex with him for six months.'

'Roxy!' I shouted.

'Tell me, Audrey,' she continued, ignoring me, 'don't you think it's a *terrible* idea? At your golden age, you of all people must know that life is short, so Alex needs to grab it, or rather grab a hot *man*, by the balls and get as much as she can whilst she's still young enough to enjoy it.'

'Roxy!' I shouted again. 'I'm *so* sorry, Audrey. My cousin doesn't have a filter or any respect, so it would seem.'

'Well,' said Audrey, raising her eyebrows. 'Roxanne, you are correct, life *is* short, so it *is* important to enjoy it.'

'I'm glad you agree with me,' said Roxy, smiling smugly.

'*But*,' added Audrey, 'I happen to think there *is* some value in waiting. To make sure that the gentleman has honourable intentions.'

'See!' I jumped in.

'Whilst life is short, in some ways, that's all the more reason to make sure you don't waste it on the wrong person. And in the grand scheme of things, six months doesn't seem like an unreasonable amount of time to exercise a little self-control.'

'No offence, Audrey,' said Roxy, rolling her eyes, 'but it's probably been a while since *you've* had any action, so *of course* you'd say it's not long.'

'Actually, I've had relations more recently than you might think young lady,' said Audrey coyly.

'You little sexpot!' said Roxy, rubbing her hands with glee. '*Really*? You're still *at it*?'

'For goodness sake, Roxy!' I winced.

'Just last Friday,' added Audrey with a telling smirk.

'Harold. A gentleman from my bridge club. He and I have an *arrangement*. It's not as wild as my heyday, obviously. We both suffer from arthritis amongst other ailments, so can no longer swing from the chandeliers, and some body parts don't function as well as they once did. But thanks to those little blue pills and a generous application of K-Y Jelly, we manage just fine.'

'Audrey!' I said, my mouth hitting the floor.

'I think I've just found my new hero, Alex!' said Roxy, holding her hand in the air for a high-five. 'I *love* this woman. Still knocking boots in her golden years. *You go, girl!*' Audrey slapped Roxy's palm enthusiastically.

'Oh, you youngsters,' she chuckled. 'You think that when we start collecting our pensions, our urges just evaporate. *Yes*, it is true for some women. Lots of my friends couldn't think of anything worse than engaging in intimate relations. They're thrilled that they don't have to feign headaches or get involved with such activities anymore. But I've always had a healthy appetite. And I'm seventy-seven, not a hundred and seven. There's still plenty of life left in me yet!' she winked.

'I'm seeing you in a *whole* new light, Audrey!' My eyes widened. 'I don't know what to say…' Whilst it was a shock, thinking about it, she would be a catch. Audrey was in good shape and always took pride in her appearance. She could pass for a woman in her sixties rather than her seventies. *Easily.*

'Oh, dear Alex. I may be older than you, but I'm not blind. I see those gentlemen who come to your home late at night and then disappear half an hour later. And I see the sadness in your eyes the morning after. I haven't read this book that Roxanne speaks of, but it's worth a try, isn't it? I waited many, many months before I went to bed with my husband, God rest his soul. I wanted to be sure that he was worthy, and he was. I don't regret it. I know things are different these days. You live in a disposable culture. Easy come, easy go. There's so much choice with these dating online things you use, but sometimes old-fashioned values are the best.' She got up and patted me gently on the shoulder. 'Anyway, I'll leave you ladies to it. There's a function at the community hall this afternoon, so I'd better go and get ready. It's been a delight chatting with you. Do have a think about it, Alex. Consider trying a different approach. I'll see myself out. Bye for now, Roxanne.'

'Bye, Audrey,' said Roxy, winking at her as she left the kitchen. 'I'd better be making a move too, Alex.' She zipped up her boots and headed out to the hallway as I followed. 'Things to do, men to screw and all that,' she cackled. 'I can chuck that book in the bin on my way out if you like?'

'*Bye, Roxy!*'

I shut the door, went into the bedroom and flopped onto the duvet. My head was spinning. It was encouraging to hear that Audrey was in agreement, but Roxy had also made some valid points. What if I spent all that time getting to know a guy, only to discover that we got on brilliantly outside the bedroom, but inside it we just didn't connect? I really didn't know what to make of it all.

My phone chimed.

Gosh. Doorbells ringing, my mobile pinging. It's all go today.

I touched the screen.

Mark?

Who's Mark?

Oh…I remember Mark. But I hadn't heard from him in what? Two months? What did he want?

I opened the message.

Mark
Hey, babe. How's it going? Can I come over?

I chucked my phone across the bed.

Enough!

I picked up a pillow, buried my face into it and screamed.

I'm so sick of this.

I was tired of all these guys zombieing, ghosting, breadcrumbing and whatever-ing me. Only contacting me when they wanted to get their leg over.

I didn't want this anymore. I needed to make a change.

There's a saying: *if you keep doing what you've always done, you'll get what you've always got.* Stacey and Audrey were right. I needed to give this a try.

No more one-night stands. No more sleeping with guys without commitment. No more feeling like shit.

I'd decided. I was going to do it, or rather *not*. No sex for six months. I was keeping my legs closed and my treasure chest firmly locked. *I now declare my body a man-free zone.*

SEPTEMBER

CHAPTER SEVEN

I t had been an interesting ten days. After I'd decided that Saturday night to do this *Six Months to Love* challenge, I'd gone to bed early so that I could wake up at the crack of dawn on Sunday to get started. I'd made myself a giant mug of coffee and some fried eggs with beans on toast, climbed back under the duvet with Laurie's book beside me and the fresh green notepad Audrey had bought me for Christmas placed firmly on my lap, and got to work.

I pushed myself through Step One. I had finally accepted the challenge. I was up for it. Ready to try. The whole self-love thing wasn't something I could tackle in a day; that would need to be a work in progress. With that in mind, I'd started focusing on Steps Two and Three.

As part of the *Visualisation and Goals* process, I had taken a deep breath, then pushed my doubts and sceptical thoughts to one side. I dug deep and decided that I had to be honest with myself. The truth was, I *did* want the happy ever after. I *did* want to get married and have children. I was just afraid that it wasn't possible for me. But with the book's help, I was determined to take a leap of faith and believe.

I'd turned to another fresh page in my notepad. I say *another* because I had made several attempts at writing my Mr Right wish list. The first version went a little something like this:

1. Tall, dark and handsome, preferably with stubble or a nice soft beard. *Mmm*. Oh, and a lovely full head of hair.
2. Good body. You know, all strong and manly like Dwayne Johnson. *Yum.*
3. Charming like George Clooney.
4. Funny like Will Smith.
5. Doting dad like David Beckham.
6. Hung like a Chippendale.
7. A generous and highly skilled lover. *Double yum.*
8. Has a decent job. Doesn't need to be a high flyer, just earn enough to pay his own way.
9. Doesn't live too far away, ideally within fifteen miles.
10. Will listen to me talk about my day without complaining.
11. Caring.
12. Kind.
13. Likes cats, films (including romcoms), the gym and reading.
14. Gives good foot rubs and massages.
15. Good cook.
16. Loves me. Not in a stalker-ish, suffocating way.

More like in romantic, perfect book boyfriend way. *That would be a dream.*

17. Doesn't want to wait ages to marry me.
18. Wants kids.
19. Comes from a normal family, i.e., the complete opposite of mine.
20. Healthy and takes care of himself.
21. Has nice friends.
22. Doesn't spend the whole weekend watching football.
23. Not too messy.
24. Doesn't leave the toilet seat up. Actually, forget this point. That's *definitely* asking for the impossible.

As the hours had passed and I'd thought about it more, I'd realised I was being *way* too picky, or *overscreening* as Laurie would say. So after several more attempts to whittle it down, I finally settled on the following list of qualities I'd like my soul mate to have. I said I would like a man who:

1. Is kind.
2. Makes me laugh.
3. Shares my interests and goals in life.
4. Will be supportive.
5. Will love me.
6. Will commit to marry me within the first year of our relationship.
7. Will want us to spend the rest of our lives together.

That wasn't too much to ask, was it? I hoped not. When I was writing it down, it felt like a lot. Particularly given my track record. But Stacey said to put everything out to the universe and allow it to answer. I prayed that she was right. She'd been *amazing*. Talking me through the process and giving me advice. Stacey was becoming a really good friend, which I was very grateful for, as ever since Karen had moved, with the time difference and her busy schedule, I've been short of a bestie to talk to. Currently my female circle only consisted of Roxy and Audrey. Of course I'd love to have more friends as sometimes it could get lonely, but it wasn't easy to strike up good friendships in a big city like London. In fact, it was almost as hard as finding a decent man...

As well as making a list of my goals, I'd thought about what conditions needed to be met before I would sleep with a guy and decided there would be no sex until he showed he wanted to commit to me fully. That he was in it for the long haul. Marriage, children, the whole nine yards. I also needed him to say he loved me and mean it. I was sure I would know. That I would *feel it*. I hoped so, anyway. I'd written it down as a reminder:

Only When It's Love.

Only when he said he loved me would I give myself to him. That was the requirement.

I'd also made a list of my dating deal-breakers: 1) infidelity 2) unreliability 3) lack of commitment 4) dishonesty and 5) lack of integrity. If a guy showed any signs of those, I had to be strong and walk away.

I'd laid down the groundwork for Step Three by updating my online profile.

Having completed those steps, I'd spent all of last

week working on the task of finding Mr Right by arranging the 'first interviews'. Usually I'd rush this part. Frantically swiping and saying yes to any hot guy who seemed nice enough that asked me out. But this time around, on the nights I didn't go to the gym, I sat sifting through potential candidates, not just focusing on looks but looking for signs, either from their profile or the messages we'd exchanged, that we at least had some common interests. Per Laurie's advice, I didn't overscreen. I was just a lot more thorough than normal. Then and only then did we agree to meet.

I had four 'interviews' lined up so far. I was still wrestling a bit with the multi-date approach. Mainly because I'd always somehow felt like if I'd agreed to date one guy, then it would be wrong to go on a date with another until I'd given it a chance to work out. And of course it never did, so avoiding putting all of my eggs in one basket seemed like a much more sensible approach. It also made me feel more confident. Like if things didn't work out with one guy, there would be at least three more fish in the sea to try. So after ten days of working through steps one to three to lay the groundwork, it was finally time to start Step Four: the first interviews.

My first date was with Callum, who I was meeting tonight for a quick drink before my Legs, Bums and Tums class. We'd met on Bumble, and he was tall, dark and handsome, exactly my type. I knew Laurie said that was against the rules, but he'd seemed nice enough during our chats online, and rather than sending endless messages, he had been keen to meet early on. So in the spirit of keeping myself open to opportunities, I'd thought, *Why not?*

I paused at the corner of the road, took out my make-up compact, swiped on an extra coat of hot pink lipstick and looked at my reflection in the window of a parked car. I'd worn a black-and-white patterned pencil skirt and black heels. Not the most comfortable to walk in, but they made me feel sexy. And of course, look taller. At five feet four inches, I needed all the help I could get in the height stakes.

Time to go in. I took a deep breath and then stepped through the doors.

The bar was relatively quiet, which wasn't surprising for a Tuesday evening. There were just a few guys dressed in suits ordering some drinks, and a couple in the corner, deep in conversation. I spotted him straight away, perched on the tall burnt-orange stool at the circular wooden table opposite the bar, underneath the bright spotlight.

Damn.

He was *exactly* like his profile picture. Very good-looking.

We greeted each other, ordered drinks from the waiter and began chatting about usual stuff. How our days at work had been and the common conversation starter topic for Brits: the weather.

He quickly knocked back what looked like half a bottle of beer whilst he moaned about the fact that he'd got caught out by the unexpected rain shower earlier, making his hair (which was certainly very lustrous) a 'disaster' and had considered cancelling the date altogether if he couldn't fix it at work. Then for ten minutes straight, he'd whinged about how outraged he was that the formula in his favourite gel had been changed 'without warning' and how it now took him longer to get his hair looking 'perfect' in the morning.

As I sipped on my rosé and looked at him from across the table, going on about the various gels, pomades and putties he'd experimented with before eventually 'finding one that wasn't too expensive or excessively sticky and didn't set too hard', I began to get sidetracked. I couldn't help but wonder how nice it would be to run my fingers through his thick hair. I *loved* doing that. Especially when I was kissing a guy. His lips did look good. I watched them moving as he spoke, but right now, I wasn't thinking about what he was saying. Instead I was imagining them all over me…

Oh…yes…

I looked down at his grey shirt. He'd left the top three buttons open, and I could see wisps of hair peeping out. I wondered what his chest was like. He looked like he was in good shape. As my eyes scanned his torso from left to right, I thought about what it would be like to run my hands all over it. Better still, just imagine having his chest pressed against mine…

I'd really, really, *really* like that right now. The thought of his strong, body grinding on top of me…

'Alexandra?' said Callum.

'Mmm…' I replied, still deep in my fantasy.

'Alexandra?' he repeated. 'Is everything okay?'

I snapped out of my thoughts. I'd been so busy undressing him in my mind, I had zoned out from the conversation.

'Sorry, yes, I'm, I'm f-fine, Callum,' I said, trying to compose myself.

'Is there something on my shirt?' he asked, glancing down at his chest to check. 'It's just that you were staring.'

'Oh, sorry. No…it's not that. Um, would you excuse

me, please?' I said, getting up. 'I just need to pop to the ladies.'

I rushed into the toilets, flung open a cubicle door and then stood behind it, closing my eyes firmly.

Shit.

I needed to get a grip. If I was going to do this, I couldn't go on dates and start ogling guys. I mean, yes, I know everyone checks each other out and has naughty thoughts, but clearly I'd taken myself into a whole other fantasy world and stared so much I was surprised there wasn't a puddle of drool on the table.

I need to focus.

Easier said than done, though.

A week and three days since I'd started the challenge and I was already starting to feel urges. Not because it had been ages. It hadn't even been a month since my last time, and I'd gone longer than that. The problem was, knowing that I *couldn't* have sex and shouldn't be thinking about it just made me think about it even more.

It's a bit like when you tell yourself that you need to stop eating chocolate. Suddenly you see chocolate *everywhere*. You start craving chocolate cake, giant chocolate-chip cookies and hot chocolate, you want to guzzle a whole tub of triple chocolate ice cream, then you turn on the TV to distract yourself and *Charlie and the Chocolate Factory* is on. Suddenly, the whole world is made of bloody chocolate.

Except rather than being in a chocolate universe, it was like I was living on the set of an adult movie. Everywhere I turned, I saw couples kissing, touching and caressing each other. I swear I'd even seen two dogs at it in the park the other day. It was like everyone else on the planet was getting it on except me.

On the tube home last night, one couple had been snogging and groaning so much I'd thought they were about to start humping on the carriage floor at any second. It was like they knew about my challenge and were doing it *deliberately*. As if they were taunting me, saying, 'you can't have sex, but we can, ha, ha, ha!'

Evil. Pure evil.

But it was early days. Of course it was going to be difficult. I just needed to concentrate. Focus on his conversational rather than his bedroom skills.

I exhaled, opened my eyes and glanced down at my watch—6.23. I needed to leave to make my 7.15 gym class. If I'd felt that Callum and I could have a connection outside of the bedroom, I would've considered staying longer, but it was obvious we had nothing in common.

Don't get me wrong, I know how much hair can change how you feel. Two years ago when I'd broken up with Tony—who, after four months of dating, I'd thought was the one—I had gone straight to the salon and chopped all my hair off into a pixie crop. But then I'd felt so self-conscious about it being short, I'd gone back the following week to get extensions, and I'd been doing that ever since. It was all part of my work uniform. It made me look professional and feel glamorous. Being in sales meant it was important to project the right image. Plus most guys love long, flowing locks too. So yes, I'm all for hair talk, but a twenty-minute monologue about gel was pushing the boundaries of stimulating conversation, even for me.

Then again, should I try to keep an open mind? Maybe

he was nervous and the conversation would be better next time?

As I returned to the table, I asked the waiter for the bill, then reached into my purse. Callum, on the other hand, sat still in his seat.

'Shall we just split it?' I said.

'Oh.' His face dropped. 'I thought you'd be paying? You know, seeing as we met on Bumble and women make the first move?'

'That's funny!' I chuckled, hoping he was joking.

He wasn't.

'Yeah. Sorry, Amanda, I forgot my wallet, so don't have my credit card. I've only got a fiver on me and I need to get the tube home, so if you could pay, that'd be cool.'

Who goes on a date without any money? I would always bring enough cash to at least cover the cost of my own drinks. Surely that's just good manners?

And who the hell is *Amanda*? It's *Alexandra*. He couldn't even get my name right.

Replying was pointless. I called the waiter, paid and left.

I was definitely not keeping an open mind as far as he was concerned. *No way.* But at least tomorrow was a new day, and a new day meant a new date, which I hoped would be significantly better.

Date number two was with Eddie in a small basement bar in Soho, which looked a bit seedy to be honest. Very dark, with red lighting and tacky hanging lanterns. The kind of place I'd imagine would turn into a strip club after hours.

Maybe that would explain why there were so many men here. Not the most ideal place for a first date, but I was sure it would be fine.

Eddie was a personal trainer from East London who was tall and built like a brick wall. Six foot five of pure muscle.

Yum.

It was only supposed to be a quick drink, but the conversation flowed better than with Callum, so I stuck around.

Obviously Eddie liked to work out, so we chatted a fair bit about our mutual love for the gym.

I admit, I did find my mind wandering off a few times, thinking about the fireworks that we could have in the bedroom. Being so new to this challenge, it was only natural. Especially given his physique. He was the kind of guy you could imagine picking you up in his big arms like Tarzan.

Mmm…

Focus. Focus. Focus.

Thankfully, I managed to hold myself together (just). Then, about an hour and a half into our date, Eddie leant forward.

'So, sexy Alexandra…it's getting quite noisy in here, don't you think? How about we go somewhere *quieter*?'

'Sure,' I said, keen to continue our conversation. 'I know a coffee shop not too far from here that should be pretty quiet at this time. We could go there?'

'That's nice,' he said, slipping his hand under the table and stroking my leg.

I jumped, bashing my knee.

'Ouch!' I said.

'Sorry, Alexandra. Didn't mean to startle you. I couldn't help myself. So, what do you say? Should we continue this conversation somewhere else more private, say at your place?'

He started to stroke my leg again and it actually felt good. I'd missed a man's touch. I was really attracted to him, and the prospect of Eddie coming back to my place for a good workout was the kind of offer that, ordinarily, I wouldn't be able to refuse.

I could imagine him scooping me up in his big arms, lifting me this way and that…experimenting with a plethora of positions. Mmm…

'No!' I said, coming to my senses. 'I can't!'

'Can't?' He frowned. 'Surely I didn't get the wrong end of the stick? I'm pretty sure you fancy me, don't you?'

'I *do*, Eddie, but, I *can't.*'

'Why? What's the problem?' His frown deepened. 'If you like me, then why not, babes? We'll have an *amazing* night, I promise you.'

'I-I, I just *can't,*' I stuttered.

God, this was painful. I'd never restricted myself before.

'Have you got a flatmate at home or something? I can keep the noise down if that helps. Can't promise I won't make you scream, though, darling!' He winked.

Oh God. Cringe…

'No, it's not that…'

'Time of the month? I don't mind, babes. Extra lubrication…' He winked again.

He did not *just say that*…

'Er, no. It's not that either.' I shuffled in my seat.

This was *so* uncomfortable.

'Well, then, I don't get it,' he said. 'What could possibly keep a woman like you from wanting to spend the night with a hot guy like me?'

'Fancy yourself much?' I muttered. Despite his arrogance, somehow I still felt the need to explain myself. Like it would be rude to ignore his question.

'It's just that I've started this *thing*,' I said, taking a deep breath. 'A *no-sex* thing…'

Maybe he'll accept my response and just move on?
Who am I kidding?

'A no-sex *what*? As in, you're *not* having sex? *Why?* Why would you do *that*?' he shouted in horror. A question I had asked myself many times over the past eleven days. 'What are you, a born-again Christian?'

'No…'

'So if you're not a Christian, why are you stopping yourself? And more to the point, if we're not going to fuck, then why did you bother meeting me in the first place?' he said, the vein in his forehead throbbing.

'What did you just say?' I asked, sure that he couldn't have really come here expecting that I was *guaranteed* to sleep with him.

'What a complete and utter waste of my time!' He hissed. 'I've sat here listening to you drone on about your stupid job and the stupid films you like all night, and now you decide to tell me that we're not even going to screw? This is a *joke*. A prostitute would have been cheaper than the cost of that round of drinks! And I would have saved two hours of my life that I'll never get back. A *no-sex ban*! Good luck with that, sweetheart! There may be a few idiots that are willing to wait until date number two or three, but I am definitely not one of them!'

And with that, he was gone. My mouth fell to the floor. *Speechless.*

Clearly Eddie was a major dickhead, but even knowing that I'd had a lucky escape, part of me still couldn't shake the feeling that maybe he was right. Who really waited these days unless it was for religious reasons?

I knew Laurie and Stacey insisted this would work, but guys were going to think I was a freak. And not in a kinky way. They'd think I was mad. Nuts. Bonkers. There was no way they'd stick around.

Oh God.

What the hell have I let myself in for?

CHAPTER EIGHT

'Well, that's one of the first lessons to learn from,' said Stacey as she stirred her cup of coffee. 'Avoid being too open, too soon. You don't have to tell a guy that you're not going to sleep with him or give him a reason why. Like Laurie says, going on a date and accepting his offer to buy you a drink does *not* automatically grant him an all-access pass inside your knickers!'

'I know, I know.' I winced. 'I just panicked. I'm not used to saying no. Especially to a guy who looked like that. I was *really* attracted to him.'

'Eurgh! He may have come in pretty packaging, but his personality sounds awful. And as for his arrogance! Did he really say *what would make a girl want to turn down a hot guy like me*?'

'Yep!'

'Er, perhaps your ego?' suggested Stacey. 'And that's just for starters.'

'Tell me about it! As terrible as those first two dates have been, if I put my fears to one side and think with my head, I am starting to see the benefits of the challenge. If I hadn't read the book, I probably would have fallen for his charms, got carried away because I'd fixated on his body, invited him back to my place and had sex. Then I'd be obsessing right now over whether he was going to message, and if so, when? And if he *did*, which I doubt because he seemed like the one-night-only kind of guy, I'd be worrying about what his message meant, how long I should wait to reply, if I'd see him again, how much he did or didn't like me…I'd be driving myself crazy!'

'Exactly,' she said. 'And now, because you *haven't* slept with him, we can have a calm, detached conversation because we both realise what a wanker he was. You've ruled him out of the equation, and now you can turn your attention to your next two dates.'

'Yep. And I *do* feel calm,' I said, biting into my crois- sant. 'Overall, anyway. Although I totally understand why this challenge is a good thing, at the same time, his reac- tion does make me worry. When I mentioned the no-sex thing, he automatically assumed that I just meant two or three dates. Imagine what he would have said if he'd known it was six months! I'm trying to stay positive, but I just don't think a guy is going to wait that long.'

'The wrong guy *won't*. Remember, like the book says, the wrong guys *will* give up. They'll react badly like Eddie because they're not looking for anything serious. Those are the guys you don't want. They're the ones who will bring you grief and heartbreak down the line. So it's *good* that you see their true colours now before you get in too deep and wind up hurt. But the guys who *are* serious and *do* adore you, the ones who *are* looking for marriage, *will* wait. Because they know you're worth it. I know it feels impossible right now, but hang on in there. Keep dating and you'll find the right one eventually.'

'I really, really want to believe, honestly. But I can't help but feel that I'm setting myself up to fail. If this was all reliant on my own behaviour, then I'd stand a chance, but it isn't. It also requires me finding a patient man. And based on those dates with Callum and Eddie, it's not looking likely.'

'Come on. You're, what, twelve days into this? You can't expect to strike gold on your first rodeo. You need to give it a chance. My husband was the ninth guy I dated, and I know other women that have had to wait a lot longer than that. If it was that easy, it wouldn't be called a challenge! When's your next date?'

'Tomorrow night. But I don't feel like going. I'm worried that it will be another disaster.'

'Think positive. It *will* go well.'

'You don't know that.'

'Not with absolute certainty, no, but I *do* know that if you go in thinking it will be a disaster, it won't go as well as if you went filled with hope and optimism. Remember, like us, guys are attracted to happy, positive people.'

'Okay, okay. I will be happy and smiley like I'm auditioning for a part in *The Sound of Music*.'

'Steady!' she said, picking up her mug as we walked to our desks. 'You don't want to go overboard. Otherwise, he really *will* think you're a madwoman!'

CHAPTER NINE

D ay fourteen of the challenge and I was feeling okay. Much better and more positive. Why? Because last night, I'd had a date with prospect number three and it was actually good. Well, not *good* in terms of finding *the one*, but *good* as in I'd had a nice time.

I'd gone out with Sid, who was sweet. Very polite and softly-spoken. You could tell he was nervous as his hand shook every time he took a sip of his Diet Coke, bless him.

Stocky, a little shorter than me and bald, Sid was one of my 'wild cards'. Someone that I wouldn't have swiped for ordinarily, but I'd agreed to a quick drink with him as I wanted to keep an open mind.

Unlike Callum, he actually remembered his wallet (although of course I insisted on paying for myself), and he didn't seem to expect anything more after the end of our date. Those weren't the only reasons I thought he was sweet, though. He came across as a genuine guy. The bummer is that I wasn't attracted to him. There just wasn't that spark. I knew sometimes it took time for these things to grow, but I had to be honest with myself. If we saw each other again, it would only be as friends.

What the date *had* done was to help restore my faith in men. It was a timely reminder that not all of them were sex-crazed dickheads. At least Sid didn't appear to be. I reckoned he was the kind of guy who *would* wait to sleep with the right woman. And if Sid would wait, then maybe there were other men out there that would too. He gave me hope. So whilst I doubted he was my soul mate, perhaps Sid had taken me a step closer to meeting someone who was.

The fourth date I'd arranged was with Luke, a professor. When he'd messaged, I'd thought perhaps it was too good to be true to find a hot guy with brains on a dating app, but that was *before* my newfound optimism. *Why not?* I'd thought. If there were decent women like me on apps, then why couldn't some of the men be catches too? After I'd replied, he'd quickly suggested we meet at W1 in Mayfair tonight.

I took the lift to the top floor. Very swanky. It had a huge circular bar in the centre of the floor, illuminated by a ginormous chandelier that resembled a spaceship. I half expected ET or the cast of *Star Trek* to start coming out any second.

There were a couple of tall blondes in their twenties wearing micro dresses and skyscraper heels, perched at the bar, giggling with a large group of loud city boys who looked very drunk, and then another trio of women, dressed up to the nines, who were scanning the room and seemingly comparing notes on the various guys as if they were scouting for prospects.

This was the kind of place that lots of 'cool' people

would rave about. All glossy and glam. Worlds apart from the seedy bar I'd gone to with Eddie, but not necessarily any better. To be honest, neither of these bars were really my cup of tea, but I supposed it was good to try something different.

I was wearing a black pencil skirt with shiny black heels and a tight red sleeveless peplum top. No sleeves wasn't exactly ideal for this time of year, but it looked quite dressy and sexy, which was my aim. On second thoughts, what if they turned up the air con and my nipples started showing? Might give off the wrong vibe…I pulled my long hair from my back, so that it hung neatly over my shoulders and my boobs. Best to play it safe.

I sat down on one of the cream leather seats at the candlelit glossy black table for two and checked my watch. We had said 6 p.m., right? I launched the app and checked our messages. Yep. We had. It was now ten past. *Oh God. I hope he doesn't cancel? Stay calm. It's still relatively early. Give it at least five more minutes before you start to panic.*

I looked at the menu to kill time. *Bloody hell.* At £18 for a cocktail, I wouldn't be having more than a couple of drinks. Especially as there was still two more weeks until payday. I'd stick to wine.

'Alexandra?' said a voice behind me. I turned around, and *wow*!

'That's, that's me…' I stuttered as I stood up to greet him.

Tall—I reckon around six foot three—dark hair, green eyes and lovely stubble. He was *exactly* my type (yes, I knew what Laurie said about that, but…).

Thank you, Jesus. Please, please, please *don't let him be a dick.*

'Sorry I'm late,' he said, taking off his trench coat, revealing an unmistakable Burberry printed lining, a perfectly tailored grey suit and a crisp white shirt, which clung to what looked like a very firm chest. *Mmm-mmm.* 'Got caught up in an unexpected meeting with the dean, and then the traffic getting across London was terrible.'

'Don't worry.' I smiled warmly, fighting the urge to continue undressing him with my eyes. 'I know what it's like. You're here now.'

'What are you drinking, Alexandra?' he asked as he hung his coat over the back of the chair opposite me and sat down.

'I'll have a glass of rosé, please.'

'Excuse me,' he said loudly to get the waiter's attention. 'Double brandy, and a rosé for the beautiful lady.' The waiter nodded and scurried off behind the bar.

'So,' he said, clapping his hands and leaning forward. 'Where have you been all my life, Alexandra? You're *stunning.*' I blushed. This one was clearly a charmer.

'Thank you,' I said, twirling my hair around my fingers.

'You didn't answer my question.' He smirked.

'Your question?'

'Yes. *Where have you been?* I've been on that app for weeks and I haven't seen you, so naturally when you popped up, I felt compelled to message before some other guy took you off the market.'

'You're funny,' I chuckled.

'I wasn't joking,' he said with a poker face. 'When I see something I like, I don't hold back, I go for it. Take my career, for example. I come from a very working-class background. Before me, no one in my family had ever been to university. But I knew early on that it was something I wanted to do, and I worked my butt off both in the classroom and doing two part-time jobs to pay for the fees needed to make it happen. I got my degree, my master's, then my PhD, and now here I am today: one of the most successful psychology professors in the UK. Maybe even Europe. Who knows?'

'*Impressive*,' I replied as the waiter put our drinks on the table.

'Yes. So my career's sorted. Now I'm looking for someone to share that with. I'd like a nice wife and a kid. Maybe even two. Do you want children, Alexandra?'

Blimey. He's quick off the mark.

'Yes!' I said enthusiastically. 'I mean, it depends what day it is. When I've got a pile of washing at home and a load of housework to do, sometimes I wonder how much harder it would be to do that for a husband and children too. But, yes, I do. Absolutely.'

Oh gosh. Me and my mouth. Why didn't I just give a simple *yes* instead of going into all that gibberish about washing? Must be the nerves. *He really is handsome.* Whilst I'd be happy to be a stay-at-home mum and leave the rat race behind, there was no reason why my future husband shouldn't help out with the chores. *Don't want him to think he won't have to pull his weight too.*

For goodness' sake. There I go getting ahead of myself. I've only known the guy for two seconds and I'm already thinking about the housework rota. Jesus.

And I was supposed to be selling myself—not sounding like I couldn't cope with putting the washing machine on more than once a week. FFS.

'Don't worry about that, Alexandra. I have a cleaner to

take care of those things. We won't want to waste our valuable life doing chores. There's a whole world out there. So many countries to visit and explore. Life's too short for ironing and dusting. I can pay someone to do that for us.'

Really? Gosh. That would be lovely. Every time I had to hoover or change the bed sheets, I'd always thought I could be doing better things with my Saturday mornings, but like most people, I didn't have the money to hire someone. I just had to get on and do it myself.

'Do you like to travel, Alexandra?' he added.

'Um, yes. I went to Croatia this summer, which was pretty.' I reminisced about my recent solo holiday. Would have been nicer to have gone there with someone special, though.

'Thirty-three countries and counting,' he said.

'I'm sorry?'

'I've been to thirty-three countries so far, and I haven't even scratched the surface. This summer alone, I went to India, Thailand, Australia, Germany and Iceland.'

'That's a lot of countries,' I said, wondering if my list of destinations even stretched to double figures. *Let me see: Spain, France, Greece, Croatia…er…no. Definitely single figures.*

'I know. I get long holidays, you see. I'm pretty much off from April until October. Well, there's a few bits and bobs to do between then, like research, writing papers and responding to emails, but most of that can be done from wherever I am in the world, so I pretty much have six months off. This month I have to prep and go in for a couple of meetings to get ready for the start of term in a few weeks, but at my level, it's nothing too strenuous.

Then we have a break from the first week of December until mid-Jan too, so I'll be planning the next adventure soon. Where would you like to go?'

'Go?' I frowned.

'Yes. For the Christmas and New Year break? What countries would you like to visit?'

I took a sip of my wine. I couldn't work out whether this was a hypothetical question or he was genuinely making plans for our future, ten minutes after meeting me.

'Um, I haven't really thought about it. I…'

'I'll think of somewhere,' he said, whipping his iPhone out of his suit pocket and scrolling through what looked like an album of photographs. 'I've got lots of destinations to tick off my list yet. There's obviously the sunshine spots in the Caribbean, which will be great at that time of year. I've been to the Bahamas, Barbados, St. Lucia and Jamaica already, but haven't yet made it to Cuba, so that could work. Or on the other end of the temperature scale, there's Austria, which would be very fitting for that time of the year. I'll work it out. So,' he said, clapping his hands again. 'Marriage. How do you feel about it?'

This guy was…I don't know the word. *Intense? Direct?* I'd never expected to be discussing my thoughts on marriage on a first date. And the thing was, I didn't get the sense that he was weird. He seemed like he was actually being serious.

'I believe in marriage,' I replied. 'I'd love to get married to the right guy.'

'Call off the search,' he said, slamming his hand on the table. 'You've just found him.'

'Wow!' My eyes widened. 'You're certainly forward, Professor Luke.'

'Most people call me Professor Walton, but as you're *special*, Alexandra, you can just call me Luke.' He took a large gulp of his brandy and leant forward. 'In answer to your statement, I prefer the direct approach. Saves time. That's the problem with us Brits. A lot of dilly-dallying. No point beating about the bush.'

'I guess you're right,' I said, thinking his approach was quite refreshing. 'One of the hardest things about this dating thing is knowing whether you're both on the same page. You know, if you want the same things.'

'Precisely.'

'So you're talking about marriage…I know that clearly you're not proposing to me, as we've just met,' I laughed, 'but don't you at least want to know more about me first?'

'Of course,' he said, leaning back. 'Tell me about you.'

I gave him a brief synopsis of my life. Grew up in Surrey, one older brother who now lives in Australia with his wife and three children, parents divorced, rarely saw or spoke to them, went to the University of Brighton, studied international event management, worked as a sales manager at a publishing and exhibitions company in Holborn, a place I'd been since graduating thirteen years ago, love animals, films, books…

In a way, it felt weird sitting there rattling off a mono-logue about my history, but as Laurie says, dates are like an interview. Whilst I spoke, Luke nodded and punctuated my sentences with 'I see' and 'excellent' at varying intervals.

I couldn't quite figure him out. Luke seemed serious, but also like he had another side to him. He was very mysterious.

'So we've established that we're on the same page in

terms of marriage, kids and travel. All looking good, Mrs Walton,' he winked.

Mrs Walton? Gosh. He's jumping the gun a bit isn't he? I had to admit that Mrs Alexandra Walton did have a nice ring to it, though. Or should I keep my maiden name and double-barrel it? Alexandra Adams-Walton, or maybe Alexandra Walton-Adams. Yes, much better.

WTF?

I couldn't believe this conversation was even taking place in my head. This was our first date, for God's sake. Now who was jumping the gun?

'You're very…'

'Very…?' He frowned. 'Very what? Confident?'

'Yes.'

'Why shouldn't I be? You're not looking for a man that dithers, are you? That's definitely not me. Okay. Tell me, Mrs Walton,' Luke said as he clapped his hands. 'What are you looking for in your future husband? In *me*?' He smirked.

'You're unbelievable!' I found myself blushing again. I wasn't used to a guy being so forward about the future and calling me his wife. Normally, they didn't even want to commit to sticking around for breakfast the next morning, never mind discussing long-term plans. 'Well. You're right. A man who is confident *is* appealing.'

You can say that again. Someone hose me down. All this talk of marriage, not to mention his ridiculous good looks and charm was a massive turn-on. I crossed my legs tighter, fearing that otherwise, an invitation to jump inside my knickers might fly out and drop straight into his lap.

'Compliment accepted.'

'Luke! You're so…'

'You've already said I'm *confident*, *smart* and *attractive*...what else?' he said. I rolled my eyes, partly enjoying his cocksureness.

'I don't remember calling you attractive or smart.' *Well, not out loud, anyway.*

'Why?' He smiled. 'Do you disagree?'

'*No*...but...' He had me all tongue-tied...and I was sure I was starting to perspire too. *This man...* 'What I was saying was that I would like a man who is confident and knows what he wants, but...'

'There's a *but*?'

'*But*,' I continued, 'I also want a patient man. A man that's willing to take his time and prove himself to me.'

'In what way?' He frowned. *Oh gosh. I'm definitely not getting sucked into explaining the challenge again. I've learnt my lesson.*

'A man that can stand the test of time. That's not just after a quick fix or a roll in the hay,' I added, anxiously awaiting his response.

'You mean, you want more than a one-night stand.'

'Yes,' I confirmed. He leant back in his chair and smirked again.

'A man that is looking for a one-night stand doesn't talk about marriage and kids on the first date Alexandra.'

'It's not impossible, Luke,' I said. 'It could be part of your seduction plan.'

He laughed. 'As you said yourself, I'm direct. If I wanted to have sex with you tonight, I would just say so.'

'*Really?*' I said, taken aback by his frankness.

'*Absolutely*. Anyway, back to your point. I'm sure I've got all the qualities you're looking for. I can assure you, I'm unlike any other guy you've met before.'

'If you say so, Luke,' I said, desperately trying not to get swept away with his sweet talk, but sensing it was already too late.

'Oh, I do, Alexandra, my future wife. *I do.* So,' he said, clapping his hands—he really seemed to like doing that —'where to next?'

Here we go. Knew he was too good to be true. Now he was going to suggest we go back to his place or he comes back to mine. So much for not wanting to sleep with me tonight.

'What do you mean?' I said, raising my eyebrows.

'Shall we go to another bar? I'm going to a party with my friends later, but I don't mind staying out a bit longer and spending more time with you before I head off.'

I stood corrected. He *wasn't* trying to get in my knick-ers. *Hmm.* This guy intrigues me. Smart, confident, successful and looking for commitment. He might be *exactly* what I was looking for…

Whilst my body screamed, *Stay! Go to another bar and get to know him better. See where the night leads*, my mind shouted back a line from the book.

One good date does not a husband make.

Luke might have charmed me so far, but how would he act towards me tomorrow and the days after that? Would he message me? Ask to meet again?

No. I needed to put my foot on the brakes. Before I started writing my wedding 'save the dates' in my head, I had to curb my enthusiasm. I needed him to prove himself to me first. I'd fallen for guys too quickly so many times; I had to be stronger this time around. I couldn't get sucked in.

'Tempting offer, Luke,' I said confidently, 'but I've got

plans.' He didn't need to know that I would just be heading home to snuggle up with Cuddles and a good film. 'Perhaps you'd like to walk me to the station instead?'

Delivered like a pro. Well done.

'Of course.' His face fell. Laurie said it was good to keep a man on his toes, and judging by the disappointment I detected in his voice, I was doing exactly that.

The bar was literally a stone's throw away from Bond Street station, so once we'd navigated the crowds of tipsy revellers on Oxford Street, it didn't take us long to get to the entrance.

'Thank you for this evening,' I said as we stood in front of each other.

'Are you sure you won't stay out a little longer?' he asked, tilting his head like a cute puppy.

'No...' I said, throwing a bucket of imaginary water between my legs to tame my overexcited libido. 'I better head off.'

'Well, in that case,' he said, taking my hand and kissing it gently, 'I will say goodnight, Mrs Walton.'

He held my gaze and I couldn't help but blush. Luke really was a character. He was right. I hadn't met anyone like him before. He intrigued me. It really was a good thing I was going home now, because I knew that if I stayed a moment longer, I, or rather my body, would be putty in his big manly hands...

'Goodnight, Professor Walton.' I smiled as I turned and walked down the stairs.

That was a cool date. With a very hot man. Wow.

I sat down in the tube carriage and a warm sensation rose within me. A mixture of desire, satisfaction and pride.

I'd done it. I'd met a guy who treated me well, who I

also found really attractive, and had successfully resisted the temptation to sleep with him.

I'd turned a corner.

It was early days and there was a *long* way to go yet, but for the first time, I was starting to feel that maybe, just maybe this *Six Months to Love* challenge might be helping me to find my Mr Right after all…

CHAPTER TEN

'So, here we are,' said Luke.

'Yes,' I replied. 'Here we are…'

It was the following Saturday, and Luke and I had just got out of a taxi outside of my house after our third date. Just like our second date, which had taken place earlier this week, he'd taken me somewhere fancy. Tonight we'd gone to Buddha Bar in Knightsbridge. It was all dark and sleek, with oriental décor, amber lighting, a grand staircase with floor-to-ceiling crystallised dragons on either side and a metal Buddha levitating over diners on the ground floor. Definitely another new experience for me.

The drinks and food cost a small fortune, but as always, Luke insisted on paying for it all, despite me offering to go halves. In a way I was grateful as, at those prices, I might have needed to take out another mortgage to cover the bill.

We'd spent the night discussing a topic: can a man and a woman be friends? I'd noticed that during our dates, he liked having a debate. Maybe it was the professor in him.

He'd concluded that, yes, they could, whereas I, fresh from watching *When Harry Met Sally* last week, said that from a woman's perspective, it was difficult, particularly if she found him attractive and liked his personality. On date number two, we'd talked about nature versus nurture— what has the most influence on our personalities and the people we become? A lot more interesting than discussing the composition of hair gel, that was for sure.

Last time, we'd said our goodbyes with two polite kisses on each cheek, but I was sensing that things might be different tonight. I say *sensing*, but what I think I really meant was *hoping*. I *wanted* to kiss him. I shouldn't, because I was terrified that if I started, I wouldn't want to stop. I was *really* attracted to him. Not just physically, but mentally too. He was smart and he really seemed to be into me. I was afraid to say this out loud, but I truly believed Luke could be a contender in the search for my Mr Right.

As we approached my front door, my mind raced and my heart began to pound. What would happen next? Normally, I'd be filled with anticipation, thinking about how we'd go inside, crash through my bedroom door, then rip each other's clothes off within seconds of leaping onto the bed. But that wasn't supposed to happen tonight. I wondered, would he try to kiss me? And if he did, would I have the strength to push him away? If so, how would I do it without him thinking I was weird and losing interest? Well, if he didn't understand, then he wasn't the one for me. Right?

Oh, please be understanding…

'Well, thank you for another lovely evening, Luke.'

'No, thank you, Alexandra.' He tucked a tendril of hair behind my ear. 'You really are a sight to behold. Your beautiful long hair, your sparkling eyes, with those long lashes, the way you move in those sexy skirts you wear. You're gorgeous, Alexandra. Simply gorgeous,' he said, leaning forward to kiss me.

Within seconds, he'd thrust his tongue into my mouth and was exploring inside. His kisses were as forthright and direct as his opinions.

As he pushed his lips onto mine, his hands wandered from the small of my back and crept slowly down my arse. He pulled me into him.

'Oh God,' I murmured as I felt his hard-on against my thigh.

It felt so…so…

What the hell am I doing!

'I can't!' I jumped back.

'Sorry, Alexandra. I didn't mean to get so carried away outside your front door. Would you prefer if we went inside? So it's more private?'

'No, no. You can't come inside.' *Jesus*. There would be zero chance of me resisting if he stepped over my threshold. 'I-I just need to take things slower…'

'Completely your call.' He raised his hands. 'I shall bid you goodnight,' he said, pecking me on the cheek, 'until next time…'

He didn't even protest, or question me, or…or… anything. Such a gentleman.

'Would you like me to order you a taxi or anything?' I called out to him, feeling slightly guilty.

'No need,' he said, opening the blue gate. 'See you soon, Alexandra.'

I put the key in the door, kicked off my shoes, burst into my room and collapsed on my bed.

I grabbed a pillow and screamed into it, which I often did. Usually for disappointing male-related reasons. But this time I wasn't frustrated because I'd been dumped. I was frustrated because I'd found a guy who liked me, plus treated me well, and I really, really wanted to sleep with him, but couldn't.

I reckoned Luke would be good in bed too. The way a guy kisses is often an indicator of what he's going to be like. Luke's kisses were firm and definite. You could tell he'd like to be in control. He would ravish me. He would be insatiable. He'd give me such a good seeing-to, I'd be longing for more…

Oh God.

Why? Why did I have to go through this torture? He seemed like a good guy.

Why can't I just have sex with him? Tonight?

I hate you right now, Laurie. And hate is a strong word that I don't use lightly. Aaaarghh! Damn you and your stupid rules!

I closed my eyes and rolled around on the bed like I was in agony.

In a way, I was. My loins longed for him.

My phone pinged. I jumped off the bed, almost tripping over Cuddles, who had come into the room, and picked my bag up off the hallway floor. Maybe it was Luke saying he'd got home already. Impossible, though, unless he got a helicopter as he lived in Canary Wharf, which was at least ten miles away. Or maybe he was messaging me *just because*?

I'm so falling for him.

I unzipped my bag and fished out my phone.

Oh. It's *her*.

My so-called mother.

My mood immediately plummeted.

I tossed my phone on my bed.

I hadn't heard from her for, what, four months? Maybe more. I was so done with her and her intermittent 'parenting'. Flitting in and out of my life whenever she felt like it. So disruptive. I guessed it had always been that way. My relationship with both my parents had always been erratic. Maybe that was why, deep down, I had always secretly craved stability and my own family, because my home life was so far away from that ideal.

My mother was definitely *not* maternal and far from affectionate towards me or my older brother Nick. Dad was always working, and on the rare occasions that he *did* make an appearance, he spent most of the time arguing with Mum. It had come as no big surprise that they got divorced when I was nine and he ran off with his secretary. Such a cliché.

Cue Mum then going wild. She was like a caged animal who had been set free. She went out often and came back late, especially at the weekends, and left Nick and me to fend for ourselves. It wasn't unusual to find a strange man sneaking out of our house at odd times in the morning.

I remember one night, I must have been around ten, I heard her moaning. It sounded like she was in pain. I called out to her, to ask if she was okay. She didn't answer, so I got worried. I climbed out of bed, rubbing my eyes. As I drew closer to her room, the moans grew louder. I called out again, but there was still no answer, so I cracked her door and saw a man moving up and down on top of her. I was shocked. I'd seen men and women doing that on

TV a few times before, but understandably not in real life. I was really embarrassed. I crept back to bed, buried my head under the covers and tried to erase the unexpected scene from my mind.

I'm not sure if she'd seen me or not, but it wasn't long afterwards that Mum sat me down to have *the talk* about the birds and the bees. Cue more embarrassment.

She explained in probably far too much detail that sex was 'a wonderful, natural experience that adults should enjoy as much as possible', and she certainly stayed true to her word. That wasn't the first or the last time I heard noises coming from her room. It happened at least twice a week. *At least.* As the years passed, I just learnt to block out the screams and loud moans. But I still hated hearing them.

As Mum had never really let the men stay over, we didn't know whether she had a string of different lovers or the same ones over and over again. Whatever the case, her words and actions gave me my first lesson on the subject. *Sex is for enjoyment. A fun, disposable fix that should be engaged in regularly.*

When I was fifteen, she met Larry and began what could I guess in her terms be classed as a *relationship*. He *did* stay over. Often. And those were noises you couldn't block out. Their sex was wild and passionate, and clearly she didn't care who heard her. She'd come down to the kitchen in the morning after keeping us up for the entire night, tying her dressing gown and exhaling. Gushing about what an *amazing lover* he was. It's hard enough to think of your mother getting it on at the best of times. But at our age? Even for Nick, who was seventeen by then, it was a lot. The way it was thrown in our faces was horrible.

To me, it just didn't seem like appropriate behaviour or the kind of thing a mum should say or do in front of her children. Either she didn't care, or to her it felt entirely normal.

She'd often quiz me on whether I'd *done the deed* yet. 'What are you waiting for?' she'd say. 'It's *amazing*. I lost my virginity at fourteen. You're almost sixteen, Alexandra. It's time to become a woman! Experiment early. Sex is a *skill*. An *art*. The more you practise, the better you become. But do it safely, of course,' she'd said.

Finally, I'd thought. *She's shown an ounce of good parenting.*

Likely story.

'I'm too young to be a grandmother,' she'd added. 'I couldn't *bear* to be saddled with snotty-nosed screaming kids again. I'll book you an appointment at the doctor's. Get you on the pill ASAP.'

Always thinking of herself.

That was my role model. A woman who was desperate for her daughter to lose her virginity and become 'a woman' as quickly as possible.

As the months progressed and her relationship with Larry began to crumble, she taught me my second lesson: *sex solves everything.*

You know when you watch a traditional British soap opera and one of the characters has a problem, a concerned friend or relative will often tell them to sit down and have 'a nice cup of tea', as it will miraculously help make everything okay again? Well, that was kind of the strategy Mum used. But with sex.

Whenever she wanted something from Larry, or he was leaving to go somewhere and she was trying to persuade him to stay longer, or they'd had a blazing row and she wanted Larry to calm down, she'd put on a whole seduction routine, which would inevitably end with them disappearing into the bedroom. They'd then emerge again minutes or sometimes hours later as if nothing had happened.

Just like coconut oil that can supposedly cure every ailment under the sun, my mother's actions had taught me that if you wanted something from a man, giving your body to them was the magic answer.

Of course, I knew now that she was completely wrong. It didn't solve everything, and it certainly wasn't always amazing.

When I did lose my virginity a few months later after my sixteenth birthday, it was far from the *wonderful experience* she'd promised it would be. The same held true today.

Sure, I enjoyed the moment, but afterwards, once the guy had left—and they always did—I just felt so flat. So empty inside. Annoyingly, the sex that was most enjoyable was always with the ones who didn't stick around. The Connors of this world. But even with him, I was left feeling cold. Because I knew, sooner or later, he was going to leave me. Let me down. And there was no enjoyment in that.

Looking back, was it any wonder that I had grown up thinking that spreading my legs for a man would make him stay with me? Maybe if Mother hadn't put sex on such a pedestal when I was younger, I wouldn't have given it so freely to the guys I met in the hope that it would make them stay and like me more.

Thinking about it, my relationship or lack thereof with

my parents was probably why I had never truly felt worthy of love. How could I expect a man to love me when my own mum and dad clearly didn't? Once Dad had shacked up with his secretary and got her pregnant, all he cared about was his new family. If we were lucky, we got a stilted phone call once in a blue moon. He'd send money for birthdays and Christmas, but affection was more elusive than a unicorn. As for Mum, all she seemed to love was her freedom and men.

She was part of the swinging sixties' sexual revolution, and she told us she'd rejoiced when books like *The Joy of Sex* (which she often referred to as *The Bible*) were released. Mum really believed that for women, having lots of nookie was liberating. You know *my body, my choice*. She never tired of telling me how lucky we were, as with the pill and condoms widely available, women could now go at it like rabbits without the fear of getting pregnant or catching diseases.

And I guessed, up until recently, I must have bought into that. Surely that was why I'd always given it up so easily. Why deny myself? If I wanted to do it, then why shouldn't I? But now I understood. Yeah, we could take the pill to stop us from getting pregnant, but I'd realised that there was no pill that you could take to stop your brain from getting hooked on a man, developing feelings and getting hurt. Most women didn't have any control over that natural connection—the biological things that happened in our body that made us feel attached, even when we knew a man was no good for us.

'No!' I said out loud as I sat up straight in the bed. This challenge was hard, and although I really did want to sleep with Luke tonight, I couldn't give up. I had to give this a proper go. I had more to offer than what was between my legs, and if he was the right man, he would appreciate that.

As the saying goes, no pain, no gain. If crossing my legs and resisting temptation was going to help me to find that stability I had always craved, then it was a sacrifice I was willing to endure.

CHAPTER ELEVEN

'So how was your *third* date with Luke?' said Stacey, biting into her toast.

'Good, thanks,' I replied, grinning like a Cheshire cat. 'We went to Buddha Bar.'

'Oooh, fancy.'

'Yeah,' I said, stirring my coffee. 'With fancy prices to match!'

'I bet!' She perched on the kitchen stool. Stacey had quickly learnt not to get too comfortable, as Steve could come in at any minute and order us back to our desks.

'Luke chose it. I did offer to go Dutch, but he insisted on paying for all the drinks and the taxi home.'

'*Home?*'

'Yeah. Back to my place,' I said. Stacey raised her eyebrows. 'No! Don't worry! I didn't let him come in. But I've got to be honest, I'm not sure how much longer I can hold out for. Last night, our goodnight kiss quickly escalated to a full-on snog, with tongues, and his hands started to wander all over me. Even though I wanted him to continue, somehow, *God knows how*, I pulled away and told him that I wanted to take things slowly…'

'And how did he react?'

'Good. Okay. Really understanding. I could tell he was disappointed, but he was a gentleman. Said it was *my call* and then wished me goodnight. He messaged this morning about meeting up again, so I think we're cool. I even gave myself a pep talk last night and told myself that I was determined to stick with it, but now, in the cold light of day, I'm not so sure. I'm worried I'll crumble next time.'

'You'll be fine,' she said, wiping the crumbs from around her mouth. 'You're much stronger than you think, and as long as you keep going out in public places and don't let him step foot inside your house, then you're already halfway to abstaining. Unless, of course, you're one of those exhibitionists who likes to do it on pavements or in the toilets of a swanky bar?'

'Thought about it last night, but I haven't tried either. Ask me again in a month when I'm even hornier than I am now,' I chuckled.

'Your strength might surprise you Alex. In some ways, what you're going through now is the hardest part. It's the cold turkey stage where you're trying to change a habit. In a month's time, you should be used to not having it, so in theory, it should be easier.'

'In *theory*,' I said. 'I know we can't go all the way, but surely we must be able to do more than just peck on the lips? Laurie's rules are *so* strict. No tongues and not even any vibrators! I've had to lock mine in the garden shed as I didn't trust myself. What about touching a bit? Using hands? *Fingers?* Either Luke's or my own?' I pleaded. Stacey raised her eyebrows. 'No? Perhaps a banana, then? Cucumber? Any other phallic-shaped vegetables? Anything…? *Please…*?'

Gosh. What was wrong with me? I felt like I'd turned into a raving nymphomaniac. I'm sure I never used to think about sex half as much as I did now. It's like since I'd begun this challenge, it had started to dominate my thoughts.

'Nope, sorry, Alex. None of that's allowed. Look, I know it's difficult. The book *does* recommend going to the gym to release the happy hormones that give us the rush we normally get from an orgasm, so you could try and go more often. I took up karate. Maybe you could get some new hobbies to help take your mind off it?'

'Props for doing karate. Remind me not to get on the wrong side of you!' I pretended to cower, then chuckled. 'I think the gym thing, I can try, though. I'll increase my sessions. See if that helps calm me down.'

'Good plan. Oh yeah!' Stacey's eyes widened like she'd just had a flash of inspiration. 'I just remembered that one of the women I know who did the challenge also recommended vitamins.'

'*Vitamins?*' I spat out my coffee. 'I hardly think that popping some Vitamin C is going to help when I can feel Luke's dick rubbing against me.'

'I know! Sounds left-field, but she swore by it! Actually, it wasn't a vitamin, it was a herb. Chasteberry, I think it was called. Apparently, monks used to take it to decrease their sex drive.'

How ridiculous! I wasn't feeling the idea of popping pills, but my gym didn't close until midnight, so maybe instead of going home after my dates with Luke, I could do half an hour on the treadmill to run off my frustrations. I'd read some articles online that said some women even had orgasms whilst working out. Apparently running, weight training, sit-ups and cycling were particularly good for giving pleasure. Now *that* was something I could get on board with.

Then again, sometimes the gym could be a hotbed of temptation. There had been some very fit men working out there lately, and when they were grunting and groaning as they flexed their muscles, it could be hard to stay focused. I was embarrassed to admit it, but that was why I always wore make-up and a nice pair of leggings, just in case I met someone there. *I know, I know.* I was there to sweat and keep fit, not to meet men, and after some disastrous dates with guys from my gym in the past, I really should have known better. But remember, Laurie did say in Step Three that I should keep myself open to *all* possibilities…

'Thanks for the suggestion but, vitamin or herb, whatever it is, I think I'm going to need more than that.'

'Fair enough! Okay, well, when I started having naughty thoughts and felt my resolve weakening, I used to imagine Bobby straining on the toilet, doing a gigantic, super-smelly number two. Now, if that doesn't dampen your libido, then I don't know what will,' she laughed.

'Gross!' I winced. 'That vision might actually cause me to throw up, which wouldn't create the best impression.'

'No…but unless you have some sort of faeces fetish, it should help. If not, just think of the happily ever after that could become your destiny if you wait, or the stress you'll have to go through if you sleep with him and then he doesn't call the next day. *That* should be enough of a deterrent to help you keep your knickers on.'

'Hah! You reckon? Thinking about guys not calling hasn't stopped me from getting screwed over in the past. And as for my knickers, I think the elastic is getting looser with every date!'

'Funny! But you're a different person now. You're enlightened and thinking differently. You're doing great, Alex. Just keep going.'

'Thanks, Stacey.'

I *was* proud of myself. And as hard as the whole abstinence thing was, I was enjoying the excitement of going out on these dates. Following the challenge made me feel like I had a plan. Like I was working towards something concrete. Like there was hope. There was even another new interesting prospect on the horizon who had been messaging me.

I'd been debating about meeting this other guy, Miles, though. Mainly because things were going so well with Luke. I was trying not to get carried away, but I couldn't help it. Luke was smart, attractive, and confident—and he didn't shy away from talking about commitment. I was really falling for him. When I mentioned it to Stacey, though, she was adamant.

'You know the rules. Multi-date until you get a commitment. Whilst Luke is talking about marriage, you have to still keep yourself in the game until he makes a firm declaration.'

'Yeah, I know. He's just dreamy, though,' I said. Stacey folded her arms and gave me a stern *pull yourself together* look. 'Yes, yes. Point taken. I'll message this Miles guy later and agree to meet.'

'*That's the spirit.* Oh, and another thing. This trying to always pay for yourself stuff that you're so fond of, best to put it on the backburner. Men like to pay for a woman when they take them out.'

'Pff! Callum certainly didn't!'

'Let me rephrase. *Gentlemen* like to pay for a woman when they take them out.'

'That's one of the things I didn't like about the book. Don't you think that's a bit sexist? A bit 1917?'

'Why? What happened in 1917?' she laughed.

'You know what I mean!' I said. 'I don't like that rule. Women have been fighting for equal rights for years, and I'm all for equality, so why shouldn't I pay my own way?'

'I know it sounds antiquated, but remember, this is about old-fashioned values. And trust me, Alex, it works better that way. It makes them feel like a man.'

'Should I tie myself to the kitchen sink like a good, obedient wife and stop voting at the same time too?' I scoffed.

'Okay, okay,' she said, rolling her eyes. 'What about this as a compromise, then? If they offer to pay, don't refuse. Accept graciously and let them. Can you work with that, at least?'

'Ugh. I suppose so. Sometimes I just can't help but feel that if they pay for you, they expect something in return. Look at Eddie. He bought me one cocktail, which I *did* of course initially offer to pay for, and he seemed to believe that came with an all-inclusive Alex buffet.'

'Like I said, *gentlemen* like to pay and normally expect nothing more than the pleasure of your fully clothed company. Most don't expect anything straightaway.'

I thought about what she'd said. I supposed Luke is

proof of that. He'd been a real gentleman on all of our dates and hadn't pushed it when I'd said I wanted to take things slowly.

'Okay, Mrs Dark Ages.' I stood up and pushed the stool under the breakfast bar. 'I'll give it a try for future dates. Anyway, better go back to my desk. I've got a mountain of calls to make, and any minute now Steve will be on the warpath.'

'Yeah, he's been breathing down my neck too. But work can wait. Message the new guy first!' she said, following me out of the kitchen.

'Look at you! You've only been working here five minutes and you're already rebelling. I'll think about it…'

'Do it *now*!'

I headed back to my desk and plucked my phone out of my bag. Maybe it wouldn't hurt to meet him for a quick drink. At least then I could say I'd tried everything.

That was the strategy I had taken when I'd met Kyle and Leo, from one of the apps last week, for coffee during my lunch break. Neither of them had amounted to anything. I could just tell they were looking for no-strings fun, so for both dates, I'd only stayed for about twenty minutes and said I had to get back to the office. I hadn't heard from either of them since, so they must have also realised that we weren't compatible—or, more likely they saw I wasn't going to give up the goods. I was glad I went along and tried, though. Which was exactly what I should do with this new guy.

Yes. I'd better do it now before I changed my mind again.

Me

Hello, Miles, thanks for your message. I'd love to meet for a drink. 7.30 p.m. on Friday is perfect.

Sorted. Done. Another date and another potential prospect on the cards. He probably wouldn't measure up to Luke, but it was worth a shot. After all, as the saying goes, *nothing ventured, nothing gained.*

CHAPTER TWELVE

I was on my way to Mr Fogg's Tavern, a pub in Covent Garden, to meet Miles, and despite knowing that multi-dating was perfectly fine as long as there was no sex involved and you hadn't made a commitment to go exclusive, I was still feeling a little guilty. Mainly because lovely Luke had messaged yesterday to ask if I wanted to meet up tonight and I'd had to tell him I was *busy*. I guessed it made a change, *me* turning a guy down. Normally, whenever they messaged, I was so accommodating and always tried to bend over backwards to please *them*, which as we've established, usually then ended with me on my back, in their bed, legs akimbo.

But that was the *old* Alex. The new improved Alex was fast approaching the one-month mark of this challenge, having reached day number twenty-seven, and was feeling pretty damn pleased. Frustrated, *yes*, but still pleased with the achievement. As long as an attractive guy didn't look at me, touch me or get too close to me (which is a challenge in itself on the packed tube during rush hour), then I was totally fine.

Yep. All good.

Totally!

Maybe…

Not.

My phone pinged. My heart started thumping. Whenever I got a message just before a date, I instantly assumed that it was the guy messaging to cancel. I held my breath as I took my phone out of my bag. *Phew.* It was Roxy.

Roxy

How's the challenge going? I'm swimming in a sea of dicks at the moment, so let me know if you've changed your mind and fancy some cock and I'll send some your way!

She really was incorrigible! And crude.

Me

All fine, thanks, Roxy! Thanks for the tempting offer, but I'll pass…

I added some crying-myself-laughing emojis to keep it light-hearted.

Roxy

If you say so, sweetheart. In that case, I'll call the local convent and see if they've got space for you.

She added a winky face. So cheeky! Still love her to pieces, though.

Me

Ha ha! Anyway, better go, Rox. Off to a hot date. Hope all's well with you? x

Roxy

Okay, my love. All good my end. Happy leg crossing! xxx

Indeed. Well, how much I needed to cross my legs all depended on what the date was like, I guessed. I didn't know that much about Miles, to be honest. All I remembered was that he was a thirty-seven-year-old doctor who liked films and eating out, and one of the photos on his profile picture was with a cute Labrador, so he either had a dog or liked animals, which was definitely a thumbs-up from me.

We had a good match score, but I'd also scored highly with Eddie and one of the guys last week and those dates had been major flops, so sometimes you had to look beyond the numbers, past their profile and the pictures, then just take a chance and meet in person to see if there was that connection in real life.

I was wearing a rich blue pencil skirt, skintight cream top, sheer tights and my heels. I nearly always wore fitted pencil skirts. Sometimes clingy dresses too, but never trousers. I wanted to, but Mum had always drilled it into me that men liked women to look feminine and sexy, so I guess it was still ingrained in my brain and I couldn't seem to shake it. Even though deep down, I knew I'd be more comfortable in a pair of jeans or those nice loose trousers that Stacey always wore, I still couldn't seem to help myself from believing that I'd stand a better chance of attracting a guy if I stuck to my uniform of skirts and figure-hugging tops.

I'd arrived ten minutes early to give myself time to go to the loo and compose myself, but as I walked through the door of the dark green brick building, which was decorated with bright flowers and gas lamps, I felt a tap on my shoulder.

'Hi, Alexandra, I'm Miles.'

'Oh, hi!' I said, surprised that he was also early and that he instantly recognised me. I guessed, looking around, there weren't that many women with long dark hair.

It was like I'd entered another era. This pub had a Victorian feel. Made sense as I remembered reading when I'd googled it earlier that it had been inspired by *Around the World in Eighty Days*, hence why it was overflowing with Phileas Fogg regalia. There were ageing souvenirs, knickknacks and even a boat swinging merrily from the ceiling. Vintage music played in the background, and all of the staff were dressed in period costumes. Very cool. It was busy, but not overcrowded, and the atmosphere was lovely and relaxed.

'Nice to meet you,' I added as Miles leant forward and gave me a kiss on each cheek.

'You too. I've saved us a table over here,' he said, pointing to an area past the curtains against the back wall.

'Thought it would be better than sitting too close to the bar. Is this okay for you?'

'It's perfect. Thanks.'

'Great!' he said, pulling out a chair for me to sit down.

'Oh, thank you,' I said. *How nice.* I knew I was perfectly capable of doing that myself, but there was something romantic about it being done by a guy. What could I say? I was easily pleased.

'You look lovely,' he said, moving to stand opposite me.

'Thanks,' I said, conscious that I'd said *thank you* what felt like a dozen times in the past thirty seconds. All for good reason, though. He looked great too.

As another of my 'wild cards', apart from his short, dark neatly trimmed hair, Miles wasn't my normal type. He was clean-shaven, whereas I'd developed a penchant for guys with stubble or beards. He also wore glasses, and I'd never dated a guy with specs before. His dress sense was quite smart. Not *suit-smart* like Luke was on our first date. A little more relaxed, but still very polished.

He was wearing black trousers, very shiny shoes (they were that sparkly, I could probably do my make-up in them) and a sky-blue shirt underneath a navy-blue jumper. *My favourite colour.* Some of my male friends had told me they often wore a jumper as a second layer when they couldn't be bothered to iron the whole shirt, as then they only needed to press the collar and cuffs, but Miles didn't strike me as that kind of guy. Either that or he was just cold and wanted extra padding. After all, we were now in October.

'What can I get you to drink, Alexandra? Being a

humble pub, this place doesn't have table service, so I'll just go and get them.'

'It's lovely here,' I said, looking around. I did love a good pub, and even though I'd only been here a few minutes, I could tell I'd like to come here again. As well as being really unique, it was very intimate, warm and cosy. 'I'll have a glass of rosé, please, Miles,' I said, and he smiled and headed over to the bar. I was about to reach into my bag to get my purse, and then I remembered Stacey's advice. *Let the man pay.* It grated at me, but I left him to go up and do his *man's thing* and get the drinks. Maybe I'd offer him the money when he got back to the table. Didn't want him thinking I couldn't pay my own way.

I glanced at the menu. *Now that's more like it.* Most drinks were under a tenner. Much more reasonable than the prices I'd seen on a lot of these dates. They even did some cool snacks here. Depending on how the date went, maybe we could order some later.

As Miles stood against the bar with his back to me, I studied him carefully. It was hard to tell exactly what his body was like. Unlike jeans, which the guys I dated typically wore, his trousers hung fairly loosely so didn't show as much of an outline. And with the multi-layer shirt/jumper combo, I couldn't really work out the shape and definition of his arms and chest either. No ogling tonight, then.

'So, Alexandra,' he said, placing the drinks down on the table and taking his seat. 'Thanks for meeting me tonight. I was chuffed to get your message.'

'No probs. Thanks for messaging.' Gosh, this was all so polite.

'To tell you the truth, I was *this* close to throwing in the towel and kissing goodbye to the whole online dating thing, and then I spotted your profile and I thought, *Okay, let's give this one more roll of the dice.*'

'So what you're saying is your future membership for all online dating sites rests entirely on my shoulders? If it goes badly, you'll abandon the apps altogether? No pressure, then!' I laughed.

'Yep. That's pretty much the size of it. But, Alexandra, there's always the alternative, which is that if it goes well, I'd *also* need to abandon the apps so that we can sail off into the sunset together. Either way, I'd like to delete them, but would prefer to do that because I've found someone special.'

'Aha!' my eyes widened. 'So are you a *romantic*, then, Miles?'

'I'd like to think so…I mean, it's not for me to say that I'm a big romantic, as I believe in many ways being romantic is down to how you make a woman feel, so it's for her to decide whether I am or not. But, even though I know it's not very cool to admit it, I like romance. Who wouldn't want to fall madly in love?'

'A *lot* of the guys I've been dating over the years, for starters.'

Oops, not sure if I was supposed to talk about other guys and failed relationships…*Sorry, Laurie.*

'Sounds like some of the women I've met too, but I'm sensing you're different…'

'Of course I am!' I said, remembering to sell myself this time. 'Well, like you, I'll be modest and say that I also think so, but ultimately, it's for *you* to find out.'

'Well, I look forward to doing that, Alexandra.' He smiled.

Wow. What a beautiful smile he had. His whole face beamed and his big brown eyes sparkled brightly. Maybe the reflection of his glasses amplified the glow. I felt my stomach flip.

'I look forward to sharing, Miles,' I said as I began playing with my hair.

'Great. Well, let's start that now, shall we? I'd love to hear *everything* about you, Alexandra.'

'Really?' I said, surprised that he was immediately interested in chatting about me.

'*Absolutely!*' he said, flashing his smile.

'Well, how long have you got, Miles?'

'All night.'

'Then again, I could probably summarise my life in ten minutes, so we could still make it home in time to catch the evening soaps on TV.'

Ugh. Now I'd made myself sound like a woman whose life revolved around watching television. It was hard following all these rules about not saying this and that.

'Oh, I doubt it. You seem like you'd be someone I could talk to for hours,' said Miles, rescuing my faux pas and instantly making me feel at ease. 'And I'd much rather be here finding out about you than watching soaps. Not that there's anything wrong with watching soaps if that's what you enjoy.' He laughed again. At least I wasn't the only one putting their foot in it.

'It's okay!' I laughed again. 'I'm more of a romantic film buff than a soaps or TV person.'

'*See!*' His face lit up like the Eiffel Tower at night. 'I

knew I liked you, Alexandra. So come on, then: favourite romcom?'

'Ooooh!' I gasped. 'That's like asking me to choose my favourite child. Not that I have children, just to clarify, but you know what I mean.'

'I do, I do. But stop stalling. Come on,' he pressed. 'Which one?'

'Not fair!' I said, desperately trying to think of all the great films I'd watched in my lifetime and compile a mental shortlist. 'You can't pressure me for a quick answer. That's too hard a question! You might as well have asked me to spend the evening explaining algebra in Dutch.'

'Well, you can do that if you prefer? Can't promise I'll be able to stay awake or understand what you're saying, though,' he chuckled.

'Very funny! I can't even speak Dutch!'

'You're *stalling*!' He crossed his arms, pretending to be serious, but his cheeky grin said otherwise.

'Okay, okay. What about top *five* romcoms?' I fluttered my eyelashes in the hope that I could persuade him.

'Cop-out.'

'That's all I can offer you right now, I'm afraid. This is what happens when you put people on the spot,' I laughed.

'Go on, then. But they'd better be good!'

'They will be, Miles. Anyway'—I frowned—'what would *you* know about romcoms? You're a guy?'

'So sexist!' he huffed. 'Beneath this rugged male exterior is a soft-hearted metrosexual who isn't completely averse to the idea of snuggling up on the sofa on a Sunday afternoon to watch a good romantic comedy with a glass of wine and a bowl of popcorn.'

Really? Now that was interesting. Most guys I'd dated would only watch my favourite films with me under duress and tended to either fall asleep or moan all the way through about how soppy they were.

'Sweet or salty?' I asked.

'You're deflecting and stalling *again*!' He raised his eyebrow. Miles had nice brows. Thick, dark and natural. I wasn't keen on the male eyebrow-shaping thing. Good to take pride in your appearance, but personally I preferred them to look how nature intended. Untamed, uneven and perfectly imperfect. 'I'll tell you my preferred variety of popcorn when you tell me your favourite romcom films. I've already stretched it to five choices and you're *still* playing for time!'

'Alright. Let me see…' I rested my finger on my chin as I pondered. 'In no particular order: *When Harry Met Sally…*'

'Classic. Okay. Next?'

'*The Holiday…*'

'Yes, yes. Absolutely!' His eyes widened. '*Love* that film! Carry on…'

'*Pretty Woman…*'

'Yeah. Can't have a romcom list without Julia Roberts.'

'Number four: *Notting Hill* or maybe *Love Actually*. I can't decide,' I replied.

'Cop-out! *Love Actually* is a controversial one, but we can debate that another time, Alexandra. What's the last one, then, in your top five?'

'Um…this is *so* hard!' I took a swig of my rosé, hoping it would give me some inspiration.

'You said you're a film buff and that you love

romance, so now's the time to prove it. You can do it, Alexandra!' He beamed.

'Okay, okay. It's a toss-up between *Sleepless in Seattle*, one of the three *Bridget Jones' Diary* films, *You've Got Mail* and *To All the Boys I've Loved Before*.'

'That's cheating!' He threw his arms up in the air in mock-protest. 'You're trying to cram six films into one slot! Get off the fence and choose!'

'I just *can't*! Anyway,' I said, trying to take the spotlight away from my blatant cop-out, 'didn't *you* claim to be a romantic, Miles? So why am *I* doing all the film choosing? Bet you can't even name *three* great romcoms, never mind five. And they can't be any that I've already mentioned, *obviously*.'

'Easy!' he said calmly, like I'd just asked him to say the first few letters of the alphabet.

'Go on, then. Or are you just *stalling*?' I smirked.

'As you'll get to know Alexandra, I am a man of my word. And unlike *someone* I've just met, I'm decisive too. No sitting on the fence. Here we go: three romcoms I like, also in no particular order. Drum roll, please,' he said, slapping his hands on the table as I joined in. '*The Proposal*, *Crazy Stupid Love* and *It's Complicated*.'

'Ah, dammit!' I slapped my hand on my forehead. 'Forgot about those! Excellent choices!'

'Thanks,' he said, taking a bow.

'You really *do* know your romcoms. And you were right, you did come up with three very quickly.'

'Why, thank you!'

'Then again,' I said, 'you did have *much* longer to think about it than I did. And it was *your* question, so maybe you've been thinking about it all day…'

'Ah! So cynical. You're not a sore loser, are you?'

'Are you calling me a loser?' I chuckled.

'Of course not, Alexandra. No winners or losers here. Just two film fans exchanging notes. What about the old romcoms? You know, from the 1950s? Have you ever seen any of those?'

'I haven't, actually,' I said.

'A lot of people our age haven't. We tend to watch more modern films,' he said. 'I only discovered some old Cary Grant films by chance when I was channel surfing one Christmas and loved them.'

'I'll have to look some up on Netflix,' I replied.

'I don't think there's many on there, but I've got some DVDs. Maybe one day we can watch them together?'

'That would be lovely!' I caught myself saying without even thinking. What about Luke? Surely I shouldn't be agreeing to watch DVDs with another man when Luke was already practically planning our nuptials?

It would be nice though. Romantic. And *sexy*.

Oh God...

I tried to push away the vision of Miles and me snuggled up on the sofa, watching a romcom. The credits would roll, and we'd kiss passionately and end up making love on the sofa...

Stop it. Stop it. Stop it! *Stop thinking about bloody sex!*

I thought Stacey said it got easier after the first month...

Now where was I? Rolling around naked on the sofa with Miles and feeling guilty about Luke...

Sod it. I was supposed to be keeping my options open until he committed properly, so maybe I just needed to worry about it *if* and *when* the time came.

'Great!' said Miles. 'And you can bring the popcorn. Sweet and salty will be just fine.'

'I thought you didn't sit on the fence?' I laughed. 'Pick one or the other!'

'Touché, Alexandra. *Touché!* Sweet popcorn it is.'

From that point on, we talked non-stop. What was supposed to be my standard thirty-minute drink ended up being over a three-and-a-half-hour date. And I honestly had no idea where the time went.

We spoke about films a lot, I did remember that. He knew so much about them, and he gave me loads of recommendations for ones I hadn't even heard of. I thought that would be my evenings sorted for the next few years.

Probably contrary to Laurie's suggestions, we talked about relationships for a while, and whilst I vented (not too much, though) about guys who were just after fun (which I thought would also highlight the fact that if that *was* what he was after, he was barking up the wrong tree, although I sensed that wasn't the case), he gave me an insight into some of the women he'd met.

He sounded more exasperated and disillusioned than I was. Miles had been on dating apps for the last four months, ever since he'd broken up with his ex-girlfriend of two years (I knew the rules said not to date guys that had come out of a serious relationship less than six months ago, but she'd left the country and he seemed cool about it, so it was fine). He said a lot of women were just into the fantasy of being with a doctor. One had even asked why he hadn't come on the date in a doctor's coat so they could do *role-play* later. A couple, he said, were mainly interested in how much he earned and if it was enough to give them a champagne lifestyle.

It was funny. As I listened to him and protested that those few examples were not representative of womankind as a whole and certainly not me, I also got a greater appreciation of how frustrating it must be for a decent guy when a woman judged them by the bad experiences she'd had with men. It helped to remind me of the importance of keeping an open mind.

What else did we speak about? Our shared love for animals was definitely a topic we covered. I just remembered laughing. *A lot*. At one point, it felt like I'd done two hundred sit-ups because my stomach ached so much. And every time he smiled, my heart started beating faster.

Not only was his smile electric, but his mouth, his *lips*, were amazing too. Equally sized top and bottom, smooth and very juicy.

We had a few *moments* too. I felt it. The *connection*. We'd belly laugh about something or other and then we'd catch each other's gaze and just sit there smiling. Silently. It was only for a few seconds each time, but there was just *something* there. Something indescribable. Like a *force*. An *energy*. Pulling us together. Wild card or not, I was *definitely* attracted to him.

The bell rang. We looked up and saw the barman stood on the counter.

'Thank you for joining us, ladies and gentlemen. Our time to part has come. Last orders!' he said jovially. It was very theatrical here. I loved it.

'Wow!' said Miles, glancing down at his watch. 'Closing time already? I didn't even get to show you the Gin Parlour upstairs with all the chaise longues, quirky furniture and cool trinkets on the walls. I feel like we just got here.'

'I know—it's mad!' I said, pulling my phone out of my handbag and touching the screen to check. Yep. It was indeed almost 11 p.m. 'The time has just flown. And *I* didn't even get to ask you about your job or, I don't know…all the hundreds of things we're supposed to talk about on first dates.'

'Well, that's easily solved.' He smirked.

'Yeah, I guess we could start talking about it now before they chuck us out.'

'*Or*'—Miles leant forward—'we *could* just talk about it on a *second* date. If you'd like to see me, again that is?'

'Of course!' I said, a little too keenly. 'Yeah, I mean, that would be cool. If you'd like to.' *Well, he wouldn't have asked if he didn't.* One day I'd get the hang of this dating and saying the right thing.

'I've had an *amazing* evening with you, Alexandra, so I'd *love* to. How about tomorrow night?'

'Tomorrow?' My stomach plummeted.

Shit. Shit. *Shit.*

I was meeting Luke tomorrow night. Dammit. I mean, not *dammit* as in I didn't want to. Of *course* I wanted to see Luke. Luke was *great*. Why wouldn't I want to see him? It was just that I really liked Miles now too.

Christ. I'd told Stacey this multi-dating thing would be messy…

'Yeah, tomorrow night,' he repeated.

'I'm really sorry, Miles, but I've got plans tomorrow night.'

Gutted. Who knew when he'd be free again? You hear

about doctors working long shifts day after day. Maybe it would be another week until he was free.

'Okay.' He paused. 'How about tomorrow afternoon, then?'

Oh! That could work…I normally did the housework on a Saturday, but I could often get it all finished by noon. And anyway, as Luke had said on our first date, life's too short to spend it doing chores. I could see Miles in the afternoon and then Luke in the evening. Two guys in one day? Well, I wasn't sleeping with them and we weren't committed… *Remember, it's fine. It's totally fine…*

'Tomorrow afternoon is good, actually,' I confirmed.

'Great! In that case, I've already thought of the perfect place to take you.'

'Really?' I said.

'Yep.' He grinned.

'Where?'

'It's a surprise.'

'No! You've *got* to tell me, Miles!' I pleaded.

'No can do, Alexandra,' he teased.

'Okay, then, I'll just guess.'

'No guessing allowed.' He waved his finger. 'It will ruin the surprise.'

'Another pub?'

'No! We're at a pub now. What kind of boring romcom will our story be if we went to the pub on both our first and our second date?' he laughed.

'Ha ha! So we're starring in our own romantic comedy, then?'

'Of *course* we are. I told you I'm a romantic! Haven't you noticed the cameras and the extras coming and going? The director and I are going to edit the footage later.'

'Well, now that you mention it, I *did* see a few people acting a bit suspiciously earlier,' I joked. 'Okay, if it's not the pub, then it *must* be the cinema?'

'Too obvious. I can confirm that it is *not* the cinema. Because we talked a lot about films today, tomorrow we can chat about something different. Got to mix things up a bit. For the sake of our film, of course. Want to keep the audience entertained so the next scene, i.e., our second date tomorrow, should make them happy. And you, of course. I need to ensure the leading lady is happy at all times…' There went that killer smile again, and the elastic in my knickers.

Dear God.

'That's good to hear,' I said, regaining my composure.

'Alexandra,' he said, standing up and holding out his hand. I put my palm into his as we headed towards the door. 'Allow me to escort you to your chariot.'

'Thank you,' I said. 'There's no fairy-tale carriage waiting for me outside of this pub, though, unfortunately.'

'Ha-ha! Well, I can hail a taxi for you if you like. Make sure you get home safely.'

'Thanks, Miles, but I'm fine. I'll just jump on the tube.'

'Sure?' he asked.

'Absolutely.' I'll admit, it had been nice getting a taxi home after my date with Luke, but it wouldn't take long to get home from here, and I didn't want to waste money.

'Well, in that case, at least let me take you down to the platform, so I know you've got on the tube okay.'

'Really, it's okay. You don't have to…' Suddenly a line from the book popped into my head: *Allow a man to treat you well.* Just like Luke had paid for the taxi, Miles was trying to be a gentleman and ensure I got on the tube safely, and here I was batting his kind advances away. 'Actually, if you're sure you're okay to, I'd *love* for you to walk me to the platform, Miles. That's really kind of you.'

'No problem at all, Alexandra.' He squeezed my hand gently. 'It would be a pleasure.'

CHAPTER THIRTEEN

A s I stepped off the tube, I felt the butterflies dancing in my stomach. I hadn't been able to stop smiling all morning as flashbacks of last night's date with Miles jumped in and out of my mind. He was so funny. So warm. So…I couldn't put my finger on it, but he just made me feel completely at ease.

It was a fairly mild October afternoon, so I'd opted to wear a black-and-white knee-length skirt which was tight around the bum, then flared out slightly at the bottom, with opaque tights and a smart fitted black polo-neck jumper with a little black cotton jacket, and I had just changed into some black suede high-heeled boots. Not the most comfortable to walk in, hence why I'd waited until the last minute to take off my flats and put them on, but I was yet to meet a man who didn't love a woman in heels, and as bad as it sounded, I wanted Miles to fancy me. Plus, I could usually manage to walk from a station to a nearby destination. Most places in London were only a few minutes' walk from the tube, so I'd be fine.

I couldn't wait to find out where we were going. We'd arranged to meet on the northbound platform of the Bakerloo line at Oxford Circus station, and with eighteen stops until the train reached its destination, it was hard to guess a potential location. Perhaps we were off to a concert at Wembley Stadium? I didn't remember us talking about music, though.

I reckoned we were going to Paddington. I'd heard there were some nice new bars and restaurants around there. Or maybe—

'Hello, leading lady!' said a voice behind me.

'Hi!' I said, turning around to see Miles flashing his megawatt smile. He leant forward to give me a kiss on each cheek. Gosh, he smelt good. All woody and manly. Oh God. I could feel the tingles starting. *Focus*.

'So, ready for scene two?'

'Sure am!' I said, trying to compose myself.

Miles was wearing tan-coloured trousers, a white-and-blue lightly chequered shirt, mint-green jumper and navy-blue blazer. Very dapper.

'Excellent. Glad to hear you're ready.'

'Can you tell me where we're going yet, then?' I said.

'Not too much longer to find out,' he said as we boarded the carriage. 'Probably not even worth sitting down as we're getting off at the next stop.'

'Regent's Park?'

'That's the one!' He held on to the handrail closest to the double doors.

My mind started racing.

'Are we going for a walk? Is there a festival there?'

'Patience, Alexandra,' he teased.

'You're so cruel!'

'Come on. Off we get,' he said, holding out his hand. We took the lift to the exit. 'So,' he said as we stepped outside, 'would you like to know where we're going now?'

'Yes!' I shouted. 'You *know* I do!'

He stood in front of me, grinning.

'We…are…going…to…'

'Stop teasing!'

'The *zoo*!'

'The zoo?' I repeated. 'That's actually pretty cool!'

'Yeah?'

'*Hell* yeah!' I gushed. 'I *love* animals and I haven't been to the zoo for years!'

'Phew! I hoped that you'd like the idea. It's just that when I was listening to you last night, your face really seemed to light up during our conversation about Cuddles and my family's dog Bouncer. Then when you said that sometimes you felt you liked animals more than humans, I thought *bingo*!'

'Wow, you remembered what we talked about and put all that thought into a date? For *me*?'

'Yeah…' He blushed. 'I just thought it would be nice. Different to just taking you to a bar or pub. The weather isn't too bad today, so I thought we could have a nice stroll through the park, which will take about twenty minutes, and then spend a couple of hours at the zoo. Maybe even have a quick drink afterwards. Depends on what time you're going out tonight, of course.'

'Oh, er, I should probably head off around five,' I said, trying not to feel guilty about my drink with Luke at 6.15.

'Cool. Well, that gives us a good few hours, then. Shall we start walking?'

'Yes, let's,' I said.

'Great!'

As we approached the park, it suddenly dawned on me. We were going to the park. *Walking* through the park. Twenty minutes, he said it would take. *Walking* in high-heeled boots. *For twenty whole minutes*. Then walking around a zoo for hours. *Shit*. My bunions, feet and my ankles were going to be totally fucked. If I'd known where we were going, then I would have…I would have…

Actually, I didn't know what I would have done, or what I would have worn. My beige ballet shoes, which were the only flats that I owned, weren't exactly sexy. I hadn't bought them with dates in mind. Just comfort. Nothing I could do about it now. I just had to block the pain out and try and enjoy the date.

'So,' I said, taking a deep breath and trying not to focus on my toes, which were already beginning to burn, 'last night, I didn't get to ask you much about you and your work.'

'That's okay. I'm not that fussed about talking about it. I'm happy to, though, of course, if you want to.'

'Thanks. I'm really interested to know what you do. What kind of doctor are you?'

'A paediatrician.'

'That's really cool,' I said, moving slightly to the left to let a woman with a pushchair and three kids pass along the walkway. 'Do you work really long hours?'

'It's not too bad. I'm fortunate. I generally work Monday to Friday, around fifty hours a week. Sometimes more if extra shifts are needed, and we rotate being on call overnight. Could be much worse.'

Oh, that was interesting. I'd assumed he'd constantly

be on call and need to work long shifts. Then again, fifty hours was still a lot.

'And do you enjoy it?'

'I *love* it.' His face lit up, and then it became overshadowed with sadness. 'Don't get me wrong. It can be draining emotionally—especially when you're dealing with sick or dying children. That's tough. Particularly when I first started. It's still hard now, but you've just got to find a way to get through it and help as many of the kids as you can.'

'A real-life hero.' I smiled.

'Oh, I don't know about that…' He shrugged his shoulders. 'I do the best that I can, but we're a team. We pull together. We all want to help. I'm just a doctor doing his job. I wish I could do more. I'd really love to carry out some relief work overseas. Help more children in need.'

'Well, I think it's brilliant.'

'Thank you, Alexandra,' he said, staring into my eyes and causing my heart to flutter. 'That's really kind.'

'Please,' I replied. 'Call me Alex.'

Our eyes locked once more, and I felt the same spark and tingles as I'd experienced last night. The connection. The magnetic energy.

'Okay, *Alex*,' said Miles, breaking the spell. 'So, which animals do you fancy seeing today, then?'

'Ooooh…I don't know. How about *everything*!'

'Excellent!' He rubbed his hands together excitedly. 'Love your enthusiasm.'

'Well, you make it very easy for me to be enthusiastic. So,' I said, quickly changing the subject in case he thought I was being too gushy, 'what made you become a doctor, then?' His face fell. 'Oh, sorry. Do you not want to talk about it?'

'It's okay. Just wondering whether the story's a bit heavy for a second date, that's all.'

'Don't worry. I don't want to make you feel uncomfortable, Miles. I was just interested to find out more about you. But we can talk about something lighter if you prefer.'

'No, no, it's fine,' he said. 'If it feels too dreary, then just pinch my arm and I can dance for you or something. That will definitely make you laugh and help lighten the mood!'

'Why? Are you not a good dancer?'

'Two giant left feet,' Miles laughed.

I looked down at the ground, which, true to the season, was covered with russet, yellow and brown leaves. His brown shoes glistened, and they were indeed large. *You know what they say about men with big feet…*

'I'm not much of a dancer either,' I said, removing my mind from the gutter.

'That's a relief. At least if I invite you to a party, you won't show me up on the dance floor.'

'Definitely no chance of that, Miles!'

'So,' he said, taking a deep breath. 'Getting to the serious stuff…I had a difficult childhood. Dad left when I was five, Mum started drinking heavily and became an alcoholic. Things got pretty bad. I still have vivid memories of when I was six or seven, waiting at the school gates for her to pick me up, then having to try and find my own way home, using the key under the mat to open the door and then seeing her passed out drunk on the sofa. I also remember the stench of whisky on her breath. I always wondered why other adults didn't have that. Because I'd gotten so used to Mum stinking of alcohol, I'd just thought it was how all adults smelt. The more time passed, the more my health deteriorated, as I'd lost so much weight.'

'Weren't you eating? Didn't she feed you?'

'No. Not really. If she was having a good day, then maybe I'd get dinner. Sometimes even toast for breakfast, but that was rare. When she was really out of it, which was most of the time, she wouldn't cook or go shopping. I'd be left scrambling around the house, looking for enough pennies to buy a packet of crisps from the corner shop for dinner. The free school lunches I was lucky enough to have were often the only food I ate all day. Teachers noticed that I was getting thinner and thinner and were always asking if everything was okay at home. Especially as I always looked scruffy. Sometimes I'd go weeks without my clothes being washed or ironed. The kids would tease me, saying I smelt, so I remember trying to wash my uniform in the bath with soap. Which was fine, but then one morning, when I tried to iron my shirt on the floor—I was too small to put up the ironing board up, you see—I burnt myself. So when I turned up at school, the teachers immediately called social services.'

'Jesus, Miles. That's awful,' I said, trying to imagine what he must have gone through. Even though we'd known each other less than twenty-four hours, it was strange to see such sadness in his eyes. I'd already become used to his smile and the warmth that seemed to radiate from him.

'Yeah. It was pretty bad.' His shoulders dropped. 'So then I spent years in care. In and out of different homes, then with different foster carers until I was eleven and was finally adopted by my amazing parents who changed my life. They saved me. They really took care of me and gave me a loving, stable home, which I believe made me the man I am today.'

'They must be so proud of you.'

'Yeah. They are,' he said, the brightness returning to his eyes. 'I owe everything to them. So in answer to your question, the reason I became a doctor was because I wanted to help children. To nurture them. I guess to help them. The way that I was helped and saved by my mum and dad. I don't know if that makes any sense…'

'It *does*, Miles. It makes a *lot* of sense.'

'I had a great upbringing from the age of eleven. A *wonderful* family life. I'm so grateful for that. That's what I'd love to have one day. A partner—a wife to love and cherish. To share my life with and to work together to provide our children with a stable home. Help them to achieve whatever it is they'd like to—support them as they pursue their dreams. So, that's me. Hope that wasn't too heavy and serious, Alex,' he said nervously, trying to gauge my reaction.

'Gosh, Miles,' I said, desperately wanting to throw my arms around him and hold him tight. 'You've been through a lot, but I actually think it's amazing the way that you haven't let it hold you back. You've had a traumatic child-hood, and instead of allowing it to bring you down, you've used it as a driver to do something positive with your life. I think that's incredibly inspirational.'

'That's really kind.' He blushed. 'Thanks, Alex.' Our eyes met again. I meant every word of what I said. I thought he was *amazing*. His strength, his positivity, his kindness. It was wonderful. 'So,' he continued, 'you didn't pinch my arm, then. That means you've missed out on my dazzling dance moves.'

'Ah, dammit! Does the offer still stand?'

'Maybe. But you'd better be quick. We're almost at the entrance…'

'Okay, then!' I reached out and gave his upper arm a squeeze with my hand. It felt *very* muscular. What else was hiding underneath all those layers of clothes…?

'Too late, Alex. We're here,' he said, turning the corner and approaching the ticket office.

'You sure you still don't want to dance? To entertain the queue?'

'*No way!* Embarrassing myself in front of you is one thing, but in front of a crowd of strangers is a definite no. Rain check!'

'Alright, then. I look forward to you showing me your moves another time,' I said, realising afterwards that could be interpreted in multiple ways. Miles smiled as if to confirm that he got the innuendo memo too. My stomach flipped again as I allowed my imagination to run away for a few enjoyable seconds.

As we queued for the tickets and talked, I couldn't seem to stop my heart from beating faster. The more I looked at Miles, the more I realised how attractive I found him. I'd loved his smile from the moment we'd met, and I although I hadn't been sure about them at first, I was really starting to dig his glasses. His beautiful eyes just sparkled beneath them. He had the whole sexy Clark Kent vibe going on. Mmm-mmm.

It was also interesting that he said that he would like to get married and have a family—although saying he'd like to have that 'one day' didn't exactly give the impression that he was in any rush to settle down anytime soon, which was a shame.

There was so much to see, we almost didn't know where to start. Miles suggested the Penguin Beach and found a spot near the wooden hut where we could sit and I could rest my feet, which by now were throbbing. Although I'd tried my best to disguise it, maybe Miles had seen me hobbling along and felt sorry for me? Either way, I was glad to take the weight off them.

For about half an hour, we just sat in the demonstration area, watching the penguins diving for food, then we headed down to the underwater viewing areas and looked on in awe as they flew underwater in the 1200-square-metre pool.

Whilst we'd been chatting away constantly, up until that point, we'd always kept a little distance. Even if it was just a few inches. It was like we were both nervous to get too close, for fear of whether the other would reciprocate. But now we'd been at the zoo for over an hour, I felt Miles begin to relax a little more.

As we headed over to the Into Africa exhibit, he linked his arm in mine and just smiled. Feeling the warmth of his body was like a bolt of lightning. I wanted to wrap my arm around his waist. Pull him in even closer to me. For our lips to meet. Maybe there would be time for that later. I hoped so.

We went to the viewing platform and were mesmerised by the elegance of the giraffes. Like the name of the exhibit suggested, the surroundings had been designed to recreate an African-esque setting. It felt quite authentic.

Next we strolled along to the Tiger Territory. As if reading my mind from earlier, Miles wrapped his arm around my back and pulled me closer. I rested my head on his shoulder as we walked and breathed in his delicious scent. I couldn't help myself. When I looked up, he was staring down at me, his glasses misting up a little. Our eyes locked, and for a moment I thought we were going to kiss, until a couple of rowdy boys pushed past us, chasing each other and screaming playfully. Kind of killed the mood.

We held hands as we watched the tigers scale the huge trees in the tropical Indonesian-style setting through the floor-to-ceiling glass windows. They looked so beautiful with their deep orange coats and thick black stripes. Miles told me that Sumatran tigers, which were the species here, were the rarest and smallest subspecies of tiger in the world and were seen as critically endangered. I'd thought I loved animals, but he seemed just as passionate. Apparently, he'd been fascinated by them ever since he'd started living with his adoptive parents, as they used to take him to the zoo every summer.

I was in my element. By the time we'd seen a couple more exhibits, we were starving so made our way to the Terrace Restaurant. Whilst Miles went to the toilet, I slipped off my boots to give my feet a breather. I shouldn't really, as they'd probably be impossible to put on after-wards, but the pain had become unbearable. I knew it was stupid to suffer like this, but it was what we women did, right? To look good and feel more confident. They'd be okay in an hour or so, once we'd finished eating.

We both opted for fish and chips and chatted about what we'd seen so far. It felt good to refuel. All that walking had certainly burnt a lot of calories.

'Ready to go?' asked Miles.

'Yeah…sort of…' I winced, reaching below the table to try and find my boots whilst still maintaining eye contact with Miles. I must have inadvertently kicked them to the side. They were practically in the walkway beside our table. I was surprised someone hadn't tripped over them. There was no way I could put them back on without him seeing me.

'You okay, Alex?' he said, looking concerned.

'Yeah, I…I've just got to put my boots back on. They were squeezing a little, so I thought I'd slip them off for a bit.'

'It's okay, I understand. Not that I wear high-heeled boots, of course…' He shook his head, realising how it sounded.

'Are you *sure*, Miles?' I chuckled.

'Well, only on Sundays, and today's Saturday, so…' We both burst into a fit of giggles. 'What I meant to say was, I know from experience, and by that I mean from exes, that wearing heels for long periods of time isn't very comfortable.'

'Yep. Unfortunately, I'm yet to find a pair that offer both style and comfort.'

'Forgive me,' he said cautiously, 'but, when you went in your bag earlier to get your phone out, did I see another pair of shoes in there? Some flats?'

I blushed. They must have fallen out of the shoe bag. He wasn't supposed to know about those. I was trying to maintain the illusion of a strong, sexy woman who wasn't fazed by wearing a pair of heels. Dammit. I couldn't lie, though.

'Yes…yes, you did.'

'Alex, I know that you might want to project this glamorous image by wearing heels—at least, that's what my ex told me when I made the mistake of asking what I thought was a simple question as to why women wear heels if they hurt so much—but I just wanted to say that if you wanted to change into those shoes, if they made you feel more comfortable, then it really wouldn't bother me. I'm not one of those guys that expects a woman to dress a certain way. Yeah, heels are nice. *Sometimes*. But a woman can look just as sexy in a pair of trainers or flats. It's about how she carries herself. Her confidence. *That's* what is attractive. To me anyway.'

I stared at him, waiting for him to say *only joking*, but he didn't. Of course, deep down I knew suffering in heels for a man was stupid and that I should be able to wear what I wanted, but I guess I'd never been brave enough to stick my middle finger up at convention and actually do it. I'd thought a man would think less of me if I did.

'Well…' I paused. 'I *could* really do with putting on my flats right now.'

'I bet you could. We've been walking for hours. Even *my* feet are hurting me.'

'Really?' My eyes widened.

'No…I just wanted to make you feel better.' He smiled. Miles really was a sweetheart.

I pulled my flats out of my bag, slid them on, closed my eyes and exhaled. They felt *heavenly*. Like walking on clouds compared to those boots. Now I knew where the term *killer heels* must have come from. *Killer* being the operative word. I think I'd definitely need to soak my feet in the bath later.

We wandered around the zoo, alternating between holding hands, linking arms and holding each other. It was magical. I must have taken at least a hundred photos on my phone along the way. Mainly selfies with the animals in the background and Miles and me posing in front. I had so much fun. It was the perfect date.

'Are you cold, Alex?'

'A little.' I shivered. Should've known this light jacket wouldn't have been warm enough for this evening.

'Here,' said Miles, taking off his blazer. 'Have this.'

'Oh, but then *you'll* be cold...' *Let a man be nice to you, Alex*, I reminded myself.

'Don't worry about me. Here,' he said, placing it over my shoulders. 'The temperature just dropped so quickly. It's getting dark too.'

'Oh, shit! What's the time?' I asked, reaching in my bag for my phone to check. As I unlocked the screen, the 5% battery symbol flashed up. Must have run it down taking all those photos and videos.

Miles hurriedly pulled his sleeve up over his watch. 'It's almost five-thirty! Sorry, Alex. I didn't realise. You said you had to leave around five. Are you going to be late? Where do you need to get to?'

'London Bridge, but it's a good twenty minutes to Regent's Park station, and then I'd need to get the tube to Waterloo, then get the Jubilee line, so that will be say another half an hour journey, and then it will probably take another five or ten minutes to get up to the bar.'

'Would it help if I got you a taxi?' asked Miles. 'Then again, the traffic is so bad around here, it would probably take even longer. Can you at least call or text them to say you're running behind?'

'Yeah. Yes...I can do that. I think my phone will die at any second, though.'

'Or, I know: bring the number up and then we can put it in my phone and text them from there? My battery's still good.'

'Erm…' I stuttered, as my mind screamed *no way*! Could you imagine? Texting Luke from Miles' phone? That did *not* seem like a good idea…*at all*. 'I'm sure it will be okay. If we hurry, I could still make it for six-fifteen, or maybe a few minutes after.'

'Okay, let's go,' he said, and we headed through the park. Walking quickly was now a possibility with these flats on, thank goodness.

My stomach sank. I'd had such a wonderful afternoon with Miles, and I didn't want it to end. It had gone far too quickly. I mean, yes, I was on my way to see Luke, which I was sure would be nice, but I just wished I could have stayed with Miles a little longer. A few more hours. Or even for the rest of the evening. If I didn't have to rush off, we could have gone for dinner. I bet we would have chatted and laughed all night. Then he would have walked me to the tube platform like he had last night. And I would have loved to stare into his beautiful eyes whilst he leant forward and kissed me. Just the thought of it made my whole body tingle…

I couldn't think about that now. Firstly because I was meeting Luke, and secondly because fantasising about Miles kissing me could quite possibly cause a tsunami to erupt in my knickers. *No*. I needed to block out all sexual thoughts. *Immediately*.

We made it to the station in good time, and thankfully the tube came pretty quickly.

'So you're off at the next stop,' said Miles.

'Yep. Thank you so much for an amazing day, Miles. I've had a brilliant time.'

'Mission accomplished, then,' he said, his glasses steaming up again slightly. So cute when they did that. 'Really glad you enjoyed it, Alex. I had a fantastic time with you and all our new furry friends too. You'll have to send me some of those photos.'

'Will do,' I said, not wanting to take my eyes off him.

'If you like, I can get off and walk you to the bar to meet your friend?'

'Thanks, Miles. That's really lovely of you.' *He's so kind*, I thought as my stomach tightened, overcome with guilt, knowing I was leaving him to meet Luke. 'I'll be okay.'

'Okay, Alex,' he said, gently stroking my arm and setting off a shockwave. 'If you're sure.'

'Oh! I almost forgot!' I said, taking off his blazer. 'Your jacket.'

'You keep it. Until next time. It'll give me an excuse to see you again.' He smiled.

'No honestly,' I said, handing it to him. 'I'll be fine. And no excuses needed. I'd *love* to see you again.'

'Really?' His face lit up.

'*Definitely.*'

'Brilliant! Well, I'll message you tomorrow to check when you're free.'

'Great! Thanks again, Miles,' I replied as I reluctantly backed away towards the doors.

'You're welcome, Alex. I think we did a pretty good job with scene number two.'

'We certainly did! This is my stop, then,' I said, staring into his eyes, wondering how we'd say goodbye.

'It is…well, see you soon.' He leaned forward and kissed me gently on the cheek.

As his lips touched my skin, I felt like I'd been struck by lightning. I wanted to stay on the train. Be close to him and feel that electricity pulsing through me again.

As the *doors closing* alert began to sound, I reluctantly stepped on to the platform.

'Bye, Miles,' I whispered. 'I hope to see you very soon.'

CHAPTER FOURTEEN

I was meeting Luke at GŎNG—the bar that was part of the Shangri-La Hotel in The Shard, which was on the fifty-second floor. Not ideal when you're running behind. I had to take not one but two separate lifts: one to the thirty-fifth floor and then another right to the top. Crikey. I reached in my jacket pocket for a tissue to mop my fore-head. I'd been rushing so much that I could feel the beads of sweat forming. I knew I wouldn't have time to go to the toilets to check my make-up and hair when I arrived, so I'd done that quickly whilst taking the escalators up to the station exit.

The lift doors opened, and wow! Even through the crowds of people, I could see that the views were breath-taking. I anxiously looked around for Luke, then spotted him seated on the soft brown leather stool right by the window, dressed in a grey checked suit with an open-neck white shirt.

'So sorry I'm a few minutes late,' I said as I rushed over.

'Thought you'd stood me up,' he said, glancing down at my shoes and frowning. *Shit*. I hadn't had a chance to change back into my boots.

'Sorry—I got held up, and my battery died. I wouldn't have stood you up, though. That would be rude,' I said, unbuttoning my coat and sitting down on the stool opposite.

'It's very difficult to get such a prime table here on a Saturday night. It's a good thing I have connections and was able to hold the space. Anyway, you're here now,' he snapped. 'What are you drinking? Rosé?'

'Yes, please,' I replied, and he got up and walked towards the bar.

Luke seemed a bit off. I reached in my bag to see if my phone was still on to check the time. I had 3% battery, and it was 6.21, which meant I must have literally been five minutes late. Surely it couldn't be that? He had been fifteen minutes late on our first date and then twenty minutes late on our second because his conference call had run over, and I hadn't complained. Not that I was condoning it, because of course it's never good to be late, but this was the first time for me.

The bar was really busy. Like every place I'd been to with Luke so far, it was very glam. Much like the people here. Even though my skirt and polo neck were fairly smart, they weren't on the same scale as the women that were done up to the nines in high heels and sparkling cocktail dresses. I felt very out of place. Especially with my flats. Ah yes. My boots. I'd squeezed them into the shoe bag and they were now hanging out of my handbag. Would it be weird to change into them now? My feet probably wouldn't fit into them, but I could try and do it quickly before Luke came back.

Too late.

'One rosé as requested.' He placed the glass on the table and sat down. 'Sorry if I was a bit short earlier, Alexandra. I had an annoying phone call before you arrived, so I was a little irritated.'

Phew. Glad he apologised. Was getting worried there.

'Sorry to hear that, Luke. Nothing too serious, I hope?'

'No. Just someone trying to negotiate my speaking fee down for a conference, so I told them where to go. I'm more than worth every penny of what I charge. Anyway'—he clapped his hands together—'pretty impressive here, isn't it?'

'It certainly is,' I replied, scanning the illuminated London skyline. Now I was seated with nobody obstructing my view, it was much easier to take it all in. I spotted so many sites in the distance. The Gherkin, City Hall, the Tower of London… from this high, it looked like I was gazing down at a toy-town city with miniature trains crossing the tracks and little boats cruising across the Thames. Everything was so small.

'Did you know, Alexandra, that this is the highest hotel bar in Western Europe?'

'I didn't, Luke,' I replied, 'but I can see how that would be true.'

'It's one hundred and eighty-two metres above ground level. And you see the bar? That was the inspiration for the restaurant's name. The name GŎNG comes from *dougong*, which is a traditional Chinese architectural element of interlocking wooden brackets, which have been featured in the bar's design.'

'I see,' I said, glancing over. It was hard to get a good look as there were lots of smartly dressed people crowded around the bar and seated on the tall, fancy red-velvet-and-mahogany stools, but from what I could see, the bar was made from green marble. As for interlocking brackets, I wouldn't have a clue. Architecture wasn't my area of expertise.

'I often come here for cocktails and caviar,' added Luke, handing me the menu for reference. 'After nine p.m., you can sit back, relax and enjoy drinks around the infinity-edge Sky Pool too, which is also the highest in Europe.'

'Oh, right, very cool,' I said, scanning the list of cocktails as he spoke. I nearly fell off my chair. *Bloody hell.* Most of them cost over £20. Talk about sky-high prices to match the views.

'So!' He clapped his hands together again. 'What did you get up to this afternoon, then?'

'I went to the zoo,' I replied. No big deal telling him that. I could have gone there with anyone.

'The *zoo*?' His face crumpled. 'That explains the shoes you're wearing then. But what would possess you to voluntarily spend your Saturday afternoon in a zoo? I remember being forced to go there on school trips. Hated it. So smelly. Those creatures are filthy and spread diseases, you know. That's why they advise you disinfect yourself thoroughly after being around them. Eurgh!' He winced.

Judging by the mention of my shoes, he was clearly not a fan of flats. Just what I'd always thought. Men generally prefer women in heels. Miles was probably just being nice as he could see I was in pain.

But how could Luke say that about animals? They're *amazing*. I was sure he didn't really mean it, though. A few minutes with my Cuddles and he'd fall madly in love.

'I actually *love* animals,' I protested, 'so it was a brilliant afternoon. That's a big exaggeration about spreading diseases. Yes, there are risks, like there are with everything, but if it wasn't safe, then we wouldn't have public zoos. Washing your hands with soap and water is fine. It's not like you need to be sprayed with industrial-strength disinfectant afterwards or be put into quarantine or anything.'

'Even so, I think it's a *bizarre* way to spend your time.' He shrugged his shoulders. 'Each to their own, I suppose.'

What was so bizarre about spending time with animals? If he could just see them up close, study them, observe them, he'd understand. I wished my battery wasn't low; then I could show him some photos that would melt his heart. Oh well, I guessed it was unrealistic to expect us to agree on everything. Perhaps it was best to change the subject. I was sure there were plenty of other things we could chat about.

'What did *you* do today, then?'

'Well,' he said, clapping his hands, 'I was liaising with some contacts in Australia. Looks like I'll be going there in a few months to do a talk. They said they wanted a professor who was the best in the field of cognitive neuropsychology, and so naturally I told them there was nobody more knowledgeable than me.'

'What, you literally said that?'

'Said what?'

'That you were "the most knowledgeable professor in your field"?'

'Yes. Why? What about it? I *am*.' He pushed his chest out proudly. 'What's the problem?'

'No, no problem. I mean, obviously, I know very little about cogno…cognitive…neuro…your psychology specialism…' I stuttered, trying and failing to remember what it was called.

'That's right, most people don't. It's a very specialist area, which is exactly my point.' He leant back and folded his arms.

'It's just, I'm sure you're great at what you do. I guess I was just wondering if you ever feel weird pretty much declaring that you're the *best in the world* at something yourself. Don't you worry that it might come across as a bit, you know, *arrogant*?'

'You see?' He huffed. 'That's the problem with this country. British people are taught not to be confident, not to celebrate achievements. If self-deprecation was an Olympic sport, Britain would win gold. That's what I love about the Americans and other nations. They *celebrate* success—the bigger the better. Over here, it's all, "oh, I can't say this or that as I'm British, and I'm so reserved and not allowed to be successful." That's ludicrous! I've worked hard to get where I am and to earn good money and travel the globe and become a world-famous professor. I believe I *am* the best, so why shouldn't I shout about it? I'm a fit, successful, solvent, handsome, highly educated man. What's so wrong with saying that? Why should I feel ashamed to admit it?'

I understood what he was saying. *To a degree*. And, yes, he was right. He was all of those things, but I guessed I wasn't used to someone blowing their own trumpet so loudly. It certainly wasn't my style. Even if I *had* achieved all of that, I'd probably be more humble about it. Let someone else say that I was *the best* rather than boasting about it myself. But that was just me.

That said, confidence *could* be an attractive quality in a man. Maybe I was just reading too much into it. He was just selling himself to get the speaking gig. Nothing wrong with that, I supposed.

'I'm not saying you shouldn't shout about your achievements,' I said. 'They're great. It's brilliant that you're *the best* and that you're getting these bookings overseas.'

'It is. Speaking of the Americans, I'm in talks with some of the top universities about going over there to lecture some of their students next year too. I'd also like to do more in Asia. Combine it with some extra travelling. I reckon I'll hit fifty countries next year. *At least.* I'm thinking maybe I should start trying to commercialise my Instagram page. No one I know has been to as many countries as me. There must be a lot of companies that would pay good money for me to stay in their hotels and fly with them, or at least give me travel and board for free, so that I could keep even more of my speaker's fee. I'd be a good advert for any brand.'

If Luke's own self-praise was anything to go by, any company he endorsed could be assured that he wouldn't be shy about saying how brilliant they were.

There was no *discuss* topic this time around. For the next couple of hours, the conversation mainly consisted of Luke talking about his travels, his work and the international speaking engagements he had lined up.

If I was honest, at times my mind drifted and I started thinking about Miles. Wondering what he was doing.

We'd only been on two dates and I'd barely known him for twenty-four hours, but it seemed like much longer. With Miles, my whole body and mind felt lighter and brighter. For some reason, I felt a bit tense with Luke tonight. Like I was walking on eggshells. Like I'd say the wrong thing. Sometimes I felt stupid because I didn't know as much about the world as he did or because I wasn't as educated as him. But I couldn't deny he was a catch. And looks wise, he was definitely my type.

That said, I didn't have the urges that I'd felt on previous dates. Back then, I'd struggled to keep my mind from thinking about what it would be like to have sex with him. But tonight, I wasn't really getting that. Maybe Stacey was right. Perhaps now that I had almost completed my fourth week, my body had calmed down and was used to the lack of activity. Actually, that couldn't be true, as I had definitely been getting the tingles this afternoon with Miles...

'So, Alexandra,' said Luke as we walked across the marble flooring of the ground floor and stepped outside into the cold air. 'How about coming back to mine for some coffee? It just arrived today. Had it shipped over from Italy. It really is the best you'll ever taste.' As he leant forward to touch my hand, I flinched. I didn't mean to. It just happened.

'I, er...sorry, Luke, not tonight. I'd like to take things slow.'

'Don't worry. We'll take it slow,' he said, stroking my hand. 'That's why I suggested meeting early this evening. We could have chilled by the pool and listened to the DJ they have playing tonight, but I thought it would be nicer if we headed home. That way we can spend the whole night together making love and then tomorrow morning too. No work to rush off to the next day. Just take our time. It'll be nice and slow and relaxed. I *guarantee* it.'

I froze. On our last date, I had practically been ready to jump him, but now I just didn't want to. Both my mind and my body told me to resist.

What should I say, though? I really didn't want to go into a big explanation...

Actually no. Why should I have to? Just because he'd taken me to some super fancy bar and we'd been on four dates, that didn't mean he should automatically expect me to drop my knickers. A month ago, that would have been the case, but not anymore.

'Maybe another time, Luke,' I said, easing my hand away. 'Like I said, I want to take things slow. It's too soon.'

'Too soon?' His brow furrowed. 'What are we up to now? Our *fourth* date?'

'Yes, that's right,' I said as confidently as I could. 'Our fourth date. And I'm not ready. I'm sure as a gentleman, you understand that—right, Luke?'

'It's always the lady's call,' he said, holding his hands up. 'Would you like me to drop you off, or are you getting the tube?'

'The tube's fine, thanks.' I could really do with jumping in a taxi, as it was freezing, but I was feeling strong and I didn't want to risk my resolve weakening.

'Okay. Well, in that case, safe travels,' he said, stepping towards one of the taxis parked at the entrance, opening the door and climbing inside. 'Goodnight, Alexandra.'

'Goodnight, Luke.'

I'd survived another date. I'd resisted. I'd successfully abstained.

The question was, how long would this newfound strength last?

CHAPTER FIFTEEN

'I reckon you're going to love this place,' said Miles as we stepped through the white double doors. He'd taken me to a boutique cinema that was showing an indie film he'd heard about called *What Are The Chances of Love?* and he was raving about how different this place was to the mainstream theatres. 'The picture quality and the sound are excellent,' he gushed, 'and because it's small, it's got a much more intimate feel. I love coming here.'

'Well, if you love it, then I'm sure I will too, Miles.' I squeezed his hand.

'And there's no need to go to the kiosk and queue up for hot dogs or popcorn. They deliver it all to you at your seat. Whatever you want. We could have mini fish and chips, or sticky toffee pudding, cocktails, wine—rosé, of course.' He smiled. 'Our dedicated waiter will bring us whatever the leading lady requests.'

'Excellent!'

Miles approached the beautiful gilt-domed box office.

The entrance had been designed to look how I'd imagined an American movie theatre to appear in, say, the 1950s. Even the popcorn was stored in a retro machine. It was so quirky and cool here. A classic, old-fashioned feel, but with a modern twist. We headed down the corridor to screen number three, and the usher, who was dressed in a smart red velvet tuxedo jacket and blue bow tie, showed us inside.

Tonight was our fourth date, and I was now five and a half weeks into my challenge. I'd got myself into a routine. Every week, I would go on one or two dates, work out at the gym three times, spend one evening at Audrey's and rest on Sundays. It was flexible, of course. Sometimes I'd go on more dates, sometimes less. It was working well and helped keep me calm so I wasn't totally focused on men.

Last week, I'd had a lot on at the office and had to work late, and as Luke was away at a conference, I'd only gone out once, on Thursday with Miles. For our third date, I'd suggested that we go bowling, which was fun, albeit a little humiliating too. Miles literally wiped the floor with me, he was that good.

'You didn't have to beat me so spectacularly,' I'd protested as we'd walked hand in hand to the station afterwards. 'I know achieving more than double my score makes you look all manly, but you could have *at least* got a few less strikes or tossed the ball into the lane next to us a couple of times, to make me feel better!'

Miles had laughed. 'But I *did*! Well, not the tossing the ball bit, as they probably would have thrown it straight back in my face, but I did *try* holding back on the strikes the best I could…'

'*Whatever,*' I'd said. 'Don't worry, Doc. I'll beat you next time.'

'*Beat me*, eh?' He'd smirked. '*Promises, promises…*'

I loved it when Miles was a little bit naughty. It didn't happen often. Most of the time, he was very respectful and never talked explicitly about sex. But occasionally, an innuendo or double-entendre would come up naturally in conversation and you'd know that those thoughts were there. Even if he didn't say them, they were floating around somewhere in his mind. *Mmm.*

Three dates in and we were still at the kissing-on-the-cheek stage, which was unheard of for me. I couldn't remember the last time I'd taken things so slowly. Perhaps when I'd first started dating when I was fifteen? *A long time ago.* I couldn't lie. I was definitely hoping we might have a snog tonight. Time would tell, though. It was better for it to happen naturally, so I'd just have to wait and see what happened…

'After you,' said Miles, stepping aside so that I could sit down first. Whilst the interior of the theatre continued the classic feel with the thick red velvet curtains covering the screen, the seating was definitely very modern. 'There's a remote-control panel on the armrest so you can recline the seat back or raise the footrest. *Please.* Make yourself comfortable.'

'Thanks, Miles.'

'Always a pleasure, Alex.'

We took off our coats and scarves and settled back into the special *love seat*: a soft red leather sofa that Miles had reserved for us. It was really comfy. Much better than the tatty hard blue chairs at the multiplex cinemas I'd been to, which often had food or drink stains engrained into the grotty fabric. Here, they even had matching red cashmere blankets to snuggle under. This was almost as good as cosying up to watch a film at home.

Miles pressed the button to call the waiter, and ordered two large glasses of wine and a bowl of popcorn to get us started, then asked for the mini portions of fish and chips to be delivered halfway through the film.

The theatre was practically empty. I guess not many people came here on a Wednesday evening, which was fine by me as, aside from a couple sitting in the middle and a few other people scattered towards the front, we practically had it to ourselves.

The lights faded and the adverts began. After the usher crept over and placed our drinks on the swivel table connected to the seat, Miles put his arm around me, and I instantly felt the tingles rushing through me. As I went to rest my head on his shoulder and breathed in his gorgeous woody scent, he lifted my chin and turned my head around to face his.

Miles took off his glasses and rested them on the table. Even though it was dark, I still saw the sparkle in his eyes. *God, he was beautiful.* As I gazed into them, I could have sworn my heart stopped for a second. Before I could catch my breath, Miles leant forward and placed his lips gently on mine.

Oh Gosh...

It was like my whole body had been struck by lightning.

Miles' lips were the softest I'd ever felt. Smoother than silk and deliciously juicy. His breath was sweet, minty and warm. He kissed me slowly like he was savouring his favourite dish and wanted to enjoy every morsel. *No rush.*

As the intensity grew and the kisses became more passionate, my heart pounded and my inner thighs trembled. *This was heavenly*.

Our mouths parted further, and he began to flick his tongue gently against mine. I knew what Laurie said about French kissing, but when something felt this good, sometimes you needed to bend the rules a little. Every kiss was so in sync. Exactly the right rhythm, the right intensity, the right amount of tongue…everything just felt so *right*.

From that point on, it was like our mouths had been cemented together. We tried a few times to break away from each other in an attempt to watch the film, but never lasted more than a few minutes before our lips locked again. The connection was just so strong.

I wanted him so badly. How we managed to stop ourselves from ripping each other's clothes off, I don't know, but we deserved a medal for keeping our composure.

In truth, it was Miles who showed the most self-control. His hands respectfully never wandered anywhere other than to stroke my face, shoulders or back. He didn't even try any sly boob or bum grazing. If it wasn't for the intensity of his kisses and the undeniable chemistry, I might have wondered if he even fancied me at all. Most men would not have been so restrained.

I, on the other hand, was not as well behaved. I couldn't help myself. I was curious. Miles was always wearing so many layers. I wanted to feel if there was a nice firm chest underneath that shirt/jumper combo, and although I'd only run my hands over the top of his clothes, I do believe there was…

Like I'd felt on our date at the zoo, his arms also

appeared to be solid, and as we got closer, I quickly discovered that they weren't the only solid thing that I could feel pressing against me. Hard to tell (pardon the pun) without actually touching it first-hand or seeing an outline, but I felt confident in confirming that Roxy's fears of me waiting six months to sleep with a guy, only to find his package was smaller than my little finger, would certainly *not* be an issue with Miles…

Whilst my sly chest and arm caressing might have scraped a PG-13 classification at best, the thoughts racing through my mind would most definitely be deemed X-rated. I was imagining all sorts of things that I wanted him to do to me on this love seat. *Oh God*…I stand corrected. Laurie was right. The more Miles French-kissed me, the more accurate her description of kissing with tongues being like a gateway drug became. With every flick, I fantasised about where I wanted to feel it next: licking my earlobes, then my neck, trailing across my chest and around my nipples, heading down past my belly button and circling my clit over and over again. *Fuck.* Just the thought of it made me want to explode.

'Erm…sir…madam…?' said a voice I didn't recognise. Miles pulled away slowly. When we looked up, the young waiter was clutching our plates, and from what I could make out from the low lighting, he was looking *very* embarrassed. I knew I should probably feel bad about us snogging each other's faces off in the backseat like a couple of horny teenagers, but the sensations pulsing through me had kicked all my inhibitions to the kerb.

'Sorry to, um…interrupt,' whispered the waiter. 'Two fish and chips?'

'Thanks.' Miles took both plates and passed one to me.

The waiter quickly headed back outside. 'Well, Alex,' he said softly, 'that was *very* enjoyable.'

'It certainly was,' I replied, pecking him on the lips again, desperate to continue.

'What are you doing to me?' he groaned, stroking my cheek. 'Maybe it's good that the food came when it did. Five minutes longer and we might have given that poor waiter a heart attack!' I burst into laughter. I couldn't help it.

'Ssshhh!' said someone a few rows in front. So much for saying we practically had the place to ourselves.

'I guess we better *try* and watch the film,' I whispered. 'Although I haven't the faintest idea what's been happening.'

'Me neither. On second thoughts, why stop our fun? I'm sure the waiter's seen worse than a couple of people kissing. As we've already missed half of it, I suggest that after we finish our food, we get back to making our own film. Can't have a romcom without a long passionate first kiss.'

'But that *was* our first kiss,' I said.

'Oh, Alex. *That* was just our dress rehearsal.' He kissed my neck. 'Just the warm-up. Wait until we start the kissing scene for real…'

We were now at Tooting Bec station and heading towards my house. Dangerous, I know. Especially after our mega-making-out cinema session. Miles wasn't joking. He really *was* just warming up. As well as receiving a trophy for restraining ourselves, Miles deserved some kind of internationally recognised award for best kisser in the universe. In fact, I was surprised I'd even made it this far, what with my knees turning completely to jelly. He only had to look at me and the tidal waves started again.

He'd left his glasses off too, which only made him harder to resist. *God, those eyes.* Those lips. In fact, *everything*.

'So, Alex, we've been to the cinema, the zoo, and bowling, which, as we've established, isn't one of your strengths…'

'Oi!' I protested, squeezing his arm. (I'd find any excuse. Couldn't help myself.) 'I just had an off day, that's all.'

'I know, I know,' he teased. '*I believe you*…but I was wondering if you'd like to try another activity tomorrow night, that I'm confident we could *both* excel at? A wine-tasting class?'

Shit. Tomorrow night? I've got a date with Luke. Dammit. And that would have been right up my street, too.

'Um, wine-tasting sounds *amazing*, Miles. I mean, I love my wine, and maybe that would help me to venture out of my White Zinfandel comfort zone for a change. So it's a *brilliant* idea, in fact, *perfect* for me, but it's just that I, I can't tomorrow night, I'm afraid.'

Gutted.

'Oh right, okay,' said Miles, looking down at the pavement before meeting my eyes again. 'I know it's short notice. It's just that I was looking it up at lunchtime and saw they had a couple of cancellations, so I thought I'd mention it. Never mind.'

'Really sorry, Miles.' My stomach plummeted.

There was a silence. We crossed the street and turned

into my road. We'd never really had a silence like that before. We always naturally moved from one conversation to the next. It was always so effortless. But for the first time ever, things felt weird. Awkward.

'Actually, Alex,' said Miles as he stopped dead in the street. 'Can I ask you something?'

Miles stared straight into my eyes. *Oh no.* He was looking very serious. I wondered what he was thinking.

'Su-sure,' I replied nervously.

'I just wondered…' He shifted on his feet a little. Like he was searching for the right words. My heart started pounding, anxious about what was about to fall out of his mouth. 'I wondered, Alex, are you just dating me, or are you seeing someone else? Other guys too?'

Oh.

I guessed it had to come sooner or later. I would have preferred *later*, but Laurie had touched on this on the book. She'd said not to raise it voluntarily, as guys would probably expect that a woman would be keeping her options open in the beginning. I guessed I just had to be straight with him, then hope and pray that he would understand.

I took a deep breath, reached out to hold his hands and retained eye contact.

'To answer your question honestly, yes, I am currently seeing other guys. *But* I just go on dates, you know, drinks and dinner. Nothing more.'

'I see.' His face fell.

Although I wasn't supposed to, I felt really bad.

'I thought so,' he said solemnly. 'I'm sure a woman like you has got men throwing themselves at her feet.' I was tempted to laugh and say *as if*, but kept quiet. 'It's just that I'd prefer to date someone exclusively. It's less complicated that way.'

Tell me about it.

I wanted to jump up and say, *So would I.* Because it was true. I really would.

'So,' he added, 'would you consider it? Dating me exclusively?'

Boom.

The million-dollar question.

In one sense, I was relieved we were having this conversation. Firstly, now it was all out in the open, maybe I'd feel less guilty about seeing Luke as I would no longer be hiding it. Secondly, because exclusivity did indicate that he was at least *considering* the possibility of taking things to the next level. And thirdly because, given how much we'd been making out at the cinema, coupled with the fact that we were now on date number four, I thought that like Luke, he'd want to move things on and sleep together, which would mean having to explain the whole sex thing. But was answering the exclusivity question harder?

There was no doubt about it. I liked Miles. In fact, whilst I was trying not to get carried away with my emotions, somehow *like* didn't feel strong enough a word to describe the feelings that were building for him. Especially after tonight. But I was torn. Because I also liked Luke, and the book said that the time when you're feeling strongly for one guy or another is the time that you should continue the multi dating, not stop it. I had to stick with it until one of them stepped forward and committed to me. *Properly.* Not just hinted at it. They needed to make their intentions clear and firm. There could be no doubt. I couldn't risk dropping one too soon.

'I just need a bit more time, please, Miles,' I said softly. 'I'm trying to take things slowly. I don't want to rush into anything until I'm sure.'

He paused.

'I understand that you have to do what's best for you, Alex,' he said as we stood facing each other. His face was still solemn. Serious. I couldn't fully read it. What was he thinking? Feeling? Disappointment, yes. That was clear. But what else?

My mind, on the other hand, was racing. Like it was competing for gold in the Overthinking Olympics. Desperately hoping Miles wasn't going to say he wanted to stop seeing me. Now he knew I was dating other men—well, technically there was only really Luke now—would Miles still be prepared to carry on?

I wanted to ask, but I was terrified.

I had to, though, didn't I? I knew it would be hard and I might not like what I heard, but I *had* to bite the bullet and pose the question.

Here goes.

'So…are you okay to still see me, then, Miles? For us to continue?'

There I did it. It's out there. And now we await his response.

He broke my gaze and there was more silence. A *long* silence. Has twenty-four hours just passed? That was how it felt, but it was probably just a few seconds.

'I'll be honest, Alex. After tonight, I think I'm going to find it hard to handle the idea of you dating me and other guys at the same time…'

My stomach plummeted. I didn't want to lose him. I *adored* Miles. I loved every single second I spent with him. But now that I'd come this far, I couldn't risk putting all of my eggs in one basket without being sure that I was making the right decision.

'Oh…I…I…understand Miles,' I'd stuttered.

'However,' he continued, 'I *would* like to continue seeing you…'

Thank you, Jesus!

I was about to do the Carlton dance in my head, then something told my excitement to wait. His sombre facial expression was telling me there was a *but* coming.

'*For the moment*,' he continued. 'But I also have to do what feels right for me too. I guess we'll just have to see how things go, but think about it, okay?'

'I will, Miles. I will.' *Thank goodness*. Something told me I wasn't out of the woods yet though.

We stood there again, just staring at each other. No doubt both of our minds whirring with thoughts and questions. To break the silence, I reached in my bag and got out my keys. 'Well, this is me,' I said, gesturing towards my house.

'Oh, right. It looks lovely, Alex. Let me walk you to your gate.'

We crossed the road and then stood outside my door.

'Thank you so much for a wonderful evening, Miles. I had a great time.'

'Me too.' He kissed me gently on the forehead. 'Goodnight, Alex.'

'Goodnight,' I said, stepping inside.

I watched him walk away, closed the door, leant against it, then slid down onto the floor and squeezed my eyes shut.

Of course I was relieved that I was still dating two

guys that I liked and who really liked me, which was amazing. More than I'd ever thought was possible when I'd started this challenge. *But* a huge wave of trepidation also washed over me. Yes, Miles and I would continue to see each other, but like he'd said, he was fine 'for the moment,' and he 'had to do what felt right' for him, which meant I was on borrowed time and that, like me, he'd also be keeping his options open. And surely it wouldn't be long before Luke asked me if I was seeing other guys too.

Oh God.

I knew I had to keep doing what I was doing and carry on seeing Miles and Luke. *I got that.* I really did. But at the same time, after tonight, I was more aware than ever that I was treading a very fine line. And if I didn't get the balance exactly right or waited too long before making my choice, rather than ending up with *the one*, I could quite easily lose them both and end up with *none*.

CHAPTER SIXTEEN

'Wow! Is it your birthday?' asked Stacey as she walked into the kitchen and handed me a massive bouquet of flowers.

'Are these for me?' I twirled it around, looking at the stunning display of yellow roses and white lilies.

'They are indeed. Lucky lady!'

'No one's ever sent me flowers before! I wonder who they're from?'

I plucked the white envelope from the arrangement, pulled it open and scanned the message. 'They're from Miles!'

'What a sweetie!' squealed Stacey. 'What does the card say?'

'"Thank you for an amazing date. The fourth scene was even better than the first, second and third. Our romcom is shaping up nicely. Looking forward to seeing you soon, Miles x." Awww, that's so lovely.'

I was a bit surprised, though. After the awkward exclusivity slash multi-dating talk, I'd thought Miles would pull back a little.

'It's *on*, baby!' Stacey rubbed her hands together.

'What is?'

'The battle for your heart has begun!'

'What do you mean?'

'Well,' she said, pulling out a stool and sitting down, 'didn't you say that when you went out with Miles yesterday, the main reason the whole multi-dating conversation came up was because he asked if he could see you tonight?'

'Yeah…'

'Well, I reckon after last night, Miles realised this is a battle to win your affections, and so he wants you to know that he's a worthy contender. He clearly knew you had a date lined up with his competitor and thought he might not be taking you out tonight, but he wanted to make sure that he was still firmly in your thoughts. That's why he arranged for a beautiful bouquet to be delivered to you just before you went out with someone else. *Smart*.'

'Mmm,' I said as I sat down to join Stacey. 'Yes, I didn't think of it like that. It's so hard, though. I know it's hypocritical, but now that he's aware that I'm dating someone else, I think it may lead him to do the same, whereas up until now, I get the impression he was only seeing me. I really like him, but as he said himself, it's early days. We've only had four dates. Then again, that didn't stop Luke. He started speaking about marriage almost immediately, which is ultimately what I'd like.'

'Well, who's to say Miles doesn't want that too? Normally if a guy talks about exclusivity, it's because he's thinking long-term.'

'Yeah,' I said, resting the flowers on the kitchen counter beside me, 'but he didn't say that explicitly. And even if he did, I don't want to just be someone's long-term girlfriend. I want them to love me and to want to marry me. Miles makes me feel *amazing*. I feel so happy when I'm with him, but what if I stop seeing Luke to go exclusive with Miles and then I find out that he wants to wait ten years before proposing or his idea of *long-term* is a year or two? I want more than that. I'd like to find someone who wants us to be together for the rest of our lives.'

'So talk to him.' Stacey rested her hand on top of mine reassuringly. 'Find out more about what he's looking for. Didn't he mention marriage and kids when you went to the zoo? Pretty sure I remember you saying that's what he said he wanted.'

'He *did*, but he was talking generally. He just said "one day". He didn't say when, so like I said, for all I know that could be in the next decade. Nor did he say that he wanted that with me. Luke was more specific.'

'Hmm, true, but remember that actions speak louder than words, and Miles' actions with these flowers are saying: *choose me*. Let's see how Luke reacts when he sees them.'

'What do you mean *sees them*?'

Just as Stacey was about to reply, she spotted Sue and Neville walking towards the door and raised her eyebrows to indicate we'd need to vacate the kitchen to continue our conversation privately. Unlike the mornings, where we could chat for a few minutes before Steve did his 9 a.m 'are you at your desk yet?' swoop, at lunchtime and after 5 p.m, it was always busier.

We slipped through the door of a nearby stairwell and sat on the steps, glancing upwards to see if anyone was coming down. The coast was clear. For now, anyway.

'So come on, then. What did you mean when you said *when Luke sees them*?' I frowned. 'That doesn't make sense.'

'I meant when you walk into the bar with a bouquet of flowers that Luke didn't send you. I can't wait to see his face!'

Never mind Luke's face. *My* face was currently more creased than a pair of linen trousers.

'I'm not taking the flowers with me on my date with Luke. That's ridiculous!'

'Are you crazy?' Stacey rolled her eyes. 'You absolutely *must* take the flowers on your date! You need to see how Luke reacts. See if it makes him up his game. We need to know that he's up for the challenge. That he's willing to fight for your heart. See if he'll *go hard or go home*.'

Hmmm. I thought it over for a second.

'I hear what you're saying but…' I just wasn't sure. I hadn't seen Luke for almost two weeks as he'd had that conference thing and other stuff on at work, so to rock up to our first date in ages with flowers from another guy felt wrong somehow.

'You don't really have a choice anyway, Alex. If you leave them in the office, they'll be gone by tomorrow morning. I can guarantee it. I left a bag of sweets on my desk last night, and sure enough they were nowhere to be found when I got in. Do you think our light-fingered colleagues, the cleaners or whoever steals our stuff won't take one look at that bouquet and bring it home with them?'

'Well, it's a lot bigger and harder to steal than a little bag of sweets, so…'

'Where there's a will, there's a way. That would easily fit into a large carrier bag or a box. It's not difficult for a determined thief.'

We heard heavy footsteps coming down the stairs, so got up to walk back to our desks.

'Point taken. Okay. I'll take the flowers on the date with me. I bet Luke will be *thrilled* to see them.'

'I'm pretty sure that he won't.' She grinned mischievously. '*But* he seems like a competitive guy, so this might be just the thing to encourage him to take more affirmative action.'

'You might be right. Okay, beautiful bunch of flowers,' I said, glancing down at the bouquet and making a mental note to message Miles on the way to say thank you. 'We'd better get ourselves together. We've got a date to go to.'

CHAPTER SEVENTEEN

'How very modern of you,' said Luke, glancing at the flowers as I sat down on the deep purple banquette seating at a bar in Piccadilly. He looked handsome as always in a dark suit, matching waistcoat and white shirt. 'It's always nice to receive flowers. In this age of equality, why shouldn't a woman show appreciation to a man? It's very sweet of you, Alexandra.'

Awkward...

'Um...' I said, shuffling in my seat. 'They're not actually for you, Luke. They were a gift. *For me*. They arrived just before I left the office, and I couldn't leave them at work, so...'

'Oh.' He scowled. 'I see. Waiter!' he shouted, clicking his fingers. 'Bottle of your best champagne. Quick as you can.'

'Very good, sir!' grinned the waiter. 'Celebrating a special occasion?'

'You don't need to be celebrating to have champagne. I'm having it just because I like it,' he snapped.

'A bottle of our finest coming up.'

'Good,' said Luke, nodding at the waiter in acknowl-edgement before turning back to face me. 'So, what's the story, then, Alexandra?'

'What's the story about what?' I frowned.

'I've been trying to figure it out since our last date, and I don't get it.' He leant forward. 'I took you to one of the most prestigious and impressive bars in London, or indeed Europe, told you I wanted us to make love and you turned me down. This has *never* happened before, and I need to understand why. Are you sleeping with this guy who got you those stupid flowers and feeling guilty? *No.* That wouldn't make sense. It *must* be something else.'

See? I'd known it was only a matter of time before he started asking questions too. I mean, obviously I had to accept that turning up to a date with flowers was kind of a giveaway. Once he'd established they weren't for him, the next natural assumption was going to be that they were sent by another guy. But at the same time, *Luke* wasn't making sense either. I'd thought he was happy to take things slowly. He'd said he was. So why bring it up if he really did accept that I wanted to wait?

'I'd rather not go into it right now, Luke,' I said.

'Alexandra…' He leant even further forward and looked me straight in the eyes. 'As you should know by now, I'm a direct person. I like you. I'm *very* attracted to you. I would like to make love to you, and I know from the way you're always looking at me, undressing me with your eyes, that you want me too. So it just doesn't add up. And it's rare that there's ever a problem that I can't solve.'

'No,' I sighed, just wanting to get off the subject. 'I didn't turn you down because I'm sleeping with someone else. I *do* go on dates with other guys, but that's it. Just dates. You know, going out, but no sex.'

'I knew it!' he said, clapping his hands. 'I *knew* it wouldn't be logical for you to sleep with him and not me. *Impossible.* What is it, then? I'm even more curious now.'

Now that it had been raised, someone like Luke wasn't going to drop the subject unless I told him. He was stubborn and determined. I supposed as we'd reached our fifth date and it had come up naturally, it made sense to tell him and see how he reacted. After all, if he wasn't willing to wait, better I found out sooner rather than later so I wasn't wasting my time.

'Okay,' I said. 'But before I tell you, Luke, I need to know how you really feel about me. I mean, do you like me? How much? Where do you see this going? *Us*?'

'I *definitely* see us going all the way,' he replied without hesitation. 'I told you. I'm a man who wants it *all*. The career, the wife and the kids. And I'm still here, aren't I? Five dates in.'

'True. Yes, you are. Okay,' I said, exhaling deeply. 'It's like this…'

I explained the challenge to him. His face remained blank throughout. I couldn't gauge whether he was shocked, horrified, intrigued or in agreement. Finally, once I'd finished, he sat up straight in his chair.

'So this is a real challenge, then?' he said, his eyes widening.

'Yes.'

'Because you believe, Alexandra, that you can abstain for six months?'

'Yes,' I replied, still trying to work out what he was thinking.

'And how far in are you now?' asked Luke.

'A couple of days shy of six weeks.'

'Interesting! So four and a half months to go? That is *indeed* a challenge. And you believe your resolve can't be broken—that you'll be able to stick to it?'

'Yes, I do, Luke. That's the plan.'

'Hmmm. I see. This is fascinating. Count me in!' he said, clapping his hands again.

'Count you in?' I said. 'Do you mean you'll wait?'

'I *love* a challenge, Alexandra. This is an interesting experiment. A test of strength. Willpower. In fact, *power*. I'm glad you told me.'

'You are?'

'Yes!' said Luke. 'Now that you've told me, I know what I need to do. I mean, I know where I stand. This will help immensely…'

'I don't follow.' I frowned.

'I can now understand you better. Understand the man you want me to be. This is *exciting*!'

'It is?' I said, not quite believing what I was hearing.

'It is indeed! I never shy away from a challenge. I've always sensed that somehow you've doubted my abilities, Alexandra. You questioned me declaring that I was the best in my field. My prowess. My powers. But this experiment of yours has presented a unique opportunity. I'm going to prove myself to you once and for all. This *boy* that sent you flowers or whoever else you're seeing is no match. You'll see. As the saying goes, may the best man win, and that man, Alexandra, as you'll soon find out, will be me.'

CHAPTER EIGHTEEN

E ven though I shouldn't have been, I was feeling nervous. My heart was pounding as I walked the final steps to the bar where I was meeting Miles.

He'd invited me to a work do. Well, I use the word *invited* very loosely. Technically it was less a case of him inviting me and more a case of me inviting *myself*.

I'd been relieved when he'd replied to the message I'd sent last Thursday thanking him for the flowers and asked if I wanted to meet for dinner that Saturday. I thought maybe he'd be weird after the way we'd left things that night after the cinema, but the date had flowed well like it normally did. Anyway, towards the end of our meal, I was trying to steer the conversation towards the future and his intentions for us. However, somehow we got sidetracked into talking about his plans for the following week, and his work gathering, which was a retirement party for one of the doctors, came up.

He was saying that he always dreaded going to these events because all of his colleagues were married or coupled up, so he often felt like a third wheel. Maybe I wasn't thinking straight, because I was trying to work out how best to ask whether he reckoned he'd be likely to fall in love with me and marry me anytime soon, without him running a mile, which he would have done if I'd phrased it like that. But before I knew it, I'd jumped in and said, 'I'll go with you!', volunteering my plus-one services even though they hadn't been requested.

As soon as the words had fallen from my mouth, I'd instantly regretted it. You don't invite yourself to some-one's work thing. You *wait* to be asked. After all, these were people that he spent most of his day with. His career was very important to him. This was his professional life. Maybe he wasn't ready to introduce me to his colleagues. Not yet, at least.

After all, inviting me along would surely lead to them wanting to know our connection or the status of our rela-tionship. Just friends? Fuckbuddies? Girlfriend? It's a natural reaction, right? And given that it was a delicate subject at the moment, which required further discussion (something I was hoping we could address tonight), in hindsight, maybe I should have kept schtum. But I hadn't.

Thankfully, though, rather than making things awkward, after a slight pause, Miles had said, 'Um, yeah, yeah! Why not? I'd love you to come. As long as you don't mind meeting a bunch of doctors?'

And I'd said, 'No! Of course not! I'm sure it will be fun!'

So here I was. About to meet his colleagues. They'd probably all be super smart and spend the whole night spouting lots of medical terminology that would sound like double Dutch to me and I'd feel really stupid, but maybe their partners would be equally bamboozled by their doctor talk and we could chat about something more generic.

Yes. It would be absolutely fine. I was used to meeting new people and making conversation. When you're in sales, you have to be good at small talk. That's why I shouldn't be nervous.

Tell that to my bloody heart, which was still beating *way* too fast…

I took a deep breath and opened the large glass double doors. There were crowds of people scattered in groups throughout the large open space. It had huge windows, high ceilings, exposed brickwork and metallic ventilation ducts. Industrial chic with a modern twist.

Miles was already here. He'd finished work at 5 p.m. and come straight to the venue. I'd hoped that I could leave the office early, but of course Steve was having none of it. I offered to have the time taken off my lunch break, but he said that we were 'a team' and that we were 'all in this together' so he couldn't start 'playing favourites' and giving me 'special treatment'. I wasn't asking for bloody special treatment. Just a bit of flexibility. You'd think that after being loyal to the company for thirteen years, leaving half an hour early wasn't too much to ask.

So now it had just gone 6.15 p.m., and it seemed like the evening was in full swing. After I'd put my coat away, I quickly popped to the toilets to check myself in the mirror. I really needed to get my extensions done again, but it was such a big expense. They'd be okay for another week, I supposed. I brushed the mid-lengths and ends to ensure it was smooth, then topped up my lipstick. I'd gone for a neutral pink colour. I'd considered a bold red lip, but then I'd thought best to play it safe. A do for doctors was likely to be quite subdued. Didn't want to draw unnecessary attention to myself. Blending in would be much better. That's why I'd opted for plain black heels and an LBD. Never could go wrong with a little black dress. I had one which was low-cut and sleeveless, but in the end I'd worn this one with the scoop neckline and three-quarter-length sleeves. Not massively sexy, but much more professional. I just wanted to make sure I made a good impression with Miles' colleagues.

I picked up a glass of wine from the waiter's tray and wandered around the curved white-and-green-tiled bar in search of Miles. I spotted him chatting away to a bald, smartly dressed man in his sixties and tapped him gently on the shoulder.

'Alex!' he said, giving me a kiss on each cheek. 'So glad you came. Alexandra, this is Dr Peters. Dr Peters, meet Alexandra.'

'Call me Gerald, please,'

'Lovely to meet you, Gerald,' I said. He certainly had a firm handshake.

'Well, good to catch up, Miles. Let's talk later,' said Gerald as he headed off to the opposite side of the room.

'Thanks for coming, Alex. You look stunning,' he said, flashing his beautiful smile. *Gets me every time.*

'Thanks. You look very dapper too,' I said, using it as an excuse to look him up and down. He was wearing a black roll-neck jumper under a navy blazer with matching trousers. No shirt underneath today, and first time I'd seen him in a full suit. He looked hot.

'Very kind of you. I did try.' He glanced at my glass. 'Glad to see you've got your priorities straight and have already got yourself a drink.'

'Of course!'

'Stepped out of your comfort zone and gone for white wine rather than rosé too, I see?'

'*Oh yes!* I'm all for living life on the edge.'

'Glad to hear it,' he chuckled.

For the next hour or so, we worked the room. Miles seemed to know everyone here, and their faces all lit up whenever he approached them. He was clearly well liked. I could see what Miles meant, though. It was very couple-centric. Most people chatted in twos, sticking with their significant others, and I was also surprised at how many of them worked together. Doctors married to other doctors, nurses or other roles in the profession. I suppose we're at work at least five days a week, so it's only natural that people find love with those they spend the most time with. Well, unless you work with the likes of Garth and Steve, that is. There was more chance of me becoming Queen of England than there was of me ever dating them.

Just as Miles and I finally got to have a chat by ourselves, Gerald swooped over. 'Terribly sorry, Alexandra, but would you mind if I stole Miles for five minutes? Just need to pop upstairs to the private lounge and introduce him to someone.'

'No, no, of course,' I replied as my stomach sank. Would we ever get some time alone to have that talk? Maybe tonight wasn't the best time or place. 'That's fine.'

'Thank you. I won't keep him long,' said Gerald, resting his hand on Miles' shoulder and leading him towards the staircase.

'Sorry, Alex!' mouthed Miles as he walked away. When your boss calls you to talk work stuff, you've got to go, I guess.

I headed over to the back wall to the table of canapés. I'd been starving all night, but it's tricky to hold a conversation with a mouthful of food and juggle a plate and glass of wine at the same time. If I was with friends or people I knew, then it wouldn't be a big deal, but I was so conscious of trying to make the best impression possible.

I rested my glass on the table, picked up a mini sausage roll, placed some fancy-looking vol-au-vents stuffed with what looked like meat of some kind and some other nibbles onto my plate, then turned around to face the crowd. More people had been arriving throughout the evening. I'd thought it was busy before, but that was nothing compared to now, it was heaving. I just needed to find someone who was on their own and strike up a conversation. But first, time to eat.

Suddenly, just when I'd taken a bite of my vegetable spring roll, the crowd parted as a woman glided across the floor. She was wearing a skintight one-shoulder red mini dress, and with every step she took, her glossy dark locks swooshed in slow motion like she was starring in a hair commercial. *Wow.* Her matching bright red full lips screamed *look at me*, which was *exactly* what everyone in the room was doing. I spotted one of the wives who'd caught her husband gawping giving him a nudge with her elbow and another actually pushing up her man's chin to close his mouth, which had fallen open when he'd laid eyes on her.

She was like an Amazonian goddess.

You could tell that she knew everyone was staring at her and was relishing every second. More power to her. If I had a figure like that, I'd walk around the streets naked, stopping every few seconds to pose like a peacock to ensure everyone got a good look. Like they say, if you've got it, flaunt it. And she was *definitely* doing that.

There I was thinking that I needed to blend in, afraid to wear colour, for fear of going against the grain, whereas Ms Confident Goddess in Red was sticking her finger up at convention and proudly standing out.

She plucked a glass of champagne from the tray (wine was probably far too lowly for the likes of her) and I swear the waitress almost curtsied when she approached. She then strutted straight over to the buffet, which surprised me. The goddess in red was actually going to eat? If I was wearing a dress like that, I'd be terrified to even sniff food for fear that I'd gain ten pounds. She must be one of the lucky ones that could eat whatever she wanted and didn't put on an ounce.

Captivated like everyone else in the room, my eyes followed her to see what she was going to pick up.

Oh. A carrot stick. Dipped in some hummus. That made sense, I supposed. Not likely to put on weight eating that.

'I'm famished!' she said, catching my eye. When I'm hungry, I normally reach for pizza or a burger, not a carrot stick. I wanted to explain that a solitary raw mini vegetable probably wasn't going to help satisfy her appetite and that she should at least opt for something more substantial like a cocktail sausage, but I thought better of it.

'I *love* your dress,' I said, falling back on the tried and tested ice-breaker of complimenting someone.

'Thanks. It's the only thing I could find in my wardrobe to put on.'

Lucky her. I had some nice dresses in my wardrobe, but what she was wearing was on a completely different level.

It must be designer or something. Probably cost the equivalent of my entire monthly salary.

'I'm Alexandra,' I said.

'Nice to meet you,' she replied. 'I'm Gabriella.'

'So, are you here with anyone tonight?' I asked, shuffling a bit as I gazed at her face. Her skin was flawless.

'Well, I came on my own, but I don't intend to leave on my own if you catch my drift.' She smiled. God, even her teeth were perfect. Probably paid a pretty penny to get them so neat and white too.

'Oh, I see.' I grinned. 'Hoping to meet a nice doctor tonight, are you?'

'*Something like that…*' She smirked. 'I already know a fair few people here, but there's one in particular I'm hoping to bump into…'

'A new romance,' I gushed. 'How lovely!'

'Not so much *new*. More like a *rekindled* romance. We have history. We were madly in love. Really serious. He was absolutely besotted with me. Would've given me the world on a silver platter, but I got cold feet and bailed. I've seen the light now, though, so I've come back to—'

'Gab-Gabby?' said Miles as he walked towards us cautiously, looking like he'd just seen a ghost. 'What are you doing here?' As Gabriella threw her long arms around him, his body stiffened and the blood appeared to rapidly drain from his face. He pulled away. 'Wh-when d-did you get back?'

'This morning,' she said, tossing her ridiculously thick, glossy hair back over her toned shoulder. Bet those locks were all natural too. Even with extensions, I could never get my hair looking that immaculate. 'I'm *so* jet-lagged, I must look *terrible*, but Gerald insisted I come along tonight, seeing as I'm going to be working at the hospital again.'

'You're…you're coming *back*?' asked Miles, as his eyes widened.

'Yes!' she shrieked, clapping her hands. 'I start Monday! I swore Gerald to secrecy. Told him I wanted to surprise you. It's only temporary to begin with as I want to see how it goes and whether any more opportunities come up to work in Africa again. Maybe you'll get to come with me this time?' Gabriella cocked her head to the side flirtatiously.

'Y-yeah…I-I mean, I wanted to…I've always wanted to go…I just…' His voice trailed off.

Oh dear. Alarm bells rang loudly in my ears. This was *not* a reunion of old colleagues. The more I stood here, seemingly invisible to both of them, and watched their body language, the more I got the feeling that these two had more than a professional relationship.

She played with her hair, pushing her pert boobs out and fluttering her eyelashes, and he was looking awkward. Kind of trying to act normal and unaffected by her presence, yet melting like an ice cream in a desert at the same time. It was like she'd cast a spell over him. He'd forgotten how to stand and how to speak and was stuttering like crazy. I'd never seen him so…so *nervous*. So tongue-tied before. He was always super-confident, but it seemed like she'd caused him to completely lose his shit.

Although part of me wanted the ground to swallow me up so that I could make a quick exit and leave them to their reunion, another part of me thought, *no*. I was here, so the least he could do was acknowledge that. Explain who she was to him. Then I could know for sure if my intuition was right or whether I was just being paranoid.

I cleared my throat loudly to remind them that I was still in the room.

'Sorry! God, I'm so sorry.' Miles winced. 'Where are my manners? Gabby, this is Alex, Alex this is Gabby: an… an…old friend,' he said.

'Oh *come, come*. We were *much* more than friends.' Gabby rolled her eyes. 'Friends…passionate lovers… all of that and *more*. Miles was my ex. The love of my life,' she said, stroking his face.

Holy shit.

This was his ex? I mean, from the way they were talking and acting, I guessed there was some history, but I didn't think that *she* was the one who'd broken his heart a few months ago.

Fucking great.

When I'd asked Miles what his ex looked like and if she was pretty, he'd just shrugged his shoulders and said *yeah, I suppose so*. Talk about understatement of the century.

The more I looked at her, the more intimidated I felt. Imagine the body of Gisele fused with Beyoncé's curves and J-Lo's bum and you kind of get a sense of how this woman looked.

How could I, a short, average-looking woman from South London, compete with someone who wouldn't look out of place as a Victoria's Secret model?

And it wasn't even like she was all style and no substance. She had brains as well as beauty. She was a doctor, for goodness' sake. She was confident and determined. What's worse, she'd just more or less told me that she was here to take her ex back, and said ex now turned out to be Miles: the guy that I was here with.

Calm down. Calm down.

This is the benefit of multi dating, remember? You don't have all of your eggs in one basket. Just as Miles has no official claim to you, you have no official claim to him either. You have no right to be jealous when you're dating another guy, so even if he does *arrange to meet up with Miss Universe, it'll be the same as you meeting up with Luke.*

Right?

Er, no.

This is his ex, for goodness' sake. They have history. It is not at all the same.

Okay, then, I said, desperately trying to reason with myself, *if they* do *end up getting back together, you will be fine. It's a* good *thing, remember? It will show that you two were not meant to be. That he didn't like you enough. That he wasn't ready to commit. It's better that this happens sooner rather than later, isn't it?*

Isn't it?

Oh God. This was a disaster.

'Look at him,' she said, turning to face me, 'I *love* it when he gets all shy. He goes all quiet. *So sweet!*' She stroked his cheek once more. I really wished she would stop fucking doing that.

'I'm just surprised to see you, that's all,' he said, starting to regain his voice.

'Well, you'll be seeing a *lot* more of me'—she turned to face me again with a fake smile—'so get used to it! I can't *wait* to start working closely with you again. See you on Monday, Poochie,' she said, kissing him gently on the cheek, and walking away, wiggling her pert bottom.

She was doing that *deliberately*.

Bitch.

I knew I wasn't supposed to get jealous because Miles and I weren't official, but I couldn't help it. I felt like I'd just been punched in the stomach. Winded. In pain. Empty. So many emotions swirled around my mind. Not to mention at least five million questions.

Poochie? Was that some sort of nickname she had for him? And did she say that she was jet-lagged and looking awful? If that was her looking awful, I'd hate to see what she looked like on a good day.

And they were going to be working *closely together*?

Great. This is just peachy, isn't it?

I had never seen Miles so tongue-tied. Was he still into her? He *must* be. No guy of sound mind would kick her out of bed…

He'd only mentioned his ex briefly before and said that they'd broken up because they both wanted different things and she'd emigrated. There I was, thinking, *Well, that's fine, then. If she's not in the country, then she's not a threat. I can ignore Laurie's rule to avoid guys that have broken up with a long-term ex less than six months ago. Miles is over her. What does Laurie know?* I'd told myself. *Every guy is different. It will be fine.*

Like hell it would.

This was a total shitstorm.

What was I to do now? Hang around and spend the whole evening watching her flirt with him and stroke his face? Get paranoid if he disappeared to the toilets, wondering if they'd arranged to have a quickie in a cubicle for old times' sake?

No. Best to bow out now with my head held high. Leave them to it. Now I was the one worried about feeling like a third wheel. I'd thought that meeting his colleagues tonight might bring us closer. Give me a sign that he was likely to want to make a proper commitment. But in fact, it had done the complete opposite. How could I even consider ending things with Luke to date Miles exclusively now that Goddess Gabriella was back on the scene?

'Is that the time?' I said, pulling my phone from my bag and feigning a yawn. 'I'm feeling a bit tired. Long day at work and everything. I'm going to head home.'

'Really? You don't have to. I'm sorry about all that. I wasn't expecting her to be here.'

Clearly.

'Yeah. Big day at work tomorrow, so best I get a good night's sleep.'

'Okay, then,' he said weakly. 'Thanks for coming, though. I'll see you soon.'

'Yeah,' I said, straining a smile and heading to the cloakroom. But the truth was, now that Gabriella was back in town, I wondered if in fact we would.

CHAPTER NINETEEN

That was unlike Miles. It was 6.04 and we'd arranged to meet at 6 p.m. He was always on time. In fact, more often than not, he was early. But today there was no sign of him.

We'd arranged to meet at a pub close to the hospital. When we were messaging last night, he'd said today wasn't ideal and had suggested catching up later in the week or over the weekend, but I had an exhibition in Manchester from Friday to Saturday, so I'd be travelling there on Thursday morning to help set up, and on Sunday I'd already agreed to meet Luke. Plus, I hadn't met up with Miles since his work do a week ago, and I was desperate to see him.

After that night, we'd messaged a few times, but the texts had felt a bit more, I don't know, *distant*. Not as chirpy and upbeat. Yes, he'd messaged me the morning after the party, apologising again for his ex turning up, and asked how I was. He'd also texted over the weekend a couple of times as he'd gone to see his parents, which I knew he'd had planned for weeks. But it was me who had messaged yesterday to ask if he wanted to meet today. I'd been fretting, you see, as I hadn't heard from him at all on Monday, which was the same day that Gabriella had returned to the hospital to start working 'closely' with him again. Coincidence? I wasn't sure.

Now it was Wednesday, they would have spent a whole three days together, and so I'll admit, as well as wanting to see Miles because I really missed him, I was also keen to find out whether her presence had changed him in some way. Had anything happened between them? Had they stolen a quick kiss in the medical cupboard (if that's even a thing)? Had she gone back to his and slept with him? *I know, I know.* This jealousy wasn't healthy or even valid. We weren't boyfriend or girlfriend, so what business was it of mine what he did? Fine in theory, but my heart wasn't feeling very theoretical right now.

This was the longest five minutes ever. In truth, Miles had said it would be difficult to meet tonight because of some stuff that had happened at work (which of course I instantly hoped wasn't Gabriella-related), which was why he'd suggested later this week would be better, but I'd been quite insistent. Not in a pushy way (well, at least I hoped not). More in an *I can meet you somewhere near the hospital in East London to save you time* way. I figured the easier I made it, the more likely he was to say yes. So that was why we were meeting here.

I recognised some of the people from the party last week, who'd smiled and nodded from across the bar. This must be where they all came after work. It was a simple, traditional British pub. Wooden bar, tables and chairs, burgundy-and-white checked carpet with matching walls. I scanned the room and realised I was the only one sitting alone. I felt like a proper Billy-no-mates. I reached in my bag to check my phone to see if there were any messages to say he was at least on his way. Just as I did, Miles came rushing through the door. Phew.

'Sorry! So sorry I'm late, Alex,' he said as he reached the table and gave me a quick kiss on my cheek. 'I was worried this would happen. I knew today would be full-on.'

'Don't worry,' I said, glancing up at his face and feeling guilty about pushing him to meet. He looked tired. Drained. His eyes weren't sparkling like they normally did. Even though he was wearing his glasses, I could still see that they seemed puffy, and dark circles cast a shadow underneath them.

'I've got to go to the gents, but I'll grab us some drinks on the way back, okay?'

'Okay, thanks,' I said as he put his coat on the chair in front and then headed off to the opposite end of the room. I should have offered to get the drinks in myself. He seemed flustered. I'd get the next round.

Oh no. That's all I need.

Just as Miles disappeared into the toilets, the pub doors swung open and in walked Gabriella. I was seriously contemplating hiding under the table, but it was so small I'd never fit, and anyway, she'd already spotted me. *Dammit.* She smiled, flashing her Colgate-perfect gnashers, and then strutted straight over to me like she was walking down the catwalk for London Fashion Week.

Gabriella's hair was tied up in a ponytail without a stray hair in sight, and even though her make-up was more understated this time, with a glossy nude shade on her lips, annoyingly, she still looked good. She was wearing a black trench coat, with a belt that had been expertly tied into a perfectly symmetrical bow around her waist to accentuate her hourglass figure, sheer tights and elegant black heels. Even though I was wearing my favourite navy body-con dress and up until thirty seconds ago had been feeling confident, in her presence, I felt like a frump.

Great. Just great.

'Cassandra!' she beamed as she approached the table and leant down to give me two kisses on the cheek. God, she smelt amazing too. All fresh and citrusy, like she'd just stepped out of a shower or had bathed in lemon-infused water and then hired an army of angels to gently massage her skin with sweet flower petals.

'Hello, Gabriella,' I said, ignoring the fact that she got my name wrong.

'Miles is here already, then, I see,' she said, glancing down at the chair. 'I'd know his coat anywhere. I helped him choose it last year. I always knew exactly what suited him,' she said, flashing a bitchy smile.

'Right,' I replied.

'I'm surprised he even came out tonight, to be honest. After these past couple of days, he's worn out, bless him. It shows, too. He looked so tired when we were together this afternoon. Still utterly gorgeous, *obviously*, but tired. He definitely needs a shot of ginger. That's what I always used to have on standby after one of our sessions.' She smirked. 'Miles was always *insatiable*. I've never met a man with such a big…*appetite*. I don't think we ever went more than forty-eight hours without it. Couldn't keep our hands off each other. That's why I call him *Poochie*. Because he always wanted to put his P in my coochie…*Oooh!*' she said, fanning herself with her hand. 'I'm getting hot just thinking about it. Speaking of the horny devil, there he is at the bar. Better go and check he's okay. Bye, Cassandra!'

As she headed over to join Miles, my cheeks grew so hot you could fry an egg on them, and I had more steam coming out of my ears than a hundred kettles.

What a bitch.

Not only did she insist on calling me the wrong name (which I was sure she'd done deliberately), but she'd also implied that they'd been doing stuff together to make him tired. Or was that my paranoia? He did look drained. I'd noticed it straightaway. Was it because they'd been fucking? And why did she feel it was appropriate to start talking about what they used to get up to in the bedroom? Telling me that they were at it like rabbits with that stupid *Poochie* nickname and practically calling him a sex addict. Did Gabriella somehow know I was doing this challenge? Did she have some sort of sixth sense? Perhaps she'd studied psychology or something and could read my body language, which was giving off a vibe that I wanted it but had to abstain? Or maybe it was her way of warning me that Miles wouldn't wait. If he never went more than two days without sex with her, how could I expect him to wait months for me?

Fuck.

And now look at her. Leaning against the bar, flirting with him again. I was fighting a losing battle, wasn't I? If he hadn't already succumbed to her charms, it was surely only a matter of time. They'd be working together for nine or ten hours every day. How would he be able to resist? In fact, was there even any point in me trying to have this conversation with him tonight about the future, when it was obvious that his future was with her? Maybe I should just bow out now.

'Here you go, Alex,' said Miles as he put the glasses of wine on the table and sat down.

'Thanks, Miles,' I said, examining his face for answers to the myriad of questions that were popping up into my head.

'Are you okay?' he asked, removing his glasses and rubbing his eyes. *Damn.* Gabriella the bitch was right. He looked knackered, but still so bloody gorgeous.

'I'm fine. I've been busy at work preparing for this Beauty & Wellbeing exhibition later this week but… anyway, how are you, Miles? How have *you* been?'

'Not great, to be honest, Alex. I'm not sure I'll be able to stay long. I'm not in a good place right now. My head's spinning. Trying to make sense of it all.'

Make sense of what? I asked myself. Was it Gabriella? What did she say to him at the bar? Or had something happened between them these past few days, and he was trying to work out whether he wanted to get back together because he still loved her or if he wanted to be with me? He wasn't the only one whose head was spinning.

'Oh?' I said. 'Why? Is there something you'd like to tell me? I mean, something you'd like to talk about? Sometimes it helps.'

I braced myself for what was to come. Perhaps it was going to be one of the 'it's not you, it's me' conversations, or one of the 'I think we should take some time apart' lines that I'd become so accustomed to over the years. *Here it comes…*

'Ordinarily, I'd agree, but not tonight. Sometimes things happen and there's no logic to them. No reasoning, no amount of discussion, reflection or *if onlys* can change it. It's done. Sometimes you just have to hold your hands up and say, I'm just a man. As much as I can try to be strong, some things are just out of my control.'

Oh gosh. He slept with her, didn't he? Shit. I knew she had him under her spell. He wasn't able to control himself. Most men wouldn't. I didn't condone his actions, but, if he was going to succumb to any woman, it was understandable that it would be her. Didn't stop it from feeling like someone had just plunged a knife in my heart, though.

'I see.' I bowed my head.

'That's the thing with death.' He rubbed his eyes again. 'It doesn't discriminate. It doesn't care if it's a wonderful little boy who has his whole life ahead of him. It just comes and takes whoever it wants. Including sweet innocent little children.' He picked up his glass, downed the wine in one and slammed it back on the table. 'It fucking sucks.'

Death?

Shit. There I was thinking he was worrying about his feelings for me and wondering whether he was sleeping with Gabriella, and he was suffering because he'd lost a patient. *That* was why he looked so drained. He was clearly upset.

'I'm so sorry, Miles,' I said, taking his hand in mine and squeezing it. 'Was he one of your patients?'

'He was. Lost him on Monday. I mean, I knew it was coming. I just hoped that…I don't even know why it's affected me like this. I should be used to this by now. It's just…for some reason, it's hit me hard. And so, I just can't be here tonight, Alex. In a pub. Smiling. Trying to laugh and joke around.'

'Miles,' I said, moving my chair closer and wrapping my arm around him. 'I don't know what to say. That's such devastating news. When you said you had a lot on at work, I didn't realise. I'm sorry I suggested meeting tonight. Of course. If you want to be alone, I completely understand.'

'Thanks. Normally I'm able to just soldier on, but there was something about him. He was different. In some ways, he reminded me a bit of me when I was younger…well, I can't go into that because of patient confidentiality. I know it's not my fault. It's none of the team's fault. We did our best. We tried. *I tried.* It's just another child I couldn't save.'

'Oh, Miles,' I said, wishing I could do something to make it better. The death of a little boy was heartbreaking. It certainly put things into perspective. 'Is there anything I can do? Would you like me to, I don't know…is there something I can do to make you feel better? Even if it's just to sit and listen to you?' I wracked my brains trying to think of the right thing to say.

'You're very kind, Alex,' he said as he stood up and put his arms in the sleeves of his coat, 'but this is something I have to work through on my own somehow. I'm really sorry, but I have to go. I'll message soon.'

He leant down and kissed me softly on the forehead, then left.

I sat there for a few minutes, just feeling numb. I was so sad for him. For his loss. I wanted to be there for him. Hold him. Comfort him. Try and make him feel better. If I was upset, I'd want someone to hold me. But people dealt with loss in different ways, I guessed, and maybe being alone was his. Perhaps he didn't want to be vulnerable and upset in front of me. Maybe it was too soon and he didn't feel close enough to me yet.

As much as I wanted to know more about his intentions and if becoming exclusive meant that he would like us to start a serious relationship, I realised that I had to give him time. Be understanding. He was going through enough right now.

I'd take a step back. I'd give him some space, and when he was feeling better, stronger, then we could have a conversation about the future, and whether he saw me in his.

CHAPTER TWENTY

I *just don't know…*
   It was 3.27 a.m. on Monday and I couldn't sleep.
My head was spinning.

For once, I wasn't being kept awake because I was trying to stop myself from dreaming about sex or resisting the temptation to pleasure myself. No, this time, it was because I just couldn't work out what decision to make. How to move forward with my love life. What to do for the best. How to know which of the two guys I was dating was most likely to be my soul mate and the one that would help me to achieve the happy life I'd dreamt of. My decision had been made even harder after yesterday's date with Luke.

Whilst I was on my way back on the train from Manchester on Saturday night, Luke had messaged about plans for Sunday. I'd mentioned how knackered I was after two days on my feet, and he'd suggested that, as I was so tired, rather than me having to drag myself into town to meet, I should have a lie-in instead and then he would come round and cook for me whilst I relaxed on the sofa. Although part of me thought maybe it was his way of getting an invite to my house to have his wicked way with me, it did sound like a lovely idea, and I could really do with a rest.

The book had said that I shouldn't cook for a man during the early stages, but it hadn't said anything about *him* cooking for *me*. I knew home visits were frowned upon by Laurie in general, especially during the first month, but as I was now eight weeks in and she was the one that was always banging on about allowing a man to be nice to me, which was exactly what Luke was trying to do, I agreed.

Talking of being nice, ever since I'd mentioned the challenge, Luke had become *more* attentive. He'd started messaging me every evening to say hi and to see what I was doing, which was great, but of course, it also made it difficult to decide which guy was the right one for me.

Luke was even really considerate about the timing of our date. He'd suggested that he'd arrive at 3.30 p.m. as that would give me more time to sleep. Also, by coming during daylight to cook me lunch, rather than in the evening to make dinner, I could feel reassured that he wasn't dropping round for a booty call. It was also his idea to have lunch at my place. He said whilst he was happy to send a taxi for me to come to his so that I wouldn't have to go on public transport, I'd feel more comfortable in my own environment, so he'd come to me, which I thought was really sweet of him.

Lunch was lovely. I mean, it was all pre-prepared by the supermarket, so he'd just removed the packaging and put the chicken and potatoes to roast in the oven and microwaved some carrots, but the point was, he'd made an effort, which was nice. We'd sat at the kitchen table and had a discussion like we often did. This time it was on the relevance of university degrees in modern society, which obviously he was all for.

He'd even asked some questions about me, my job, what I liked doing; he'd complimented me on my hair (maybe the extensions were worth the investment after all, as Luke really loved them); and when Cuddles had come in, he'd actually attempted to pat her. Although she'd run back to the bedroom when he came closer, the fact that he'd tried to be affectionate towards Cuddles because he knew how much she meant to me again showed he was trying.

When it got to about 6.30 p.m., Luke said he'd better go, as he had to prep for lectures in the morning. The surprising thing was, he was there, in my house, sitting at the table and then beside me on my sofa. The two of us were alone and he didn't try *anything*. Not once. When he was leaving, he didn't even go in for a snog or a peck on the lips. He just took my hand and kissed it. I was so shocked. He was really taking my challenge seriously. He hadn't tried to push things, which would have been so easy to do. And it sounds odd, but when he left, him *not* trying to make a pass at me drove me crazy. The fact that he knew about my vow and was willing to wait was so *sexy*. It made me want it, want *him* more. I was so confused.

That's why this wasn't easy. Never did I think when I was starting this challenge that I'd be this torn. That I'd have two eligible bachelors, two smart, handsome contenders, vying for my heart. And yet here I was in that very situation, and I had no idea what to do.

That's why I hadn't been able to return his call.

Yes. To add to the complication, Miles had called whilst Luke was here, but I hadn't heard the phone ring as I'd left it charging in the bedroom. It was only after 10.30 p.m., when I'd finished clearing up the kitchen, putting on the washing and ironing my clothes for the week, that I'd collapsed on the bed, checked my phone and seen his missed call and then the text he'd sent half an hour ago saying we needed to talk.

I panicked.

Miles and I had kept in touch since meeting up last Wednesday. Even though I'd told myself I'd give him space, I needed to check he was okay, so I'd messaged him on the Thursday on my way to Manchester to ask how he was feeling. He'd said it was still raw, but he'd be fine.

I had been at the exhibition hall from the minute I arrived on Thursday until almost midnight, then had to be back on site from 8 a.m. through to 6 p.m. on Friday. After that, it was entertaining clients until midnight again, then back at the hall from 8 a.m. all the way until the show ended on Saturday. I was lucky that I got to go home. Some of my colleagues had to stay until Sunday. Anyway, all that meant it was hard to message as much as I would have liked. But when Miles had texted on Saturday morning, he'd said that he was much better and was determined to use his grief as fuel to drive him to help even more kids.

I'd told him that it wasn't his fault, and he said he knew that, but he was looking into whether there was something extra that he could do. Even if it meant making personal sacrifices or doing things in his own time. If the boy's death made him carry out even more meaningful work, then he reasoned that at least it wouldn't be completely in vain.

I hated that I had to be hundreds of miles away from him at a stupid show, schmoozing with clients, when I could be in London checking whether Miles was okay. Holding him. Rubbing his shoulders. Trying to make him feel better.

Had it just been a missed call from Miles, I might not have worried too much. I would have thought maybe he was feeling a bit low about his patient and wanted to talk. But it was the text that concerned me.

Miles

Hi, we really need to talk. Not something I want to put on a text. Pls call me.

That was ominous. It also felt really impersonal. He hadn't mentioned my name or signed it off with a kiss or blowing kiss emoji like he normally did. It was abrupt. Curt. Short.

It sounded serious. Not grief-related or *I need a shoulder to cry on* serious. More like *it's over* serious or *I'm getting back with Gabby* serious. Why else would it not be something he could put in a text? Maybe because he knew how badly I'd been affected by guys ghosting or dumping me via messages before, he wanted to try and do the decent thing and arrange to end things in person or over the phone. I don't know. It was just a feeling in my gut that told me that whatever he had to say wasn't good news and I couldn't handle it right now.

I was just so confused. About everything. This multi dating approach was supposed to make me feel calm, but I felt anything but. I just didn't think I could continue with it anymore. Not because of the whole sex thing. It was more about what it was doing with my emotions. I had feelings for both Miles and Luke, and I couldn't carry on with this juggling. The ups and downs. The uncertainty. I needed to make a decision and stick with it. But how, and who?

On the one hand, I had Miles, who was kind, considerate and caring. We could talk about anything for hours, and I felt so comfortable around him. Happy. He made me laugh, and he was incredibly sexy. And kissing him. *Wow*. We hadn't had a moment to be that close since that date at the cinema, but I remembered it like it was five minutes ago. In fact, just thinking about it made me weak. The downside was the whole ex-girlfriend situation, and he hadn't really spoken much about commitment. Only dating exclusively. It wasn't specific enough. Just because he didn't want to share me, I couldn't assume that automatically meant he wanted to take me off the singles market *permanently*.

Plus, I always went for the guys that were great kissers and made me feel weak at the knees, and it always ended badly. So whilst I enjoyed Miles' company and fancied him like mad, I couldn't lose sight of my objective. I needed to find someone who didn't shy away from making plans for the future. Someone who wanted to have a life-long relationship with me. Not *one day* in the next century, but now. *Right now*.

I wasn't even sure if he still wanted exclusivity anyway. That had been mentioned before Gabriella was back on the scene. Maybe he'd changed his mind since then. I wouldn't know without having a proper conversation with him, which had been difficult as we hadn't had time alone to talk at his work party, then it hadn't been appropriate when we'd last met as he was grieving. If I returned his call now, we *could* maybe try discussing it, but I wasn't in the right frame of mind tonight, and I'd rather do it in person than on the phone. Facetime wouldn't cut it either. It wasn't the same.

Then there was Luke. Mysterious and moody. Very intelligent like Miles and well travelled. *Very* handsome. If I could draw my ideal type of guy physically, it would probably be Luke. Well, before I'd met Miles anyway. Luke was very confident, which could come across as arrogant sometimes, but that was just his way. No one's perfect, right? And he'd been really sweet since learning about my challenge. Cooking for me, not trying it on when he could so easily have sneaked a kiss or more when we were on the sofa. The big plus with Luke was that he had regularly spoken about commitment and marriage.

And, unlike Miles, Luke knew about the challenge and yet had chosen to stick around. In fact, if anything, it had made him keener. By the sounds of it, Miles needed lots of sex, so whilst he hadn't pushed me to take things further so far, when he found out about my vow of abstinence, that might send him running straight into Gabriella's arms, or rather jumping straight in between her legs.

That's why I'd left it.

I *wanted* to message, I really did. But then I thought he might read my text and try calling again. There would be no way I couldn't answer after that. So I decided it was better to give myself some time tonight to reach a decision, get a second opinion from Stacey at work in the morning, then call Miles back at lunchtime. That was reasonable, wasn't it? I'd be fresher tomorrow. I hoped he wouldn't think I'd left him waiting too long. Would he?

After reading his text, I'd climbed under the duvet and

tried to weigh up what to do. To-ing and fro-ing with my thoughts and feelings. Then I'd attempted to get some sleep, but couldn't.

Several hours of debating later, I *thought* I knew what I was going to do. Which guy I was leaning towards the most. *Sort of*...maybe. But I just needed to be sure, because I had the feeling that once I made my choice, there would be no going back.

CHAPTER TWENTY-ONE

'Well, personally, I know who I would choose, but it's not my life,' said Stacey, taking a sip of her coffee.

I'd texted her at the crack of dawn to ask if she could meet me in the kitchen fifteen minutes before work started so I could talk to her about my dilemma.

'I know this has to be my own decision, but I'd like a second opinion. You've been here since the beginning, so I would really value your advice. I don't want to make a mistake.'

'Okay, okay. Let's strip this back a bit. You've filled me in on your date with Luke and how gentlemanly he was, which is positive. I'm up to date with Miles, the ex and the strange text. And you've spent the night weighing up the pros and cons of each—well, you *say* you have anyway. So let's rewind and focus on the cons you listed. The main drawback with Miles was your uncertainty of his commitment and interest in marriage in the immediate future, and of course the appearance of this Gabby you seem to think is perfection personified, and you struggled to find a significant drawback with Luke because as far as you could see, he's smart, he's handsome, he declared his intention to marry you on the first date and has been attentive despite knowing about the challenge. Correct?'

'Yeah, pretty much.' I nodded.

'But what about Luke's arrogance? Doesn't that bother you?'

'Sometimes, but he explained to me that it's *confidence*. He's achieved a lot and isn't ashamed to shout about it.'

'Hmm. Yes, but hasn't Miles achieved just as much as Luke?'

'Oh, definitely. He does *amazing* work. Looking after children. Caring for the next generation. I think it's *brilliant*.'

'Yes. Miles had an awful childhood, was in and out of care, yet went on to study and become a top children's doctor. But he doesn't ram his achievements down your throat every second,' said Stacey.

'No, Miles would *never* do that,' I gushed. 'He's so humble. He hates drawing attention to himself.'

'*Exactly*. And what about Luke's brashness and self-centredness? Didn't you say that he's sometimes rude to waiters?'

'He's quite direct. He admits that, though.'

'But doesn't he spend most of the time talking about how amazing he is at his job, how many countries he's travelled to, how every man, his dog and the pope wants to invite him to give a million-dollar talk because he's just *the best* at everything?'

'Well,' I said. 'He *does* have a tendency to talk about

himself…but he doesn't always. Usually there's a topic we discuss at each date which doesn't have anything to do with either of us. Just general conversation. Like a debate. And yesterday he was asking me a lot more questions about what exactly I did for work and what I liked doing in my spare time, so he's making more of an effort.'

'And aren't all of those questions that Miles asked on your first date? Yet it's taken Luke, what, six dates to be bothered to ask you the same?'

'Um, yes…'

'In fact, didn't Miles listen so intently to what you said you liked doing on your first date that he arranged the perfect date less than twenty-four hours later by taking you to the zoo?'

'Yes, yes, *okay*!' I shouted. 'I get it! And I *know* all this. I *told* you all this. Miles is *amazing*. I love everything about him, but it's not that simple. What about Gabriella?'

'I think you're forgetting that she's his ex. People break up for a reason.'

'Yes, but from the sounds of it, he didn't want to break up with her. He loved her. Probably still does. Why did he introduce her as a "friend" and not just say she was an ex? I need to know Miles wants *me*. That he'll fall in love with *me*. That he'll want to marry *me*. Not her.'

'And how do you know he doesn't?' said Stacey. 'Not everyone is as forthright and as mouthy as Luke. Just because he hasn't said it explicitly, it doesn't mean it isn't something he's thinking about. He hasn't had the opportunity to express himself about how he feels about the future with you or give his side of the story about Gabriella.'

'Which is so frustrating! Every time I've wanted to address it, something has always come up. I want to be patient, but at the same time, I can't help but think that with Luke, by this time next year I could have settled down and be married. With Miles, I'm either going to get dumped for his ex, or maybe best-case scenario, he could choose me, but then I could be the eternal girlfriend. And how can I stay calm knowing he's spending all day working with Gabriella? There's just a big question mark hanging over my future with him. With Luke I can feel more sure. He's direct. You know where you stand with him. He says what he means. Means what he says.'

'I wouldn't be so sure.' Stacey crossed her arms. 'There's just something about him that doesn't sit right with me. His flashiness, his arrogance, his inconsistencies. One minute he's self-absorbed and questioning why you won't sleep with him on the fourth date and the next he's all sweetness and light and is willing to wait *months* to have sex with you: a woman he barely knows, as he rarely bothers to extract his head from his own arse.'

I thought Stacey was being a bit harsh. Luke could be really sweet. Perhaps it was just because initially he hadn't understood why I was turning him down, as he could tell I was attracted to him, so it didn't make sense. Maybe he'd felt I was rejecting him. But when I'd explained and he'd seen that I was striving towards a goal, being the ambitious guy that he was, he could better relate. Luke knew what it was like to set yourself a challenge and work hard to achieve it.

'He's not that bad. Luke said himself, if he just wanted to sleep with me, he would have told me from the beginning. He said he wants marriage and children and to settle down.'

'I know he did, Alex. But I wonder if he's genuine.

Miles is consistent. He's always seemed into you. He's always made the effort. He's more like you. Humble. Kind. He might not be loud and outspoken, but I'd trust what he said more than Luke. Look,' she said, resting her hand on my shoulder. 'Who can say for sure? You've spent time with them both and you know how each of them makes you feel, so only *you* can make that decision. But I would ask you this: assuming that *both* of them *were* serious about committing to you, which one could you imagine cuddling up with on a cold winter's night? If you had no money to go out to restaurants or on holiday, who would you feel happiest spending time with? In ten years' time, who wouldn't just make your body tingle but also make your heart sing and your soul dance? Which one could you see yourself growing old with? If you were stranded in the middle of nowhere, who do you think would do everything they could to find you?'

'Miles,' I replied without hesitation. 'Miles every time.'

It was funny. I'd spent all night pondering and thinking. Doing mental checklists, trying to interpret every little detail of every date with Miles and Luke. But suddenly, Stacey posed those questions, and somehow I didn't have to reflect for even a second. The answer flew out of my mouth before I'd even realised it. How was that even possible? How had I not asked myself those questions before? She'd made the decision seem so simple.

'Then there's your answer. In your defence, I think you've been asking yourself the wrong questions. You've been so fixated on this whole getting married thing that you've just homed in on the guy that's telling you what you want to hear, rather than listening to your gut and the way Miles has made you *feel*. He may not have spoken about marriage with you explicitly, but him wanting to date you exclusively is his way of saying he's interested in getting serious. He wants you to commit to him the way he wants to commit to you. I suspect he's afraid of going all in and falling for you, only for you to sail into the sunset with one of the other guys or run off and break his heart like that Gabriella. After all, you're waiting for him to show you that he wants to get serious, but what have you done or said to show him that *you* do?'

'Not much, I guess,' I replied sheepishly. 'I haven't explicitly.'

'Think about it. Miles is sending you flowers, taking you to places he knows you love, making an effort to find out about you, which is how it should be. I'm sure he's not looking for you to start organising dates to take him on, but equally, even as a guy, he'd probably also like reassurance that this is going somewhere and he's not just wasting his time.'

Shit. I'd been so afraid of getting hurt that *I'd* been the one pulling back. Too scared to show my emotions. To say how I felt and what I wanted for fear he'd run away like the other guys, or that I'd look stupid. But I should have realised sooner that Miles wasn't like those other losers I'd been out with in the past. He wasn't a fuckboy. Far from it. Miles had put himself on the line that night. By asking for exclusivity, he was trying to tell me that he wanted me. But I'd basically rejected him. Made him feel like he wasn't good enough. Even though I knew what I felt, that I had strong feelings for him and wanted to be with him, I'd ignored my gut and chosen to follow the book, rather than take a chance and follow my heart.

'I see that now. I got so obsessed with that goal. Following Laurie's rules, seeing marriage as the finishing line rather than love and happiness. I wasn't thinking clearly. I'm going to call Miles back now and ask to meet him. *Today*. Say I'd like to talk to him about going exclusive. Then I can ask him, outright, about where he sees this going. And about Gabriella. It might scare him. I mean, before this challenge, although I would have *thought* about it, there's no way I would have considered actually having a serious conversation about a long-term future after dating a guy for a month. But I need to find out. Know where I stand. Then I can take it from there.'

'Sounds like a sensible plan. And, yeah, it might seem soon, but guys know. They know from the first couple of dates whether they see you as a serious prospect or not. No time to call him now, though. You'll have to do it at lunchtime. As soon as we finish this boring meeting.'

'Oh no!' I glanced up at the clock Steve had now put up on the kitchen wall. 'I forgot about that.'

'Yep. A three-hour presentation about the new direction of the company. It's sure to be *riveting*.'

'Three hours! Not even a truckload of coffee is going to make me stay awake for that long. Especially considering I've had about four hours sleep. I should at least message Miles back though, so he knows I'm not ignoring him. I know first-hand what it's like when someone doesn't return your calls.'

'You'd better be quick, though,' she said. 'The meeting is starting in two minutes, and we've still got to get upstairs. And you know what Steve is like. He's probably already prepared the chopping block for our heads. Text Miles whilst we walk to the lift.'

I plucked my phone out of my bag.

'Shit! Two missed calls from Miles!'

'Like you said, he's probably thinking you're blanking him,' said Stacey as she pressed the button for the seventh floor.

I contemplated whether there was any way to skip the meeting so I could talk to Miles. *Nope.* As much as I hated my job, I still needed it, and being even thirty seconds late for this meeting could be a sure-fire way to guarantee my unemployment. Miles would understand.

'I'll let Miles know I'm going into a meeting and will call him back as soon as it's finished,' I said typing, into WhatsApp.

'Good idea. At least that might help you get through this presentation, knowing you've got a call and potentially a nice long date with him later to look forward to.'

'Yeah,' I said, clicking send. 'I'm feeling much more optimistic now. Whatever he was calling to tell me, I still want to meet him today. I'm determined to tell him face-to-face how I feel. Gabriella or no Gabriella, I'm convinced that Miles is the man for me, and I'm not going to give him up without a fight.'

CHAPTER TWENTY-TWO

It had been almost a week since I'd last heard from Miles. Since he'd gone.

Perhaps forever.

It was all so sudden. I still couldn't quite get my head around it. I'd come out of the meeting just before 1 p.m., fuming that it had lasted four tortuous hours rather than three, and I'd raced back downstairs so that I could go to the park around the corner and give Miles a call.

He'd phoned again after I'd sent my text and then left a voicemail just after noon. I didn't bother listening to it at first. I was just so excited to speak to him. But when his phone went straight to voicemail, I decided to play the message, and it was then that I realised I was too late.

Hi, Alex, it's me. Miles. I've been trying to reach you since yesterday. I wanted to let you know that I've been called away. To work in Africa. Remember I was telling you how I wanted to do some aid work over there? To help children overseas? That I'd been waiting ages to get the call? Well, it came. On Sunday afternoon. It all happened so quickly. I'm lucky that I was allowed to go. Normally you have to give a few months' notice, but because my bosses knew I'd been trying to do this for ages and it was another colleague on my team that dropped out at the last minute, we were able to do a swap and he could take over my patients. Luckily all my vaccinations were up to date too. Anyway, they're desperate for our help. They need us straightaway, so I'm about to get on the plane now. That's why I called yesterday. I wanted to tell you as soon as it was confirmed. I don't think my phone is going to work over there. I've got no idea, so I didn't want to just disappear without explaining. We're going for two weeks. It might be longer. I won't know until I get there, so I wanted to call and tell you that I—

Miles, we'd better go…

Okay, sorry, Alex, I've got to go. T-take care.

And then the message ended.

I tried calling again. Literally every half an hour. Then Stacey took my phone and reminded me that he was flying, so calling repeatedly wouldn't help and would only make me look like a stalker.

I hoped maybe he'd land, see my missed calls and ring back. But he'd said he didn't know whether his phone would work over there. And who was the woman who'd called out to him and told him they had to go?

Hold on.

I grabbed my phone from Stacey's desk, logged back into WhatsApp and scrubbed through Miles' message to get to the last few seconds. I pressed play and held the phone to my ear.

Miles, we'd better go…

Then I played it again:

Miles, we'd better go…

That voice sounded *very* familiar.

Oh no.

I dropped the phone onto my lap.

That voice *was* familiar. That voice was Gabriella's.

Fuck. Miles had gone on a trip for at least two weeks with his ex-girlfriend who had already made it clear to me that she wanted Miles back. The woman he had apparently been besotted with. That he couldn't keep his hands off.

It was bad enough when I'd found out that they'd be working together for nine hours a day. I'd thought then that it couldn't get any worse, but it had, because of course now they'd be spending entire days *and nights* together. Working together, eating together and probably sleeping together. And I'd be here. Thousands of miles away. *Me.* The woman who'd wanted Miles to commit to *her* but hadn't shown that she was serious enough to date *him* exclusively. Who would blame Miles for falling back into her arms?

I should have called him back that night. As soon as I'd seen his message. I shouldn't have left it. I'd just been scared. Scared of what he was going to tell me. If I'd returned his call, I could have told him how I felt, so that at least he'd have gone there knowing that I'd fallen for him. That he was the one.

I didn't even know where he'd gone in Africa, or what the relief project was. I understood why he'd gone. He'd wanted to do this for ages, and after what had happened with his patient, I knew he wanted more than ever to help kids in need. What if it was longer than a few weeks? What if he decided he needed to stay for months or even years? Whilst I would still have been devastated to see him go, I could have at least let him know that I understood. That I supported him. If I'd called that night, we could have met up. Even if it was one o'clock in the morning. I would have gone to him. We could have talked everything through.

Now he thought I didn't care. That I didn't want him. Now I'd driven him straight back to Gabriella. The very thing I had been trying to prevent was what I had encouraged. And he was about to tell me something, before she'd interrupted. And now I'd never find out what it was. I should have known when I saw two missed calls before the meeting that something was wrong. I'd just realised everything too late.

I felt sick. Like someone had taken a chainsaw to my body and cut a massive hole inside me. Like my heart had been ripped from me. On top of that, I was filled with the gut-wrenching feeling of doubt and insecurities. When I'd first started this challenge, I'd felt relatively calm. No worrying about guys calling or messaging because I had options. But none of that mattered anymore. Not now that I'd seen the light. I didn't care that Luke was still a possibility. Ever since my conversation with Stacey that morning, I'd seen everything so clearly. It was Miles that I wanted. He was the one I wanted to be with, and now I'd missed my chance.

Stacey said that obsessing over the situation wasn't going to make it better. That I just had to be patient, hope that he and Gabriella didn't get back together and that he'd return to London soon. And if he did, we'd have to meet up, have a long chat and take it from there.

I'd said that I felt helpless. Passive, just sitting back and waiting for him to return. Maybe I could go to the hospital, find out where he'd gone. Maybe I could even go there to wherever he'd gone and help.

'Absolutely *not!*' Stacey had said. 'I know it's hard, but you need to find a way to get a grip. You *cannot* go to Africa chasing after him. No matter how much you like him. Remember the famous saying? If you love some-thing, set it free. If it comes back to you, it's yours. If it doesn't, it never was. I know you're upset that you didn't get to speak to him before he left and to find out how he feels, but you still have to maintain that balance. Step back and let him come to you.'

By the Wednesday, two days after he'd left, I was going crazy. I missed Miles so much. The fact that I couldn't see or speak to him left me feeling hollow. So *empty.* I knew I should pull back, but I needed him to know how I felt. That I was thinking about him. What if he *did* get the chance to use his phone? I wanted to at least send him a message, for him to hear my voice and know that I cared. So I tried to send him a voicemail, but his phone was still switched off. I then sent a couple of What-sApp messages apologising for missing his calls. Explaining that I was in a meeting when he'd phoned, but that I *really* wanted to speak to him. That I had something *important* to tell him, hoping that would encourage him to call back, but nothing. And there was still another week to wait until he was back. *At least.*

Stacey encouraged me to continue dating *just in case.* But I didn't want to. I didn't want anyone else. I wasn't even interested in seeing Luke. He might have a lot to offer with his good looks, PhD and millions of qualifica-tions, but he wasn't the man for me.

I considered the goals I'd set at the beginning of the

challenge. Luke didn't adore me, make me laugh, or share my interests or goals, and he wasn't supportive. The only point he *did* seem to score on was that he seemed ready to commit to marry me. But I didn't want to get married for the sake of it, just so that I could tick a box. *Love* was the most important thing. That had always been the primary objective. I'd got swept up in this marriage fantasy. I wanted someone I could see myself growing old with. A person I'd always be happy to be around, even if we didn't have any money. Our love for each other would conquer all.

I thought back to my dates with Miles. When we were together, it was like we were in our own world. Our own bubble of happiness. He was reliable and honest and had integrity. All key qualities I'd wished for when setting my goals. We had so much in common. He made me smile. Made me feel like anything was possible. Like I was smart and beautiful. I felt special and *adored. Loved.* That's what I'd wanted when I'd started this challenge. And that's what I'd found with Miles. I'd just been too blinded by Luke to see it.

After dating Luke for seven of the nine weeks I'd been doing this challenge, it was now clear that we didn't have a future. And even though I hadn't heard from Miles and I didn't know what would happen with the two of us or whether he wanted to fully commit, I wasn't going to bench Luke and just keep him waiting in the wings like all those men used to do to me. I wasn't going to ghost him or send some lame text message either. Even though we weren't officially boyfriend and girlfriend, I was going to do the right thing. Meet him face-to-face and tell him the truth.

So that's what I'd arranged to do. To meet him tonight. To be honest, after work, I just wanted to sit at home with a glass of wine and snuggle up with Cuddles and a good film, but I'd been doing that for the past week and it hadn't been helping. Every film I watched just reminded me of Miles. I mean, finding a guy that liked to watch romcoms of his own volition was like gold dust in itself. What on earth was I thinking, letting him slip through my fingers?

At least meeting Luke tonight would get me out of the house, albeit to break bad news to him, which I was dreading. I was usually the one being dumped rather than ending things myself, so I wasn't sure exactly how I'd phrase it. I didn't want to be mean. Hopefully I'd be able to find the right words and handle it sensitively.

I stood by the riverside on the South Bank, admiring the view of Big Ben and the Houses of Parliament across the Thames as I waited for Luke to meet me. Late again. Perhaps we should have met inside a nearby bar, but I thought it was better to have the conversation out in the open. Finally I saw him strolling towards me like he had all the time in the world.

'Hello, Alexandra,' said Luke, leaning over to kiss me on the lips. I turned my face so his mouth met my cheek. He didn't even apologise for being ten minutes late and leaving me out in the cold. '*Long time*. Bet after not seeing me, you're chomping at the bit by now, aren't you? What is it now? Week number nine? I saw the longing in your eyes when I left your place last week without kissing you. Your resolve is weakening. Just say the word, and I'll be there…' His hand slid down my back and grazed my bum.

What the hell? Why was he acting like this? Was he drunk?

'Stop!' I said, pushing his hand away. 'We need to talk, Luke.'

'Are you sure it's only *talking* you'd like to do?' He winked.

'So much for being willing to wait!' I snapped. 'Look, Luke, I think we should stop seeing each other. Stop dating.'

'What?' His eyes popped out of his head. '*You* want to stop dating *me*? That's a joke!'

'I'm sorry?'

'*I'm* the one that should be chucking *you*!' he growled. 'All this *no-sex* nonsense. You're lucky I'm still here. Most men would have bailed weeks ago.'

My mind was racing. Why was he contradicting what he'd told me before?

'But you said you were looking for something long-term.' I frowned. 'That you saw us going all the way. That you wanted it *all*. Marriage and kids. You wanted us to get married?'

'*Oh my dear, sweet Alexandra*,' he said, resting his hand on my shoulder and talking to me like I was a four-year-old, 'you've misunderstood my sentiments. My *intentions*. When I said I saw us going *all the way*, I meant having full sex. And, yes, I said I wanted it *all*, the marriage and kids thing, but I didn't necessarily mean *with you*. The calling you my wife was just an affectionate term. You know, like calling someone *sweetheart* or *darling*. Women seem to like it. Didn't you notice I stopped calling you my wife ages ago, when I realised you might be taking it too seriously?'

I could feel my face starting to burn and my heart beating faster. None of this was making sense.

'But you said you were direct,' I replied, my forehead now resembling a wrinkled pug's. 'That if you just wanted a fuck, you would have said. That you wouldn't have spoken about marriage on the first date if you weren't serious.'

Luke looked at me chuckled. 'I *did* say that, and I meant it. If you were just a fuck, like some of my students, for example, we wouldn't have even have gone out or had a conversation. Some women you sleep with straightaway. Some you keep for longer to make things more interesting. Every woman I agree to go on a date with *technically* has the potential to be the future Mrs Walton. It's then just a case of seeing who can hold my attention. And I admit, initially I was intrigued by this *holding out* game that you were playing. Made me want you more. But now I'm bored,' he huffed.

'Seriously?' I shouted, now unable to contain my anger. '*You* were the one that said you'd wait!'

'Did I, though?' He smirked. 'You're not a very good listener, are you, Alexandra? If you paid attention, you would have heard me say that I was *up for the challenge*. I've told you on numerous occasions that I like a challenge, haven't I? The challenge I was referring to was seeing if I could be the first to get you into bed. Break your stupid vow. *Get real!* I don't have time to wait *six months* to sleep with a woman! I have women throwing themselves at me every day. Students, colleagues, even some of the parents. I wouldn't give all of that up for six months. That's ludicrous! Even when I'm married I won't give that up. I told you I want to have it *all*. *Everything*. I'll still always come home to my wife, yes. Divorces are expensive, even with a pre-nup. But men are not designed to be with one woman, Alexandra. It's a *fact*. I'm attractive, and women desire me. I've been created this way for a reason. I'd be a fool not to make the most of what God has given me,' he said smugly, running his fingers through his hair. 'In fact, it would be *selfish* to deny a woman the opportunity to spend the night with me. Provided I liked her, of course. I try to be a little discerning at least. Then again, it depends on how good the totty supply is that week. Once they're on their backs with their legs spread and I'm inside them, they pretty much all feel the same. And there's always doggy-style if I can't bear to look at their faces.'

Oh my God.

I could not believe what I'd just heard. Luke was vile. He wasn't drunk. He was just an awful, awful man who was revealing his true colours. My blood was now boiling so much that I was convinced I would spontaneously combust at any moment.

'You are *unbelievable*! I don't think I've ever met such a despicable excuse for a man. You're *horrible*. A disgusting, arrogant human being. A *liar*!'

'Now, now.' He smirked. 'That's not very nice is it Alexandra? You're throwing a load of insults and then calling *me* horrible? Seems a bit hypocritical. But then again, you *are* a hypocrite. You happily date other guys and come to meet me with flowers that one of your himbos has sent you, then get upset when you find out I've been fucking other women.'

'You've what?' I folded my arms angrily.

'*Oops...*' He grinned. 'We didn't get to that part yet, did we? *My bad.* Did you *honestly* think that every time you left me with a pathetic goodnight kiss, I was going to just go and sit at home sipping cocoa by myself? Wake up, woman! There's *no way* I could last *seven days* without sex, never mind this seven weeks of nonsense we've been doing. I don't know why you're standing there looking so shocked. It's not like we ever agreed to be exclusive. Not that I could ever do that, but you know what I mean. You saw other guys, I saw other women. What's the big deal?'

Although I knew that technically we hadn't made a formal commitment to each other, so as Laurie had mentioned in the rules, Luke was likely to be seeing other people, I still felt cheated. He'd led me to believe that he thought I was special and wanted to get serious with me. He'd said he would wait. He'd deliberately chosen his words carefully to mislead me. Surely that wasn't right?

'I saw other guys, yes, but I didn't *sleep* with them.'

'Semantics,' he scoffed. 'What's the difference? *Honestly*, Alexandra, I don't understand the problem. Did I not treat you like a lady? Did I not take you out to the finest places in London? Pay for drinks, meals and taxis home? Did I not respect your wishes to take things slow? Remember, they were *your* wishes, not mine. I said I'd take things slowly *with you*. I didn't say I'd take them slowly with other women.' He shook his head in disbelief, as if *I* was the ridiculous one. 'Like I always said every time you rebuffed my advances: it was *your call*. I can only offer you a gold bar. If you're crazy enough not to accept it, then that's up to you. There are plenty of other women that will. Most put out within hours. I don't even have to buy them a drink first. Why would I refuse? Everyone knows that once you get married, you have less sex, so why cut back before I get tied down?'

'I can't listen to this! I'm too disgusted. Your attitude towards women, is just *disgraceful*.'

'Why?' He frowned. 'I've done nothing wrong. I don't force myself on these women. You of all people should know that. Is it my fault if they don't respect themselves enough to say no? If they drop their knickers minutes after we've met? If they believe in the fairy-tale of me being their perfect man? Why are you so surprised? *I told you.* I believe in being direct. *Women!*' he huffed. 'They say they want honesty, but then when you give it to them, they get upset!'

I really needed to leave. I shouldn't have still been standing there, subjecting myself to his shit. I was getting so worked up that I would either give myself a heart attack or punch him. It was best for both of us if I got away as quickly as possible.

'Goodbye, Luke!' I snapped, wrapping my scarf tighter around my neck and pulling my hat down over my ears. 'And *good riddance*!'

'Goodbye, Alexandra,' he said, staring at me coldly with his hands in his coat pocket. 'And good luck with your challenge. You're going to need it. No guy is going to wait that long without getting at least something on the side. If I were you, I'd give up now. Save yourself the torture. It's not natural, you know. Abstinence can cause all sorts of biological complications in the future. Look it up if you don't believe me. And when you see sense, and need a good fuck, drop me a line. Maybe I'll answer. If I'm not busy screwing someone else, of course. I have to admit. I'm a bit disappointed not to have conquered you. Especially after all those weeks of effort. The cooking you a slap-up meal, the deliberately not trying anything on with you at your house to drive you wild with desire. *Such a waste.* I *hate* to lose a challenge. Sullies my perfect record.

Never mind. Maybe another time. At least seeing you in the afternoon meant I got to fuck the girl from Saturday night again on Sunday morning, then go and see that other woman who's been hounding me on Tinder after I left your place, so all in all, it was still a productive day.' He grinned. 'Don't be a stranger, eh?'

And I'd thought he was being considerate when he'd suggested meeting in the afternoon to give me a lie-in and offered to come to my place to make it easier for me, when really it was because he knew he'd have a woman staying over. So much for leaving early to prepare for his lectures too. *What a bastard.*

'If you were the last man on earth and I hadn't had sex for six *years*, I wouldn't sleep with you.' I couldn't bear to listen to him a second longer.

'*Careful*…don't want to burn all your bridges,' he shouted as I turned on my heels and began to walk away. 'If you keep up with this stupid challenge, I might well be the only man on earth that will consider giving you and your frigid pussy the time of day.'

'Aaargghh!' I screamed, storming towards the station.

Tears started streaming down my cheeks.

How could I have been so stupid? How had I not seen what a total and utter bastard he was? I'd thought those early dates with Eddie and Callum were bad. But at least they'd laid their cards on the table from the beginning. Luke was a hundred—no, a *million* times worse. He was a wolf in sheep's clothing. The ultimate snake. I should have seen the signs. He was rude. He never said please or thank you to anyone, and he talked to the waiters like they were shit on his shoes. What a disgusting human being. How could I ever *think* I could marry someone like that?

And I must have known my spirit didn't take to him. I'd never suggested that he call me Alex. I asked *all* my friends to call me Alex. *Alexandra* is always reserved for strangers. People I didn't know. That I didn't feel comfortable with. I'd asked Miles to call me Alex very early on. I remembered. Because I knew he was one of the good guys.

The more I thought about it, the more I saw that Cuddles knew too. She was always a friendly cat. She never missed an opportunity to get lavished with extra attention from visitors. But as soon as Luke had attempted to come near her, she'd run a mile.

Stacey was right. Luke was bad news. And he'd spouted more shit tonight than an overflowing sewer. I didn't need toxic people like that in my life. I needed someone good, decent and positive. And I'd already found him. In Miles.

Too bad I'd realised that too late.

CHAPTER TWENTY-THREE

I should have waited.

Not been so impatient.

I just couldn't help myself. It felt like it had been an eternity since I'd seen or heard from Miles. Two weeks had now gone by without a word.

No phone calls, and the WhatsApp messages I'd sent were still on a single grey tick. Isn't that what happens when someone blocks you?

I was *desperate* to know when he'd be back. I missed Miles so much it hurt. I couldn't bear to think of never seeing him again. Never seeing that smile that always gave me butterflies. The fact that I had a man that I was now convinced was my Mr Right in front of me and let him go because I was so caught up in the empty words that dickhead had fed me made me feel sick to the stomach. Even now, a week and a half on from that showdown with Luke, I still couldn't believe that he could be so awful. So *manipulative*. He was pure evil. Just another fuckboy.

I was feeling pretty low. I'd already messed up by not

seizing the opportunity with Miles when I'd had it, and I didn't want to let him go without feeling like I'd tried everything. Left no stone unturned. I'd obviously phoned and sent messages, but I hadn't yet attempted to call his work.

Stacey had advised against it. Told me to wait a bit longer to see if he got in contact. But I'd already waited two weeks. I needed to know. So half an hour ago, I'd done it. I'd called and asked to speak to Dr Miller.

'I'm afraid Miles is still away with Gabby,' said the bubbly receptionist. 'I think they're staying for another two weeks. I'm not sure when they'll be back. Judging by the photos, they look like they're having a great trip!'

'Photos?' I'd said, my heart racing.

'Yes! On the AFTF, Aid for the Future Facebook page!' she gushed. 'There's a *lovely* photo of them both on there. Sorry, who did you say you were? Did you need to arrange an appointment for your child? Dr Holmes is covering Dr Miller's patients whilst he's away.'

'I…I'm…sorry I have to go,' I'd replied and ended the call. Thank goodness I had withheld my number.

Photos? Of Miles with Gabriella? On Facebook? Having a great time? I thought they were supposed to be working.

My heart started thumping and beads of sweat began to form on my forehead as I launched the app. I searched for *Aid for the Future*, scrolled through the feed, and sure enough, there was a photo of Miles next to *her*, grinning with a group of children in front of them.

He looked *beautiful*. *That smile.* My stomach flipped.

Then I felt my blood run cold.

They both looked happy. *Together*. Gabriella's skin

glowed and her long hair was all glossy. How was it so shiny in that heat and without access to a cabinet full of styling products?

It's over, isn't it? I bet they've fallen madly in love again and he's completely forgotten all about me.

I slumped myself down on the empty park bench opposite the big oak tree. A gust of biting wind hit my face. It was freezing out here, but I didn't care. I felt a wave of sadness rising through my body. Tears started rolling down my cheeks. I'd blown it. I'd finally met a decent man and I'd fucked up.

'Alex? Alex, what's wrong?' I looked up to see Stacey standing in front of me, clutching a sandwich.

'I've lost him, Stacey. He's back with Gabriella.'

'What?' She frowned as she sat down beside me.

'Look at them,' I said, thrusting my phone in front of her face and pointing at the photo, which was still up on my screen. 'Together.'

'Yeah?' She looked puzzled. 'It's a photo of them and the children. I don't get it. Did you hear from Miles? Did he call and tell you he doesn't want to see you anymore?'

'No. I still haven't heard from him,' I said, hanging my head.

'So who told you they're back together?'

'The receptionist at the hospital.'

'The receptionist at the hospital told you Miles and Gabby are an item?'

'Not exactly. She said they're having a great trip. That they're staying another two weeks, at least.'

'And…?' Stacey frowned. 'Oh my God, Alex! Don't tell me that you've taken her innocent comment and are jumping to conclusions that Miles still loves Gabby?'

'Well, is it so ridiculous?' I crossed my arms like a sulking teenager. 'It *could* happen! It's not impossible!'

'Not impossible, Alex, no, but no more possible than him *not* being in love with her! They broke up, remember? You don't even know how well they do or don't get on these days. In fact, you don't know anything about this trip, so it's really dangerous to jump to such big conclusions.'

'But he hasn't returned any of my calls or messages! He can post photos on Facebook, which requires an internet connection, so why can't he call or message?'

'If this was on *his* Facebook page rather than the organisation's, I might say that you had a valid point, but anyone could have taken this photo and posted it from another location. And he did say on his voice message that he didn't know when he'd be back or if his phone would be working.'

Stacey was trying to be logical. I knew what she said *technically* made sense, but I was hurting. And a broken heart didn't care about technicalities.

'That was probably just to cover his arse. There *must* be some form of technology. He must be able to find somewhere that his phone could work. I think he's Caspering me.'

'*Caspering*?' Her frown deepened.

'Yeah. I've been doing research in the evenings about men and dating. It's supposed to be the "nicer" way to ghost someone. You let them down gently before disappearing. So Miles leaving a message to say he didn't know when he'd be back was just his way of saying he didn't want to see me again.'

'Oh my God, Alex,' said Stacey, shaking her head.

'And then there's the *Slow Fade*. When a guy isn't interested in taking things further, but instead of saying so, just gradually cuts ties. He stops responding to texts and calls, and eventually all communication ends.'

'This is *exactly* why I said you shouldn't call the hospital and that you should continue dating! You're just sitting at home night after night by yourself, going on these websites and driving yourself crazy! The internet is a dangerous place when you're vulnerable. It's like when you have an ache or pain and you google it and end up on a site that basically tells you you're dying. I know the combination of missing Miles and the run-in with that giant arsehole Luke has made you feel really shitty, but you've *got* to carry on with your life. If you're not up for dating again, fair enough, but at least find something else to do. Whether you're in a relationship or not, whether Miles comes back to you or doesn't, it's really important to keep your own interests.'

I caught myself for a second. *Shit.* Listening to Stacey's reaction, saying everything out loud, listening to myself, hearing all those words tumble from my lips made me realise how far I'd fallen. I'd got sucked into a destructive cycle of self-hatred and paranoia. I'd been obsessing over Miles. Going over and over what I should have done and what I should have said, when the reality was that it had happened, and sitting at home night after night torturing myself was only going to make things worse. I had to find a way to climb out of this hole.

I took a deep breath.

'I know I've got to get a grip.' I sighed. 'The truth is, I'm just finding this really hard, Stacey. I've really fallen for Miles, and I really felt like he liked me too.'

'I'm sure he does. He's probably just so busy over there. It really could be as simple as that.'

'Maybe…'

'You've got some eyeliner on your cheek.' Stacey pulled a mirror and a fresh tissue from her bag. I stared at my reflection.

Look at me. Fake hair, fake eyelashes and all this make-up. Who was I really? I was hiding behind a mask. Convinced that I needed to look a certain way to get a man. It hadn't helped, though, had it? And as for this self-pity, this crying, it was embarrassing. I couldn't go on like this.

'Enough!' I shouted, slapping myself round the face.

'Ouch!' said Stacey, feeling the pain for me.

'Enough of this wallowing!' I jumped up off the bench. 'Enough sitting at home stuffing my face with chocolates, watching films and surfing the internet. It's time to sort my life out. Starting with getting back in shape. I've existed on a diet of pizza, crisps, Coke and other shit for the past two weeks. No more. I look like shit and I feel like shit. *Enough of this shit!* I'm going back to the gym tonight, and I'm going to have a good workout.'

'Excellent idea, Alex. It's been ages since you've been, and I know how much you used to enjoy your classes. A gym session will help you burn off calories and frustration too.'

'I'm over it. Ever since Luke's crude comments, I've barely thought about sex. He's put me off. But, yes, a workout is just the thing I need. Then I will go home, pop in and see Audrey, as I haven't seen her for a while, and then I'll start some job hunting. I don't like the sound of the changes they're planning to make to the company and how my role is going to be affected. I think maybe it's time for me to try something new. Have a fresh start.'

I exhaled and stood up straighter. I felt better already.

'That's the spirit! Give yourself a purpose and then trust in the universe. What will be will be,' said Stacey.

'Well, the universe hasn't been good to me so far. Not when it comes to men, anyway. But no matter. No more obsessing over guys. I'm going to start focusing on loving myself for a change.'

'Great idea! Don't completely give up hope on love or trusting the universe, though, Alex. Even if it hasn't worked for you before, there's always a first time. You've come this far.'

'I'll try my best, Stacey. I'm ten and a half weeks in, and even though there doesn't seem to be much point in carrying on with this challenge now that I have *zero* male prospects on the horizon, I'll stick with it anyway. Keep myself busy, keep an open mind, and yeah, whatever. I guess I'll continue to leave my fate in the hands of the universe. God only knows what it has in store for me next.'

CHAPTER TWENTY-FOUR

I put on my fluffy pink dressing gown and flopped onto the bed.

That was a great session and very productive for a Monday too. Apart from Saturday, I'd been to the gym almost every night these past two weeks, and it was working wonders. I felt and looked *so* much better.

I'd got myself into a good routine. I would go to the gym straight after leaving the office, work out for an hour, shower, come home, make a light salad for dinner and then chill with Cuddles in bed.

On Saturday, I took a day off from the gym, and after I'd finished the housework, I'd popped round to Audrey's for lunch and stayed for a few hours. Then I'd come home, put on a face mask, turned on some soft music, sat in the bath and just relaxed. Then yesterday, I'd made myself a lovely brunch—homemade pancakes with lots of fresh fruit—gone for a leisurely walk around Tooting Common, and returned home to chill on the sofa for a bit before heading off out to the gym again.

After that conversation with Stacey in the park, it was like a switch had gone off in my head. My mindset had changed. I needed to start taking better care of myself. Appreciate my worth more. The book had definitely helped me with that. Before I'd read it, I'd thought I wasn't even worthy of love. I didn't dare believe I could have a loving relationship. Now I knew that I was and I could. I *was* lovable. I *was* worthy. There was nothing wrong with me. I had lots to offer the right guy. I was kind and caring, and I deserved better than the likes of Luke.

I'd also made some changes to my appearance. Rather than always worrying about how I *thought* I needed to look to be considered attractive by men and everyone else, I began focusing on what made *me* feel happy and beautiful. Starting with my hair.

Last weekend, I'd made an appointment at the salon to get my extensions taken out. And this time I didn't get them put back in. Instead, I got my natural hair, which was now hovering just above my shoulders, cut into a cute pixie crop, and I'd never felt freer and more beautiful. It took next to no time to style in the morning and I'd received compliments from lots of people at work. But that wasn't the point. The important thing was that *I* absolutely loved it. It had been a real turning point for me, learning that I shouldn't rely on others for approval.

Affection from my parents, or a man or the world, was secondary. The onus was on me, not them or a book, to value myself. I had to love me first before I could expect someone else to.

I wished I'd been brave enough to stick with shorter hair when I'd cut it last time, instead of believing that I had to have long, glossy hair to get a man. If a guy was only going to be into me because I had extensions down to my arse, then frankly he wasn't worth having.

Ditto for make-up. When I thought about how much time I used to spend piling it on to go to the gym just in case I might meet someone, it made my skin crawl. My pores must have been more clogged than a blocked drain. No wonder I used to get breakouts. Well, no longer. I'd started to let my skin breathe more, and already it was looking much better. I'd started removing make-up before I worked out, I no longer wore fake lashes, and I was also trying to learn to be more comfortable in my own skin and not give two hoots what anyone else thought. It wouldn't happen overnight, but on Saturday morning I even opened the door to the postman without any slap on, and that was a big deal for me. Baby steps.

New hair called for a new wardrobe too. I'd finally managed to push Mum's toxic views about how men expected women to dress out of my mind. Why shouldn't I wear trousers if I wanted to? I'd gone out and bought three pairs along with some loose blouses, jogging bottoms for the gym (which unsurprisingly were a *lot* more comfy than those tight leggings I always wore), plus a pair of flats and some cool Chelsea boots. Not a stiletto heel in sight.

I'd cut back on watching the romcoms and now just treated myself to one or two a week. Instead, I had been using my time in bed snuggled up with Cuddles to research the next phase of my future.

I had decided that I couldn't waste any more of my life doing something I hated. I wanted a job that I loved. Something that would make me excited to get up in the mornings. Something that I could feel passionate about. That would really make a difference. Obviously, I still needed to pay the bills, but with it just being me, with no kids to support, as long as I could cover my mortgage, had money for food and general expenses, plus had some left over to pay for the gym and occasional treats, that was enough. Saving the hundreds of pounds I'd normally spend on extensions every couple of months would certainly help. And anyway, I'd reached the point where I would much rather earn a little less if it meant I'd be happier overall.

I still hadn't quite worked out what this dream job could be, but the fact was, I'd started the process. Scouring job sites each night was a start. If I kept reading various descriptions of different roles that were available, eventually I'd find something that caught my eye. I was sure of it.

I'd also become much better at resisting temptation. Over the weekend whilst I was watching a film, my phone had pinged. Of course, I'd got excited, hoping it was Miles. It wasn't. I couldn't believe the name that had popped up on my screen. No, not Luke. I'd deleted his number immediately that awful night. It was Connor. Bloody Connor. *Unbelievable*. That guy rose from the dead so much, he should have been given the lead role in a zombie film.

Three months ago, I would have been sucked in. Thought there was no harm in replying to his predictable 'Hey' message. I would have opened the dialogue, which would have resulted in him saying he missed me and asking if he could come over or inviting me over to his. And I would have resisted in my head but eventually given in, only to find myself in his bed and getting ghosted again a few days later.

I'll admit, I did consider it. For a second. I was lonely.

Still missing Miles. Wondering whether there was any point in continuing this challenge. But then, I'd said *no way*. No way was I going back to that again. All the worry, the disappointment, the fretting about messages, the wondering why he didn't like me enough to stick around.

No fucking way.

Been there. Done that. No going back.

So I sat down on my bed, clicked on Connor's contact info in WhatsApp and then blocked him.

Actually, I'd thought, why not just delete his number altogether like I'd done with Luke's?

So that's what I did. I said goodbye once and for all to Connor and I felt a million times better and stronger.

Although of course I still missed Miles like crazy, I'd made my peace with the situation. If he'd chosen Gabriella, then there was nothing I could do about it. Yes, she was beautiful, but whilst I was sure she was intelligent, from what I'd seen of her personality, she was far from beautiful on the inside. If Miles valued a pretty shell more than someone like me who might not come in perfect packaging but who had a kind heart and who loved him, then it was his loss.

Yes, that's right. I loved him. I realised that now. Which sadly meant it would take even longer to get over him. Although if I'd slept with him, it surely would have been much worse. The release of oxytocin could have bonded me to him for years. At least I had that to be thankful for, I guess. *Who am I kidding?* A lifetime probably wouldn't be long enough to get over him. Miles was special. The one that got away. It hurt like hell. I felt with every fibre of my being that he was the one for me. I was gutted, but what could I do? It was too late now. That ship had sailed. I couldn't waste any more of my life worrying about *what ifs*.

Maybe one day I'd have a happily-ever-after, and if I did, I'd be better for it because at least now I had learnt to love myself for the first time in my life. Until that day did or didn't come, I had to find a way to accept that it was just me and Cuddles now. As difficult as it was, I'd much rather be a single, sexually frustrated, stereotypical cat lady than waste my days and nights obsessing over someone who didn't want me, or go back to engaging in a series of empty, meaningless encounters, getting my head fucked over repeatedly.

I climbed under the covers. Cuddles was having a catnap beside me. She looked sooooo adorable. Life could be so much worse.

Time to start the job hunting again.

Just as I unlocked my iPad, the doorbell rang.

It was 9.45 p.m. No one called round this late. Not even Audrey. If that was bloody Connor trying his luck after I'd ignored his message and deleted his number, I'd be so mad.

As I slid out of bed, Cuddles stirred. I skulked into the hallway to the front door, looked in the peephole and nearly fainted.

It can't be.

Oh my God!

I unlocked the door and flung it open in what felt like a millisecond.

'Miles!' I screamed, throwing my arms around him.

'Alex!' he said, squeezing me tightly.

We stood there for what must have been at least five minutes, just holding each other. I couldn't believe he was there. Here. In London. At my front door. I was *so* happy.

As the crisp night air struck my skin, reality began to hit me, and a wave of questions flooded my brain.

'You're shivering,' said Miles. 'Maybe we should go inside. If that's okay with you, Alex?'

'Sure, come in, Miles,' I said, stepping back into the hallway and closing the door behind him.

'You've got no idea how happy I am to see you, Alex.' He beamed. 'And to see that you're happy to see me too.'

There weren't enough positive adjectives in the dictionary to express how I felt right now. My heart was singing. It felt like there were a million butterflies dancing in my stomach, and looking at him dressed in his signature white shirt, navy jumper and tanned trousers combo made my knees weak. He was even more gorgeous than I remembered. The sun had given his skin an incredible glow. His brown eyes sparkled. When I'd held him, his chest had felt so firm, so warm and welcoming. His scent. How I'd missed it. He smelt like heaven. Oh, and his lips. Those juicy lips. Looking at them, I couldn't help but reminisce about that night in the cinema and our passionate kisses. My mouth craved his. My whole body was crying out for him. Right now I just wanted him to hold me and never let go, but I had to try and push my emotions to one side. There was so much I still needed to know.

'What happened, Miles? You've been gone for so long. You didn't call. You didn't reply to any of my messages. I thought you'd forgotten about me.'

'Forget about *you*? Impossible! Alex, I love you,' he

said, pulling me into him. 'I could never, ever forget about you. *Never*.'

'You, you love me?' I said as my body began to melt.

'Alex.' He looked me straight in the eyes. 'I've loved you from the first night we met. But I was scared. I wanted to tell you, but I couldn't. You would have thought I was crazy. Who falls in love with someone on the first date? All that love at first sight stuff just happens in the films, right? You would have thought that I wasn't genuine. That I'd found out that you love romcoms and was just trying to score brownie points. Sell you a fake happily-ever-after. But I really felt it. I just *knew* that you were the one. I wanted to tell you. So many times. But then you told me you were dating other guys, and I thought you couldn't feel the same way about me if you wanted to keep seeing them.' His face fell.

'I couldn't even *consider* seeing another woman, knowing the way that I felt. So that's why I asked you about dating me exclusively. To see if you'd give me a chance. To prove that I was the man for you. I wanted to talk to you about it again, but things didn't work out at the party. After that, my head wasn't in the right place with my patient dying, you were away for the exhibition, and then of course I got the call for the trip. I decided I *had* to tell you before I left. I called you on the Sunday and so many times that Monday morning. I *had* to let you know how I felt. I didn't want to do it on a voicemail, but I couldn't reach you, so I had no choice. But just as I was about to tell you that I loved you, we had to board the flight and I didn't get the chance.'

'You...you love me?' The butterflies were now

dancing so hard I literally felt like my stomach would burst with joy.

'Yes! *So much*. This past month has been *torture*. Absolute hell. Not being able to see you. To talk to you. Not knowing if you'd got serious with another guy and forgotten about me.'

'*No way!*' I said, squeezing him tightly, burying my head in his neck, then gazing up to stare at his face again. 'I couldn't get you out of my mind, Miles. I called, I messaged...I've missed you so much. When you asked about going exclusive, I wasn't sure what to do. I was confused. I was looking for something serious. Someone to commit to me, and I wasn't sure that was what you wanted. I thought maybe you just wanted to date me, maybe as a long-term girlfriend, but not get into anything serious like marriage.'

'But I did! I *do*! That's why I told you I wanted us to be exclusive. I wanted us to take things to the next stage.'

Flashbacks of Luke and the ways he'd chosen his words carefully to imply he meant something serious but actually didn't flooded my mind.

'You mean the *next stage*, as in to have sex?'

'No! No! Not at all, Alex! I mean, yes, I'd *love* to have sex with you, but it's not like that. I'd like to experience *everything* with you right there beside me. For there to be no ceilings. No limits. Marriage, children, the whole thing. For us to spend the rest of our lives together. That's all I've wanted from the beginning. I told you that on our second date. When we were walking through the park on the way to the zoo. When I was telling you about my childhood. But I thought maybe you found the idea too scary, that I was getting too serious too soon. So I thought I better not push it. I thought that if you agreed to being exclusive, if you felt strongly enough about me, that we could talk about it more then. But I couldn't leave it to chance any longer. I couldn't stop thinking about you whilst I was away. And then they begged us to extend our trip. It was torture. Don't get me wrong, I'm proud of the work we did over there. But I missed you terribly.'

I pulled back slowly from Miles' embrace. He seemed genuine. I wanted to believe what he said. But after Luke, I was wary. Luke had also said he wanted marriage, and I'd believed him. I remembered him laughing at me the last time we saw each other. 'Oh, dear, sweet Alexandra, you've misunderstood my sentiments. My intentions,' he'd said in his condescending voice. I'd got so sucked in and heard what I'd wanted to hear. Who was to say that Miles wasn't doing the same? That he wasn't just telling me he loved me and wanted to marry me because he was trying to take advantage of me? My gut said Miles was nothing like Luke, but I had to be sure. I had to be careful. I couldn't be made a fool of again.

'If you missed me so much, Miles'—I crossed my arms—'why didn't you call? I know that by the sounds of things you were somewhere remote, but surely there must have been *somewhere* you could have used your phone to reach me. Even a letter could have got here in a month, surely?'

'You're right. You're absolutely right, Alex. That all would have been feasible if I hadn't lost my phone at the airport. Or got it stolen. I don't know what happened. I had it with me when I got off the plane, but everything was so chaotic when we arrived because it was so last-minute. I remember putting my phone down to fill out some paperwork, I got my suitcase, and then that was the last I saw of it. That was the only place I had your number. If I had your address, then *of course* I would have sent you a letter. But the only time I've been here was when I walked you home that night, and I didn't write down the road or the house number. At the time, I had no need to. And for the life of me, I couldn't remember the name of the company you worked at.'

'But you sent me flowers at work that time,' I said.

'Yes, I know, but everything was on my phone. The name of your company, the address and the florist. Without my phone I had nothing. If I'd been able to remember any of that, then on the couple of occasions that we went to the main town, I could have tried to find a phone box or some-thing to track you down. But we literally didn't stop from the moment we landed. And it really was remote where we were based. Honestly.'

'So how did you post on Facebook, then?'

'On Facebook?' His face crumpled. 'I didn't go on Facebook. How could I? There was no internet.'

'There was a photo of you and that Gabriella on Face-book. On the Aid for the Future page.'

'Oh! Maybe that was Joe, the fundraising manager. He had to fly back before us. He'd brought a camera with him, so maybe he uploaded that when he got back? I've got no idea. Please believe me, Alex. I've wanted nothing more than to see you. I got home a few hours ago. Took a shower and have been thinking all evening what to do for the best. I was going to wait until tomorrow, when I'd had time to speak to the mobile phone company to order a new phone or retrieve my messages to see if you'd been in contact, whether you'd reached a decision about dating me exclusively, but I couldn't hold out any longer. I had to know. And without my phone, I had no way of reaching you, other than trying to remember where you lived. Please apologise to your neighbour for me. I thought it was her door we stopped at that night, so I rang her bell by mistake. I'm surprised I even got the right road, to be honest! But here I am. Here to tell you that I love you, Alex, and that I want to be with you. I'd like you to be my girlfriend and then, in the very near future, my wife. And I had to tell you that. Even if you didn't feel the same, I just needed you to know…'

Before he could finish his sentence, I leapt forward, threw my arms around him and planted my lips firmly on his. As our mouths met, I felt like a thousand fireworks had been set off all at once inside my heart. My head and whole body felt light. If Miles hadn't pulled me into him so tightly, I was sure I could have just floated away.

'Alex, I love you so, so, so much,' he said, taking one of his arms from my waist to remove his glasses so that he could look at me more closely, then holding me tight once more. 'I never want to be without you again.'

'I love you too, Miles,' I said, staring into his eyes and running my fingers through his hair. 'That's what I was calling to tell you. I called you weeks ago to let you know that I wanted to be exclusive with you and that I was going to stop dating other guys. Your phone was switched off, and so I sent messages. Multiple messages, but I didn't hear from you and I was devastated. I even called the hospital, and the lady at reception gave the impression that you and Gabriella were an item, so I just thought I was too late.'

'No, no, no!' His eyes widened. 'It's *you*, Alex. It's

only ever been you. It will only ever *be* you. I've got no interest in Gabby whatsoever. That was over before I met you.'

'But you weren't tempted? She told me at the party that she was determined to get you back. That you were besotted with her.'

'I was. A long time ago. Before I saw the light. Breaking up with her was the best thing I could have done. She wasn't right for me. We're completely different people. Outside of our passion for helping children, we have nothing in common. She can be really superficial, insecure and high-maintenance.' Gabriella was insecure? I thought that someone like her would be super confident. I guessed everyone, no matter what they looked like, had their hang-ups. 'Did she make advances at me whilst we were away? Yes. But I rebuffed them straightaway and told her I was in love with someone else, which made things really awkward for a while, until she realised that I wasn't going to change my mind and got over it. Our relationship is and will only ever be purely professional. Nothing more. I believe in monogamy, in fidelity, in marriage, in family. Commitment to one person. And I want to be committed. Completely and utterly to *you* and only you, Alex. *Forever.*'

We kissed again and I felt it. He meant it. This was all I'd ever wanted to hear from a man. But more than just the words, this time, I knew—through his actions, through the way he'd behaved towards me since we'd met, through his consistency, through the feeling in my gut—that this time it was real. Miles was the one.

And then I remembered. The vow. The challenge.

Miles didn't know about it.

He said he loves me, but how was he going to react when he heard that there was no sex on offer? Every guy I'd mentioned this to had laughed in my face. Thought it was a joke. That *I* was a joke. A weirdo with unrealistic expectations. What if Luke was right? What if I'd gone through all this—missing Miles, him coming back to me, him saying he loves me—only to find that he also thought it was ludicrous and wasn't prepared to wait?

Shit, shit, *shit*!

I pulled away.

'Alex? What's wrong?' said Miles.

'You said you love me, right?'

'That's right…'

'Well…I'm really happy to hear you say that, Miles.' I bowed my head, terrified to look him in the eye. 'Because, you see, the thing is, my situation, my personal life is a little bit, um, complicated at the moment…and when you hear about it, you might change your mind.'

'Why?' he said as his shoulders grew tense. 'What is it? I thought you said you weren't dating anyone else anymore.'

'That's right, I'm not.'

'So what's the problem?' he said.

'Well, it's just that, I'm, um, kind of halfway through a challenge, and now I've started it, I'm determined to finish.'

'What sort of a challenge?' Miles frowned.

'A challenge which means that I can't, I can't, I've chosen not to have sex for six months. It's been just over twelve weeks, so I have another three months left to go.'

'Right…'

'*See!*' I crossed my arms. 'Told you that you wouldn't be interested.'

'Who said I wasn't? Tell me more about it, Alex. I'd like to know.'

'Oh…okay.' I relaxed a little. 'Well, in a nutshell, I was tired of men sleeping with me and then running off, so now I don't want to have uncommitted sex. I won't sleep with a guy until I get a commitment.'

'Fair enough.' He shrugged his shoulders.

'What? You don't think I'm weird?'

'Weird? No. Of course not, Alex! I actually think it makes a lot of sense.'

'You do?' My eyes widened.

'Yeah. Remember, I'm a guy. I have friends. Both male and female. Most men, and I stress that I *exclude* myself from this section of my gender, will take sex if it's offered to them, and then they'll move on. Then I've got some female friends who think that sleeping with a man will make them stay, but it won't. There needs to be more than that. Yes, sex is an important part of a relationship, but it can't just be physical. A lot of my relationship with Gabby was based around that, and in the end that wasn't enough for me. I actually respect a woman *more* if she wants to wait. I think what you're doing, Alex, is admirable, not weird. It makes you *special*. It will make *everything* more special. Because of the sacrifice that's led up to that moment. It's actually a good idea.'

'Really?' I said, resisting the temptation to start jumping up and down on the spot.

'Yes! Really, Alex.'

'So, you'll wait? You'll wait to have sex with me? You don't mind? You won't sleep with other women either?'

Please say yes. Please say yes. Please, please, please.

'Yes, Alex. I'll wait. Absolutely. And, no, I won't sleep with other women. You're more than worth it. I mean, don't get me wrong, I'm only human. You're *gorgeous*, especially with your stunning new haircut. It really suits you, by the way. Brings out your beautiful eyes,' he said, running his fingers through my crop and flashing the smile I'd missed so much.

Oh God! I'd just realised. I was standing here in front of Miles without a scrap of make-up and with my new haircut. Last time he'd seen me, I'd had long, flowing hair and a full face of make-up, and now I was barefaced with hair that wasn't much longer than his. Ordinarily I would have been mortified for him to see me like this, but I felt fine. Great, in fact.

'Thank you!' I replied.

'You look incredibly sexy, Alex...mmm. I'd *love* to remove that delightful bright pink fluffy dressing gown of yours and those matching slippers and ravish you right now, here on your hallway floor, but I can wait.'

'Hey!' I said, putting my hands on my hips and laughing. 'It may not be the most attractive item of clothing I own, but I happen to love my comfy dressing gown. Nothing wrong with my slippers either!'

'Of course there isn't!' he chuckled. 'They're adorable. *You're* adorable. That's why I love you. That's why I'm happy to wait. If a life with you is the reward, then it's *more* than worth it. I've waited a lifetime for you, Alex, so what's a few more months?'

And right there in that moment, as we wrapped our arms around each other and Cuddles ran into the hallway and snuggled up right beside Miles' feet, I knew for sure that I'd found him. A man who cherished me. Who loved me so much, he was willing to wait. Who said that he wanted to spend the rest of his life with me and actually meant it.

Finally.

I'd taken a chance, not given up hope, trusted the universe and it had delivered.

It had sent me my Mr Right. The love of my life.

MARCH

CHAPTER TWENTY-FIVE

'So is tonight the night, then?' said Stacey as we walked out of the office doors.

'It is indeed.' I buttoned up my coat. 'I'm *so* nervous!'

'Relax, Alex, you'll be fine.'

'How do you know? It's been soooo long! I doubt I'll even remember what to do!'

'Oh, you will, don't worry.' She placed her hand reassuringly on my shoulder. 'I felt the same when I was about to sleep with Bobby for the first time. In the end it was amazing, and I'm sure it will be the same for you and Miles too.'

'I really, really hope so. I'm amazed that we've even managed to hold out for this long, so now that we have, I can't help but feel a certain pressure for it to be perfect. There's so much riding on it. It's tonight that we find out whether the wait has been worthwhile. Whether we click in *all* areas of our relationship. I'm terrified that my cousin Roxy will be right. That we won't have that connection.

That we'll finally sleep together and it will be this huge let-down. A massive disappointment.'

'Think positive, Alex,' she said as we stopped at the lights and waited to cross the road to the station. 'In fact, speaking from experience, it's probably best that you *don't* think too much about it at all. The more you do, the more you'll worry about what it will be like, the more pressure you'll put on yourself and the more likely that will cause the disappointment you want to avoid. Just try and treat it like a normal date, and if the sex happens, it happens. Don't expect too much. Just go with the flow and it will all work out.'

'Yeah, you're right. That's why we didn't want to create a big fanfare by going away for the weekend, or making it a big event. I mean, don't get me wrong, it *is* a big deal. It's *huge*, but we thought doing anything too grand could build it up too much.'

'I agree. Keep it low-key. You've done really well, Alex. Without sounding patronising, I'm incredibly proud of you.' She smiled. 'I *knew* you could do it! Every time I've seen the two of you together, you can tell that Miles absolutely adores you. He's a great guy. I'm so pleased you took the challenge and met someone amazing.'

'Thank you!' I blushed. I was proud of myself for being able to hold out this long too. I also remembered when Stacey had first told me about the challenge and how she'd gushed about Bobby, and now I was feeling exactly the same way about Miles. He was incredible, and I felt like shouting it from the rooftops. Telling everyone how happy and in love I was. I still couldn't quite believe it. 'There were days and particularly nights that I didn't think I could do it. But here I am, and I tell you what, Stacey, I am *so* ready. Poor Miles is not going to know what's hit him.'

'I bet he feels the same.'

'Probably. He'd better! And I hope he's been drinking lots of coffee today, because I plan to keep him up all night.'

'*Go, girl*! Well, good luck,' she said as we entered the station. 'And I look forward to a full report on Monday. That's if you've left his bedroom by then, of course. Who knows if you'll even be able to make it into the office? You might be hospitalised with severe exhaustion!'

'So true!' I took my Oyster card from my bag. 'I'd gladly take a day off to recover from a hot and heavy weekend with Miles. Talking of which, better run! Got to go home and get myself and my body ready for the big night!'

I gave Stacey a hug and then went through the ticket barriers. As I walked down the escalators, I had a massive spring in my step. I really was beyond excited about tonight. I'd never thought this day would come. That a guy would wait for me. In fact, I even remembered joking that there was more chance of finding a unicorn and an alien chilling on my sofa. *Ha! That showed me.* Clearly great things can happen when you have a little faith. Think I also said that if a man held out, I'd get a gold sculpture of his privates made in his honour. Maybe I'd get on the case with that on Monday…

Miles and I had been inseparable these past three months. After his time away in Africa and not seeing him for those four long weeks, we'd had so much time to make up for.

Initially, we'd seen each other almost every night after

work and all weekend. But the more we were together face-to-face, the harder it was to stop the passionate kisses from going further. Especially if he'd come round to my place to watch a film. Every time our bodies were less than a few inches apart, we wanted to rip each other's clothes off. Miles was usually much stronger than me. If my hands started heading too far south, he'd jump up off the sofa, kiss me quickly on the forehead and say, 'And that's my cue to leave. I'll call you later, Alex.'

I questioned so many times why I was still going through with this. My goal at the beginning was clear. No uncommitted sex. I wouldn't sleep with a man until he said he loved me and meant it. Miles had said those three big words when he'd returned from Africa twelve weeks ago, so technically, I could have slept with him then, right? But when we'd discussed it, Miles had said that I'd made a commitment to myself and set a goal, so it was important to see it through. He'd read the book too (he'd asked if he could, to give himself a better understanding of women's experiences and the recommended 'rules'), and neither of us were sure if we were supposed to be abstaining for six months from the point that we officially became a couple or from the time I'd started the challenge in September.

Although it was probably from when we'd started dating, I said that I'd count it from the date I'd taken the vow, partly because there was no way I could go without for nine months—he was too tempting. We'd decided that if we could hold on until March, which would mark six whole months of abstinence for me, it would be fair to declare the challenge had been successfully completed.

Miles was a hundred percent behind me. As well as being a huge achievement, he said it would be character building. That it represented the old-fashioned values that his adoptive grandparents had built their marriage on. They'd just celebrated their sixtieth wedding anniversary, so they were great role models.

And so we'd decided to wait. It hadn't been easy. We'd had to muster up the willpower of a hundred devout nuns and priests. But by creating a routine and a series of rituals, we'd managed to do it.

For example, rather than seeing each other face-to-face every day, we'd switched to three times a week. The other four days, we would Facetime, usually after I got back from the gym. With video calls, there was zero chance of things getting out of control, although sometimes we did find other ways to keep each other entertained...

During our conversations, we'd chat about everything from light-hearted things like the top ten best actresses of all time to serious stuff like brainstorming potential options for my new career direction. Miles had suggested I do something with animals, as I loved them so much. As well as firing off CVs to recruitment agencies, I'd spent a long time writing personalised speculative letters and emails to zoos and animal centres on the off chance they had any vacancies, and I was really excited as next week I had an interview for a fundraising manager role at Battersea Dogs & Cats Home, which sounded ideal for me. I'd finally get to use my sales experience and skills to do something worthwhile. Fingers, toes and everything crossed that I got the job.

When Miles and I did see each other, which was typically two days in the week and one day at the weekend, at least two of the dates had to be external and in busy, bright, public places. So no more backseat snogging at the cinema, because at this stage, we wouldn't be able to hold back from going all the way. The theatre was fine, though, as long as we were close to the stage and in full view of most of the audience. We knew we'd be too embarrassed for any big displays of affection there.

At the weekend, we often did a day trip somewhere in the UK. We'd been for walks along Brighton Beach, to Bath, Cambridge, York, Manchester, Edinburgh...those trips alone took up almost two months' worth of Saturdays and Sundays.

In between that, at Christmas I went to meet his parents, Ron and Mary (and their adorable Labrador, Bouncer) in Kent, who were lovely. They were so warm and welcoming. I could understand why Miles loved them so much and why he was such a gentleman, as they were great, genuine, humble people.

I'd stayed over for two nights, but only in the spare room. As much as we would have loved to have been together, Miles had far too much respect for them to sneak into my bed. And after holding out for so long, I was sure if we'd given in to temptation, we wouldn't be able to indulge ourselves quietly. We'd wake up everyone in the village. I had a wonderful few days staying there. I felt at home. Like part of the family.

After seeing his parents, we'd returned to London for New Year's Eve and huddled together in the cold along the Thames as we watched the fireworks display.

Because we had a plan in place and shared so many interests, it actually wasn't that hard to find things to do to pass the time. And the more activities we did together, the closer we became as a couple and the less time we spent thinking about sex. Don't get me wrong. We still both thought about it. But if you're engrossed in watching a play, are busy in a cocktail making class or out at a party with his friends, there's less opportunity for your brain to think about getting naked. If we went round to each other's houses all the time and didn't have anything to do or talk about, then it would have been much easier to just fall into bed. That was the problem with all the guys I'd been with before. The only thing we'd shared was saliva and sweat. And as I'd discovered, that was definitely not the basis for a long-lasting relationship.

Gabriella was a distant memory. After they'd returned from Africa, she'd hung around for a few weeks and then decided to go and work abroad again. Even if she'd stayed, I can honestly say it wouldn't have bothered me. I trusted Miles and knew that he loved me. We had a bond that nobody could break. I was sure of it.

Yes, as challenging as this experience had been, now that the finishing line was in sight, I could say that I was definitely glad I had done it. The experience wasn't over yet, though. The main event was yet to happen. In approximately two hours, I would know if my gut feeling was right. If Miles and I connected physically as well as emotionally and mentally.

Like I'd said to Stacey earlier, I was absolutely shitting myself. Nervous and excited in equal measures. Miles, on the other hand, had seemed really cool and relaxed about the whole thing.

We'd agreed to go to the clinic a few weeks ago to get our sexual health checked out, and thankfully, we both got the all clear last Monday.

Miles had also sent me a copy of his diary so I'd know what time he'd be home each night, then gave me a key to his house and told me to just drop by whenever I felt ready to *come over*. 'No pressure,' he'd said. 'Doing it off the cuff will be better, rather than plotting and planning a specific date and time.'

I'd decided that this evening, Friday night, would be best. Miles generally didn't work weekends, so we could both have two whole days off to look forward to. No need to worry about getting up early. Hopefully that would help us to be more relaxed.

Before I'd left for work this morning, I'd taken out a sexy new black lingerie set I'd bought last month in antici-pation of tonight and laid it out on the bed, ready to slip into when I got home. I was also going to wear my favourite fitted V-neck navy dress. I'd worn it to a work gathering Miles had invited me to before Christmas, and he was also a fan, saying I looked 'smoking hot' in it. Although I now rarely wore heels when we went out, usually opting for Converse or flats unless I felt like dressing up, tonight I wanted to wear some black patent stilettos. The occasion definitely called for it.

I'd packed a bag to bring with me, including a change of clothes (although I hoped I'd be spending most of the weekend naked…), more lingerie, toiletries, some wine I'd bought at lunchtime and a bottle of massage oil Audrey had dropped off to me this morning, saying it might come in handy for my *special night*. So sweet of her. She was fully up to date with my challenge and said she was proud of me. Even Karen had messaged earlier in the week, wishing me good luck. Everyone was rooting for me. Funny, really. It was like I was graduating or about to take my driving test rather than about to have sex. It was a landmark, though. Although it might have sounded strange to some people, this was a big deal for me.

Just over an hour and a half later, I had been home, showered, dressed and was climbing into the Uber I'd booked to take me to Miles' place in Balham so I could arrive feeling relaxed.

This was it. It was finally happening.

I unzipped my handbag to check I had the key to Miles' house. Yep. All good.

God. I was *so* nervous. I could feel the butterflies building in my stomach.

My phone pinged. *Oh no.* What if that was him saying his schedule changed or he had to work late?

No. He would have let me know earlier. Miles was always reliable.

I pulled it out of my bag. It was Roxy. I opened the message.

Roxy

Happy bonkday!

Make sure you don't leave his house until you've fucked his brains out! Good luck, darling! xxx

Classic Roxy. I quickly typed out a reply.

Me

Thank you!

Well, that's the plan! I'll let you know how it goes…

Roxy replied immediately sending a row of banana, baguette and hot dog emojis and a winking face. *Honestly!*

Speaking of food (which of course was definitely not what Roxy was referring to), should I order some? A take-away, maybe? Would he be hungry? I hadn't eaten much. The last thing I wanted when I was getting naked in front of him for the first time was to be all bloated. Not that Miles would care. I knew he'd love me however I looked. But *I* wanted to feel comfortable. To feel *sexy*. I'd also been paranoid about eating something, getting food poisoning and then spending our first night together on the toilet. That wouldn't be romantic at all. So I'd just opted for a chicken salad using the leftovers from a roast I'd cooked last night. I felt okay, though. The protein should give me enough energy. I'd bought some nuts and snacks with me too, just in case I got peckish.

Not long to go now. Miles' road was just a few streets away.

Shit, shit, shit.

I can't believe this is it.

I thought about everything that had happened over the last six months. The ghosting with idiots like Connor. All the bad dates with those guys. Eddie and Carl, was it? No, *Callum*. Plus the others whose names I couldn't recall. It wasn't important now. That awful excuse for a man, Luke. I'd fallen for his charms hook, line and sinker. But I'd learnt from it. Then there was the gut-wrenching turmoil of not knowing whether or not I still had a chance with Miles, once I'd realised that he was the one. Seemed so obvious now, but at the time, I'd felt so confused. And then of course our reconciliation, when he'd returned to London. We still talk about that now. And then there'd been the last three months, which in contrast to all the years of uncertainty, stress and heartache, had just been so joyful. Sometimes physically frustrating, yes, but blissful at the same time. *Calm*.

I never needed to worry about whether Miles would call or message or turn up. I didn't have to think about what to do or say in front of him. He got me. Accepted me. Loved me for who I was. And there really was no greater feeling than that.

I'd arrived.

I stepped out of the cab, reached into my bag for the keys and opened the door.

I could hear soft music coming from his large living room. I switched on the hallway light.

Oh my goodness!

As I glanced down, I saw that pink rose petals had been scattered along the wooden flooring.

I smiled. How had he known I was coming this evening? I followed them like breadcrumbs as they led me to the bedroom.

I stepped inside, where red and pink petals had also been spread across the crisp white sheets on his king-size bed. Sweet citrus-smelling candles had been lit around the room, and a bottle of champagne sat in an ice bucket on the stylish oak bedside table with two champagne flutes and a large pink heart-shaped box of chocolates.

Wow.

I *loved* it.

Although we'd said we didn't want to make a big fanfare, he'd still tried to make it special. Done all of this. *For me*.

'Good evening, my darling Alex,' said Miles as he

walked up behind me and wrapped his arms around my waist.

'Mmmm,' I said, turning to face him and breathing in his beautiful scent. 'Good evening, my darling Miles. This…the rose petals…*everything*, is incredible. How did you know I'd come tonight?'

'I didn't! I've been sprinkling these petals everywhere, lighting candles and putting the champagne on ice for the past five days!'

'You sweetheart. Well, it all looks amazing!'

'Not as amazing and as stunning as you, Alex. That dress. Mmm. So hot.'

'Thank you,' I said, running my fingers through his hair. 'You're looking pretty damn hot yourself. In fact, so hot, I think I better get you out of all of those clothes.'

'Mmm,' he said, kissing me on the lips. 'I like the sound of that. I'd like that very, very much.'

As we kissed, my hands slid under his jumper, pulling it upwards, our mouths parting for a microsecond as I pulled it up over his head. One layer down… one layer closer to finally discovering what lay beneath.

I undid the buttons of his shirt, slowly. Like I suspected, it was immaculately pressed. As he slid his arms out of his sleeves and his bare chest was exposed, I felt my knees buckle.

Goddamn.

What a magnificent chest.

All this time he'd been hiding this away. *All this time*. My eyes bulged as I surveyed it, inch by inch. His chest was broad, solid and smooth. He had an outline of a six-pack. I knew he liked to keep fit and healthy, but I was *not* expecting a body like this. And his *arms*. As I'd suspected every time I'd held on to them, they were firm and muscular. I couldn't *wait* to feel him on top of me. Our skin and our bodies against one another.

I unbuckled his belt. His kisses grew firmer and more passionate. Miles unzipped my dress and it fell to the floor, revealing my black lingerie.

'Holy shit. Alex…you are a *goddess*! You are so *beautiful*.'

Fuck this slow unbuttoning. I wanted him. I needed him. *Now*. I pulled down his trousers, and then his black boxer shorts.

Jesus Christ.

'Now it's my turn to say holy shit, Miles. *How…? Where?* How did you get *that* to fit in your pants?'

'I managed…it wasn't easy, though, as he was and still is very, very, *very* excited to see you, Alex. He's been in hiding for a *long* time.'

'Well, I hope *he* is now ready to be released into the wild…'

'Oh, he *is*, Alex.' He smirked. 'He is *more* than ready.'

Miles tossed his pants and trousers to the side, scooped me up in his arms and carried me over to the bed.

I lay down and he climbed on top of me.

'*My God, Alex*,' said Miles, burying his head in my chest before unbuttoning my bra and taking my nipple in his mouth. 'You're *so* beautiful, I can't decide where I want to start. I want to do *so* much with you. I want to lick and suck every inch of you. I want to be inside you. I want *all* of you.'

'Me too,' I whispered as I moved my hand up and down him, 'and we've got all night and all weekend to do that. But I beg you, I *implore* you, *please*. I *need* you inside me. Normally, I love the build-up, the touching, the anticipation, but we've had *months* of foreplay and so I just need you to make love to me. *Right now*.'

'Your wish is my command.'

Miles entered me without hesitation.

'*Oh...*' I moaned as I felt the first thrust. The initial sensation and feeling of discomfort caught me by surprise. Understandable, though. It had been a while. Only natural that my body needed time to adjust.

We rocked backwards and forwards and quickly found our rhythm. As the blood pumped furiously through my veins, I began to really get into it. To *love* it.

Our bodies moved perfectly in sync. Any concerns I'd had earlier about our compatibility instantly washed away.

Every time his skin brushed against mine, I felt sparks of electricity flying. He leant forward, started sucking on my breasts, then teasing my nipples in and out of his mouth. His heart was beating faster and faster as he grinded into me.

I grabbed onto his firm arse and pushed him further and further inside. I groaned with pleasure. I wanted him to go deeper. For this to go on all night.

'Alex...oh, Alex...you feel fucking *amazing*.'

'So do you, Miles, so do you.'

I lifted my legs into the air, then wrapped them around his neck as he thrust harder and harder. Next, he rolled me on to my side as he slid in and out of me, making my body tremble with every stroke.

After six months of abstinence, six long months of longing to be touched, the sudden flood of emotions and sensations became too much.

'Miles, I think I'm...I'm about to come...'

'Join the club,' he panted, 'I've wanted to come since I saw you in your underwear. Hold on a few more seconds, baby. Let's try and come together. Roll onto your front and get up on your knees, please,' he commanded. 'I'm gonna pull out really quickly, so I can enter from behind. I want to get a good view of that magnificent arse of yours.'

I rolled over and gasped as he entered me. Miles didn't hold back. His hands grabbed my breasts, and we rocked back and forth, faster and faster, his thrusts growing stronger with every movement. Harder and harder, and harder...

As I felt him explode inside of me, my heart raced and my body shook uncontrollably until it happened. Like a crescendo, the sensations built and built and built until I couldn't hold on any longer and I collapsed on the bed.

Miles rested on my back. Our bodies both dripping with sweat from our long-awaited workout.

We lay there, our chests heaving, both trying to catch our breath. Trying to muster up the energy, the strength to speak. But right at that moment, no words were necessary. Our bodies had done all of the talking.

That was not like normal first-time sex. That was so much more. It was as if we'd been sleeping together for months. *Years.* I had never, ever felt so connected physically to someone before. *Ever.*

I couldn't even describe it. Even though we'd never slept together before, somehow our bodies just knew what worked. What we liked. What we needed. It was incredible.

'So,' said Miles, regaining his composure and kissing my back, 'worth the wait?'

'Hell *yes*!' I said, 'You?'

'Abso-fucking-lutely!' he said.

'Phew!'

'Come here,' he said, rolling off me onto his back and patting his chest for me to lie on. 'I want to look at your beautiful face and run my hands all over your gorgeous body. I cannot wait to make love to you again.'

'Me neither. I do not want to leave this room for the next two days. *At least*.'

'I will be more than happy to stay here with you. Not just for the next few days, or few months or years, but *forever*, Alex. I mean it. This was it. The final piece of the puzzle. The part that would make our relationship complete. Confirm what I'd felt from that first night, our first date. That we were made for each other.'

'You're right, Miles. Everything just felt so natural. Like it was meant to be.'

'That's because it *was*,' he said.

Just at that moment, I felt something sticking to me. *What the hell?*

'You okay, Alex?'

'Yeah,' I said, straining my neck to look down and see what it was. 'Oh! Just rose petals stuck between my bum cheeks, that's all.'

'Oh!' he chuckled. 'You have no idea the fun and games I've had with these rose petals this week.'

'Really?'

'Yup. I sprinkled them on the bed on Monday and fell asleep on top of them, only to wake up and find the dastardly things had completely stained the white sheets. It looked like a crime scene.' He laughed.

'Oh my God, seriously? Sorry about your sheets, but that's kind of hilarious! Not the bit about it looking like someone had been murdered obviously, but you know what I mean.' I giggled.

'I do, and I admit, I found it funny too. It always looks so romantic in the films. I had no idea. I got the hang of it, though. I worked out that if I slept in the spare room every night until you came round and bought a few extra white duvet covers to have on standby just in case, I'd be fine. So feel free to roll around the bed to your heart's content.'

'*My hero!*' I said, showering his chest with kisses. 'If it's any consolation, it was *very* romantic. Thank you for persevering with those pesky petals.'

'Anything for you, my dear.' He kissed me on my neck.

'*So,*' I said, lifting my head from his chest to gaze into his eyes. Miles had started wearing contacts, which meant I now had a glorious, unrestricted view. 'If we'd slept together, say, the first night we met or even the first weekend, do you think we'd still be together now?' I asked.

'I'd like to hope so, but I think waiting and everything we've been through has made the whole experience better. It's brought us closer. Not just emotionally, but it's made the physical connection more intense too. Made it more special.'

'I agree. It really has. Who'd have thought a six-month sex ban would help me find my Mr Right! If I'd known that, I would've abstained years ago.'

'Aha, if only it was that simple,' said Miles, stroking my face. 'Everything happens in its right place at the right time. The universe wasn't ready for us to meet yet. If you'd started your challenge a year earlier or even a week later than you did, we may never have met.'

'Very true. Well, either way, I'm glad the universe

worked its magic, as I've never been happier and felt more excited about the future.'

'Me too, Alex. Me too. Every good romcom needs a happy ever after, and we've got ours. This is only the beginning, though. The first instalment. The next chapter of our lives will be an even happier sequel.'

'Sounds great! Sign me up!' I said as Miles popped open the champagne and poured it into the two glasses.

'Cheers, Alex,' he said, kissing me on the lips then taking a sip. 'Here's to a long and very happy future together, filled with laughter, marriage, kids, and of course, *lots* of amazing sex. Speaking of which, buckle up, young lady. We've got six months of abstinence to make up for, starting right now…'

The End

GET A FREE BOOK AND EXCLUSIVE BONUS MATERIAL

Building a relationship with my readers is one of the best things about being an author. I occasionally send out fun newsletters to members of my VIP club with details of new releases, special offers, expert dating and relationship tips, interesting news and other exclusive freebies.

If you sign up to join my special VIP club, I'll send you the following, for free:

1) Yellow Book Of Love: a handy little guide, which features essential dating and relationship tips from multiple experts, including the Dating Expert of the Year 2017.

2) A list of *Alex's Top 25 Romcoms*: a definitive guide highlighting her must-watch romantic films. Exclusive to my VIP Club – you can't get this anywhere else.

You can get the book and the list of top romcoms, **for free,** by signing up at: www.oliviaspring.com/vip-club/

ENJOYED THIS BOOK? YOU CAN MAKE A BIG DIFFERENCE.

When it comes to getting attention for my novels, reviews are the most powerful tools in my arsenal. As much as I'd like to, I don't have the financial muscle of big New York publishers to take out full-page newspaper ads or invest in billboard posters. Well, not yet anyway!

But I *do* have something much more powerful and effective than that: **loyal readers like you.**

You see, by leaving an honest review of my books, you'll be helping to bring them to the attention of other readers and hearing your thoughts will make them more likely to give my novel a try. As a result, it will help me to build my career, which means I'll get to write more books!

If you've enjoyed *Only When It's Love*, I'd be so very grateful if you could spare two minutes to leave a review (it can be as short or as long as you like) on Amazon and Goodreads or anywhere that readers visit.

Thank you so much. As well as making a huge difference, you've also just made my day!

Olivia x

The Middle-Aged Virgin

Have you read my debut novel *The Middle-Aged Virgin*? It includes the feisty character Roxy from *Only When It's Love*, too! Here's what it's about:

Newly Single And Seeking Spine-Tingles…

Sophia Huntingdon seems to have it all: a high-flying job running London's coolest beauty PR agency, a lovely boyfriend and a dressing room filled with Louboutins.

But when tragedy strikes, Sophia realises that rather than living the dream, she's actually in a monotonous relationship, with zero personal life. Her lack of activity in the bedroom is so apparent that her best friend declares her a MARGIN, or *Middle-Aged Virgin*—a term used for adults who have experienced a drought so long that they can't remember the last time they had sex.

Determined to transform her life whilst she's still young enough to enjoy it, Sophia hatches a plan to work less, live more and embark on exciting adventures, including rediscovering the electrifying passion she's been craving.

But after finding the courage to end her fifteen-year relationship, how will Sophia, a self-confessed control freak, handle being newly single and navigating the unpredictable world of online dating?

If she *does* meet someone new, will she even remember what to do? And as an independent career woman, how much is Sophia really prepared to sacrifice for love?

The Middle-Aged Virgin is a funny, uplifting story of a smart single woman on a mission to find love and happiness and live life to the full.

Here's what readers are saying about it:

"I couldn't put the book down. It's **one of the best romantic comedies I've read**." Amazon reader

"Life-affirming and empowering." Chicklit Club

"Perfect holiday read." Saira Khan, TV presenter & newspaper columnist

"Absolutely hilarious! A diverse, wise and poignant novel." The Writing Garnet

Buy *The Middle-Aged Virgin* on Amazon today!

AN EXTRACT FROM THE MIDDLE-AGED VIRGIN

Prologue

'It's over.'

I did it.

I said it.

Fuck.

I'd rehearsed those two words approximately ten million times in my head—whilst I was in the shower, in front of the mirror, on my way to and from work…probably even in my sleep. But saying them out loud was far more difficult than I'd imagined.

'What the fuck, Sophia?' snapped Rich, nostrils flaring. 'What do you mean, it's over?'

As I stared into his hazel eyes, I started to ask myself the same question.

How could I be ending the fifteen-year relationship with the guy I'd always considered to be the one?

I felt the beads of sweat forming on my powdered forehead and warm, salty tears trickling down my rouged cheeks, which now felt like they were on fire. This was serious. This was actually happening.

Shit. I said I'd be strong.

'Earth to Sophia!' screamed Rich, stomping his feet.

I snapped out of my thoughts. Now would probably be a good time to start explaining myself. Not least because the veins currently throbbing on Rich's forehead appeared to indicate that he was on the verge of spontaneous combustion. Easier said than done, though, as with every second that passed, I realised the enormity of what I was doing.

The man standing in front of me wasn't just a guy that came in pretty packaging. Rich was kind, intelligent, successful, financially secure, and faithful. He was a great listener and had been there for me through thick and thin. Qualities that, after numerous failed Tinder dates, my single friends had repeatedly vented, appeared to be rare in men these days.

Most women would have given their right and probably their left arm too for a man like him. So why the hell was I suddenly about to throw it all away?

Want to find out what happens next? Buy _The Middle-Aged Virgin_ by Olivia Spring on Amazon.

ACKNOWLEDGMENTS

The acknowledgments page for my second book – yay! I love this part as I get to thank the wonderful people that helped make this possible. Drumroll please...

Huge thanks to my amazing mum for reading over multiple drafts and giving very honest and incredibly useful feedback.

Jas, DWT, Cams, Brad and Loz, grazie mille for your continued feedback, enthusiasm, encouragement and amazing positivity. You rock!

To my 'character career consultants': Mich, thanks for your psychology expertise and Jo, merci beaucoup for your insights into the medical profession and unwavering support.

Thanks to my editor Eliza, proofreader Lily, cover designer Rachel and web designer Dawn for all doing such an amazing job.

Big thanks to all the book bloggers and celebrities that have read, reviewed and helped spread the word about both *Only When It's Love* and *The Middle-Aged Virgin*. I really appreciate the support that you've given me.

Last, but by no means least, to each and every one of the brilliant readers who have taken the time to buy and read my books, I give you the biggest thank you of all. It's because of you that I'm able to pursue a career that I love and for that, I am eternally grateful.

Well, that was fun! Thanks for reading. I'm off to finish the next novel. Yep, it's coming very soon, which means I'll get to write another acknowledgments page. Can't wait!

Olivia x

ABOUT THE AUTHOR

Olivia Spring lives in London, England. When she's not making regular trips to Italy to indulge in pasta, pizza and gelato, she can be found at her desk, writing new sexy chick-lit novels, whilst consuming large bowls of her mum's delicious apple crumble and custard.

If you'd like to say hi, email olivia@oliviaspring.com or connect on social media.

facebook.com/ospringauthor

twitter.com/ospringauthor

instagram.com/ospringauthor

Printed in Great Britain
by Amazon